S0-BFC-050

BONEYARD

DATE DUE

PRINTED IN U.S.A.

WITHDRAWN

GRAPHIC NOVEL
MOORE, R
BONE
V. 7

ISBN: 978-1-56163-583-2
© 2010 Richard Moore
Printed in Canada

BONEYARD

VOLUME SEVEN
RICHARD MOORE

HIGHLAND PARK PUBLIC LIBRARY
494 LAUREL AVE.
HIGHLAND PARK, IL 60035-2690
847-432-0216

NANTIER · BEALL · MINOUSTCHINE
Publishing inc.
new york

Also by Richard Moore:
Boneyard in color, vol. 1, $12.99; vol. 2, $11.95;
vol. 3, $12.95; vol. 4, $13.95
Boneyard in B&W, vols. 5, 6 , $9.95 each
Horny Tails (adults only), $12.95
Short Strokes, vol. 1 (adults only), $11.95

See more on these at our website:
www.nbmpublishing.com

P&H: $4 1st item, $1 each addt'l.

We have over 200 titles,
write for our color catalog:
NBM
40 Exchange Pl., Ste. 1308
New York, NY. 10005

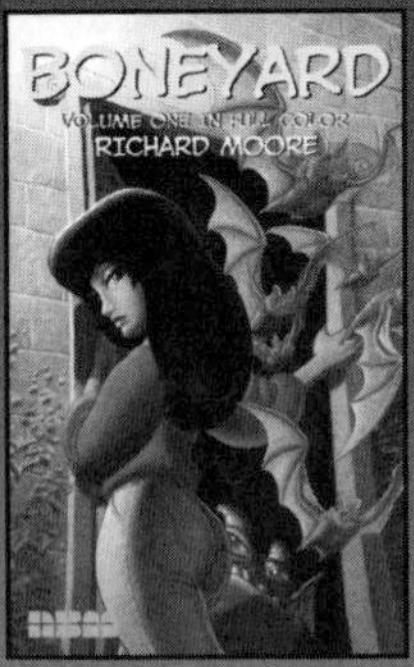
BONEYARD
RICHARD MOORE

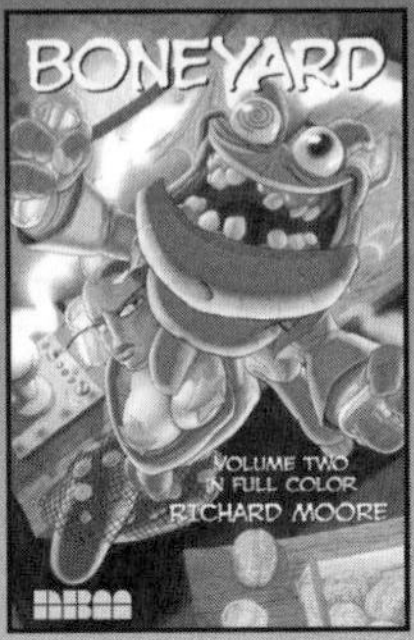
BONEYARD
VOLUME TWO
IN FULL COLOR
RICHARD MOORE

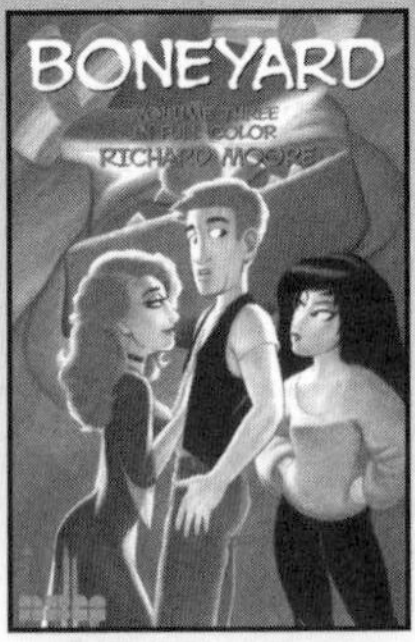
BONEYARD

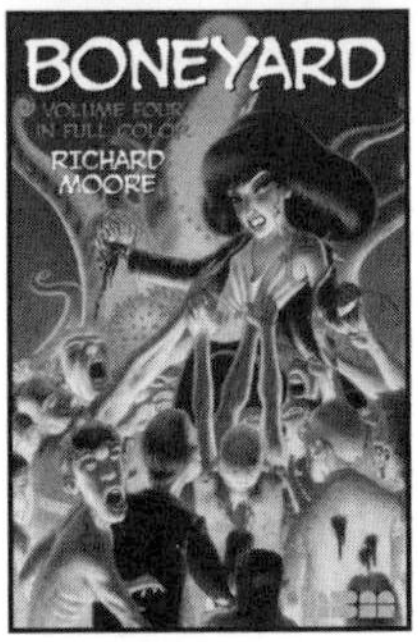
BONEYARD
RICHARD
MOORE

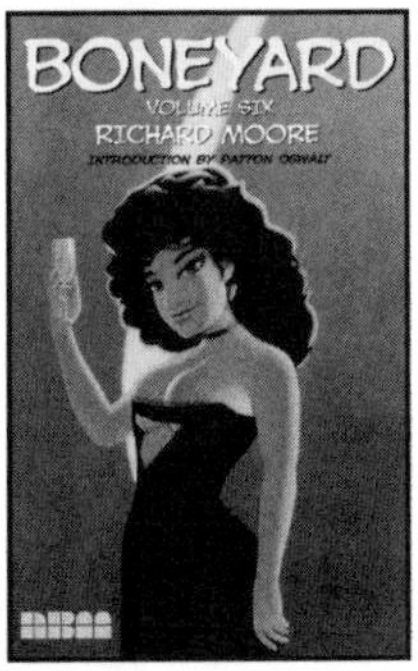
BONEYARD
RICHARD MOORE

Summary

Michael Paris has inherited a nightmare: a cemetery filled with
monsters, one of them the fetching vampiress Abbey, a whom
he befriends. And as we learned in the first story arc, the real
danger was not the monsters, but the fear and prejudice of the
regular townsfolk. Mayor Wormwood--ultimately revealed to
be the Devil himself--failed to oust Paris and the Boneyard folk
from the cemetery. The magnetism between Abbey the vam-
pire and Michael is palpable but Nessie the luscious swamp
girl fancies him as well…

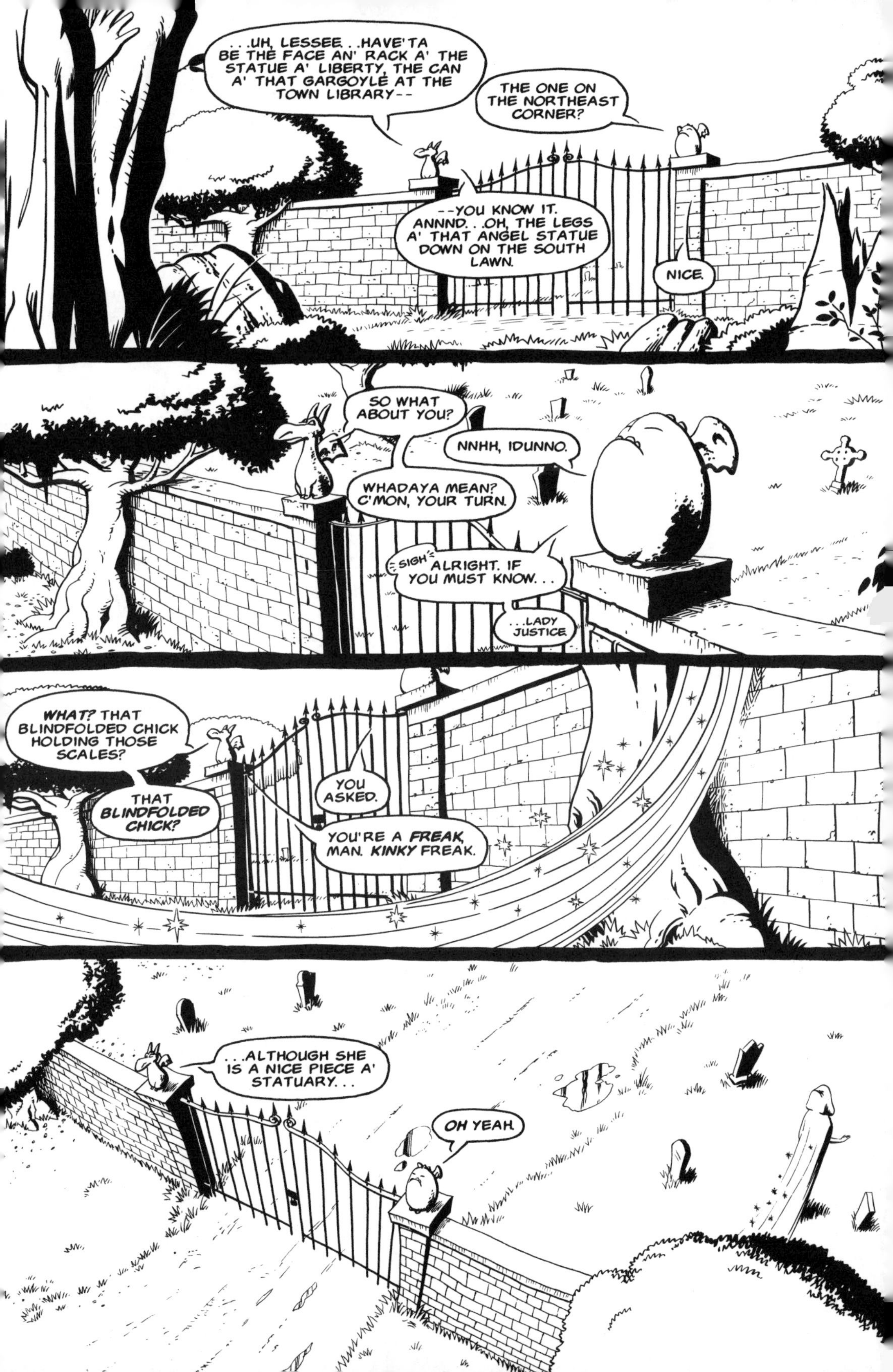

. . .UH, LESSEE. . .HAVE'TA BE THE FACE AN' RACK A' THE STATUE A' LIBERTY, THE CAN A' THAT GARGOYLE AT THE TOWN LIBRARY--
THE ONE ON THE NORTHEAST CORNER?
--YOU KNOW IT. ANNND. . .OH, THE LEGS A' THAT ANGEL STATUE DOWN ON THE SOUTH LAWN.
NICE.
SO WHAT ABOUT YOU?
NNHH, IDUNNO.
WHADAYA MEAN? C'MON, YOUR TURN.
SIGH ALRIGHT. IF YOU MUST KNOW. . .
. . .LADY JUSTICE.
WHAT? THAT BLINDFOLDED CHICK HOLDING THOSE SCALES?
THAT BLINDFOLDED CHICK?
YOU ASKED.
YOU'RE A FREAK, MAN. KINKY FREAK.
. . .ALTHOUGH SHE IS A NICE PIECE A' STATUARY. . .
OH YEAH.

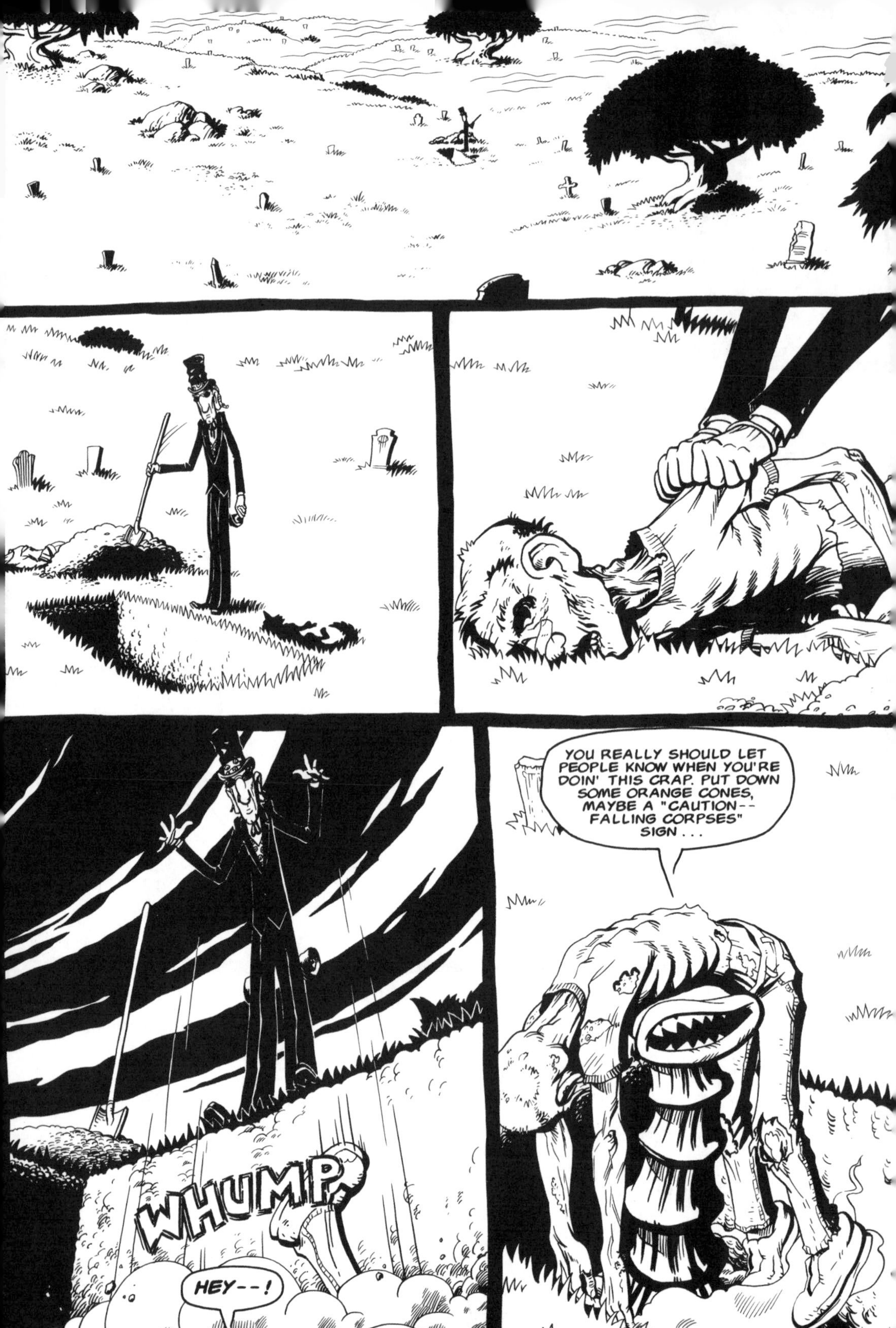
WHUMP
HEY--!
YOU REALLY SHOULD LET PEOPLE KNOW WHEN YOU'RE DOIN' THIS CRAP. PUT DOWN SOME ORANGE CONES, MAYBE A "CAUTION-- FALLING CORPSES" SIGN . . .

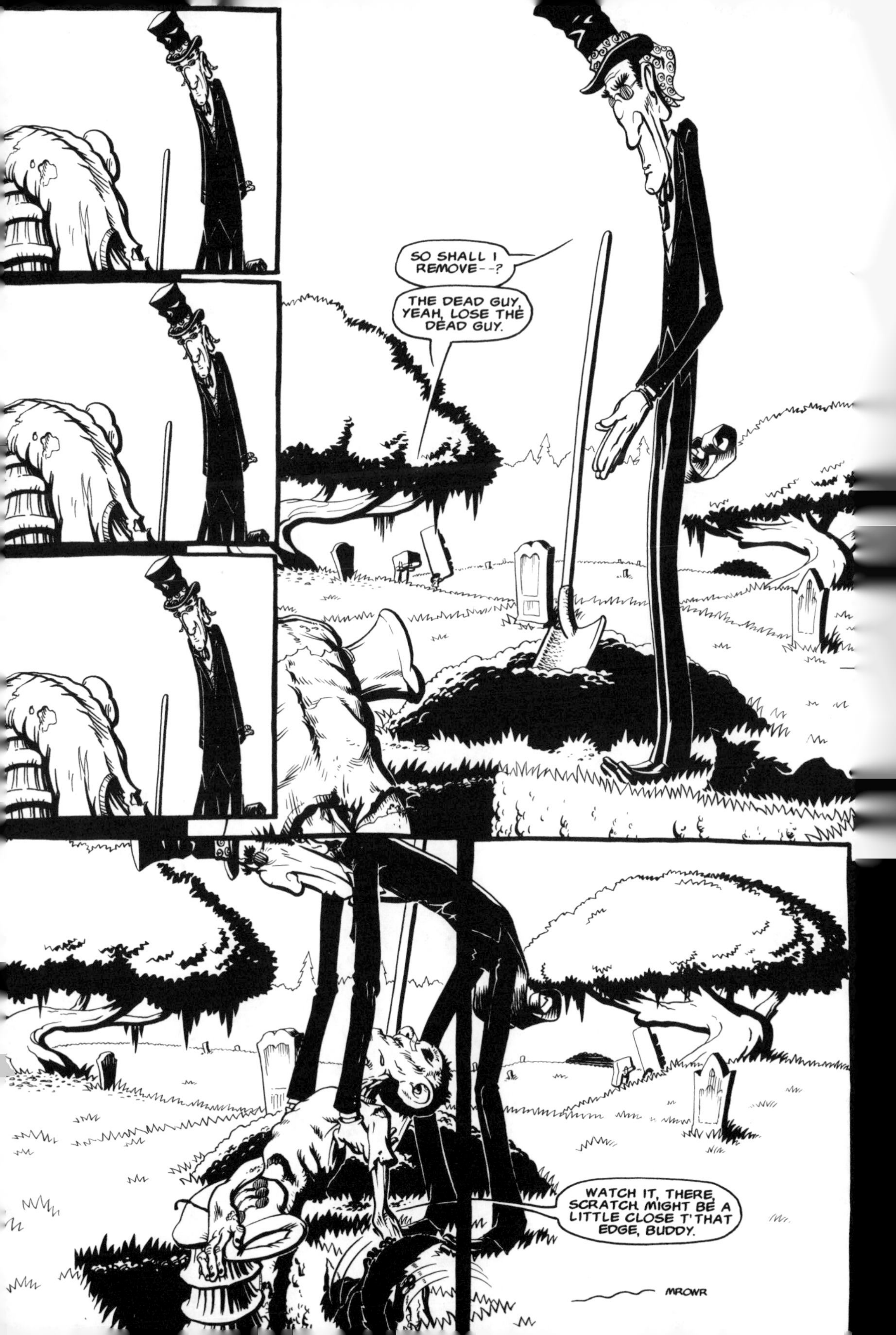
SO SHALL I REMOVE--?
THE DEAD GUY, YEAH, LOSE THE DEAD GUY.
WATCH IT, THERE, SCRATCH MIGHT BE A LITTLE CLOSE T'THAT EDGE, BUDDY.
MROWR

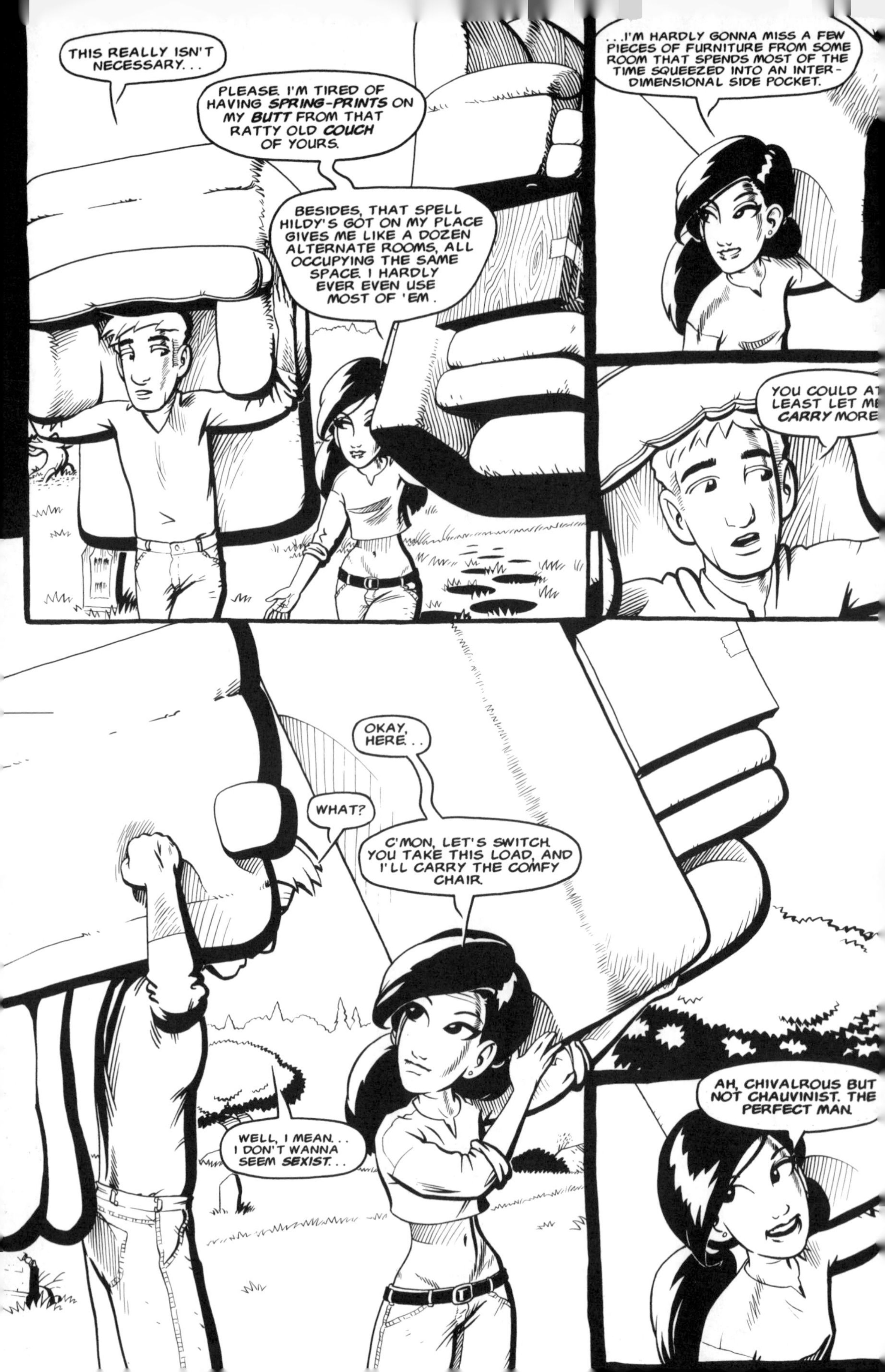
THIS REALLY ISN'T NECESSARY...
PLEASE. I'M TIRED OF HAVING SPRING-PRINTS ON MY BUTT FROM THAT RATTY OLD COUCH OF YOURS.
BESIDES, THAT SPELL HILDY'S GOT ON MY PLACE GIVES ME LIKE A DOZEN ALTERNATE ROOMS, ALL OCCUPYING THE SAME SPACE. I HARDLY EVER EVEN USE MOST OF 'EM.
...I'M HARDLY GONNA MISS A FEW PIECES OF FURNITURE FROM SOME ROOM THAT SPENDS MOST OF THE TIME SQUEEZED INTO AN INTER-DIMENSIONAL SIDE POCKET.
YOU COULD AT LEAST LET ME CARRY MORE
OKAY, HERE...
WHAT?
C'MON, LET'S SWITCH. YOU TAKE THIS LOAD, AND I'LL CARRY THE COMFY CHAIR.
WELL, I MEAN... I DON'T WANNA SEEM SEXIST...
AH, CHIVALROUS BUT NOT CHAUVINIST. THE PERFECT MAN.

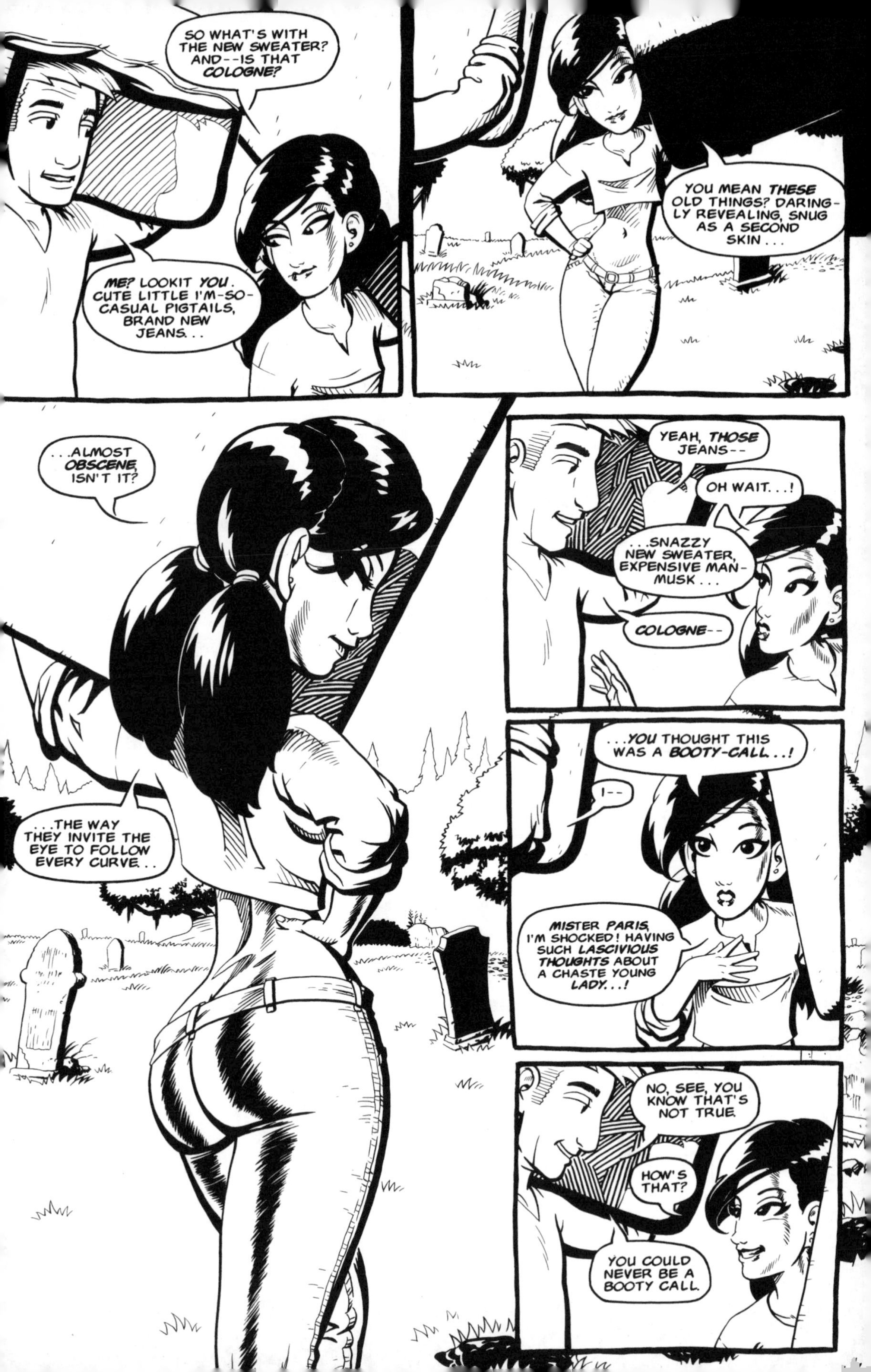
SO WHAT'S WITH THE NEW SWEATER? AND--IS THAT *COLOGNE?*
ME? LOOKIT *YOU*. CUTE LITTLE I'M-SO-CASUAL PIGTAILS, BRAND NEW JEANS...
YOU MEAN *THESE* OLD THINGS? DARING-LY REVEALING, SNUG AS A SECOND SKIN...
...ALMOST *OBSCENE*, ISN'T IT?
...THE WAY THEY INVITE THE EYE TO FOLLOW EVERY CURVE...
YEAH, *THOSE* JEANS--
OH WAIT...!
...SNAZZY NEW SWEATER, EXPENSIVE MAN-MUSK...
COLOGNE--
...*YOU* THOUGHT THIS WAS A *BOOTY-CALL*...!
I--
MISTER PARIS, I'M SHOCKED! HAVING SUCH *LASCIVIOUS THOUGHTS* ABOUT A CHASTE YOUNG *LADY*...!
NO, SEE, YOU KNOW THAT'S NOT TRUE.
HOW'S THAT?
YOU COULD NEVER BE A BOOTY CALL.

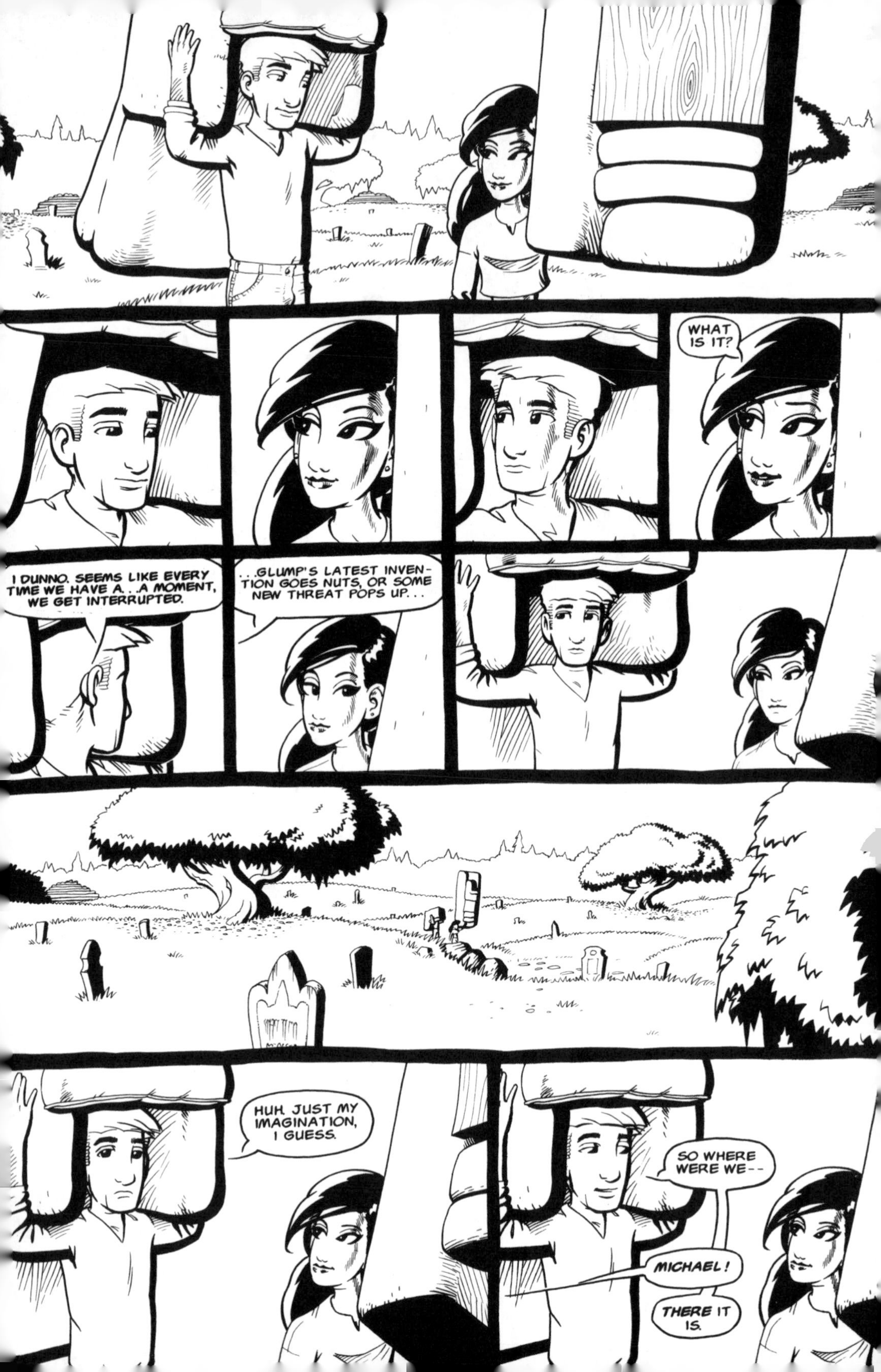
WHAT IS IT?
I DUNNO. SEEMS LIKE EVERY TIME WE HAVE A. . .A MOMENT, WE GET INTERRUPTED.
. . .GLUMP'S LATEST INVENTION GOES NUTS, OR SOME NEW THREAT POPS UP. . .
HUH. JUST MY IMAGINATION, I GUESS.
SO WHERE WERE WE--
MICHAEL!
THERE IT IS.

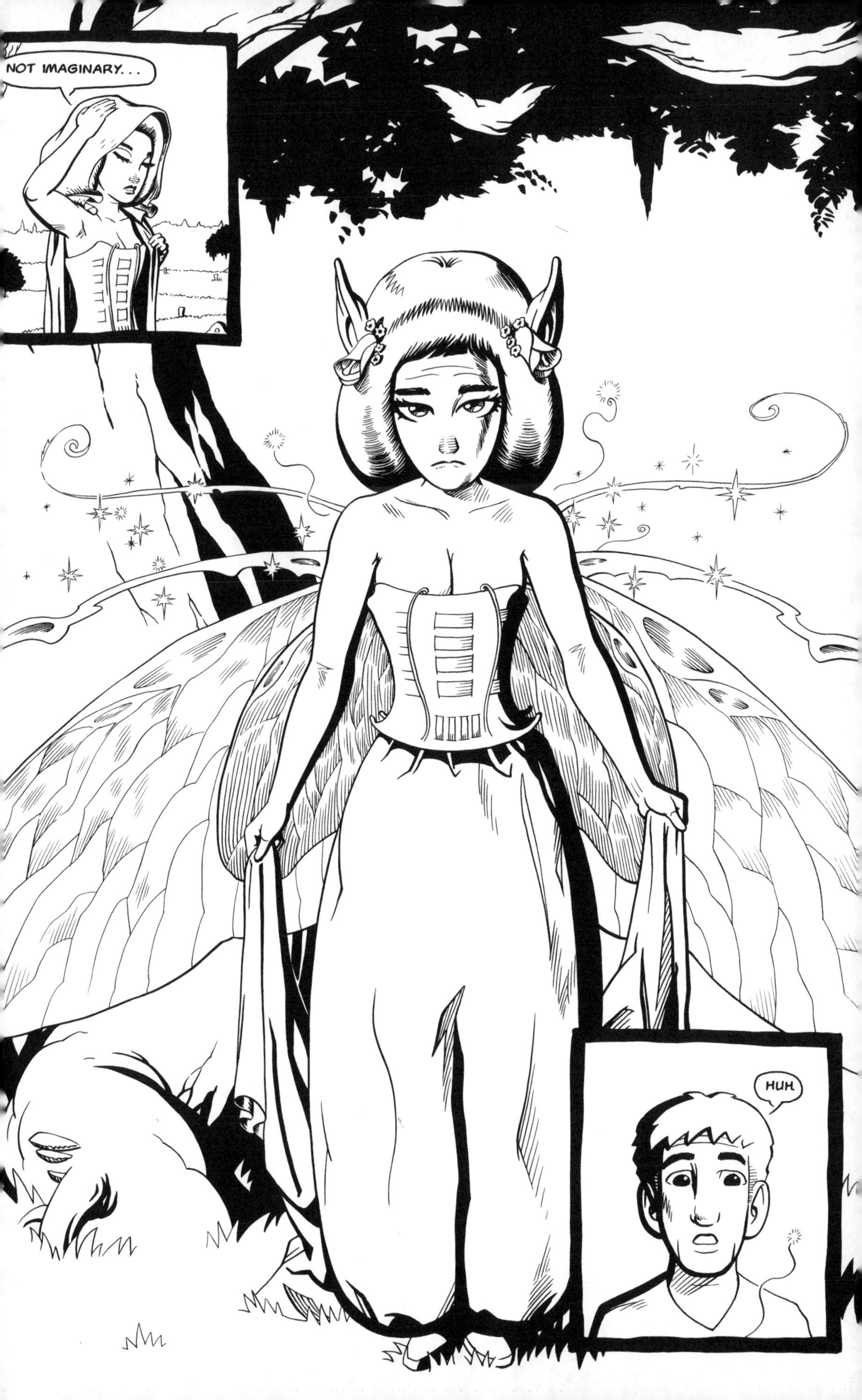
NOT IMAGINARY...
HUH.

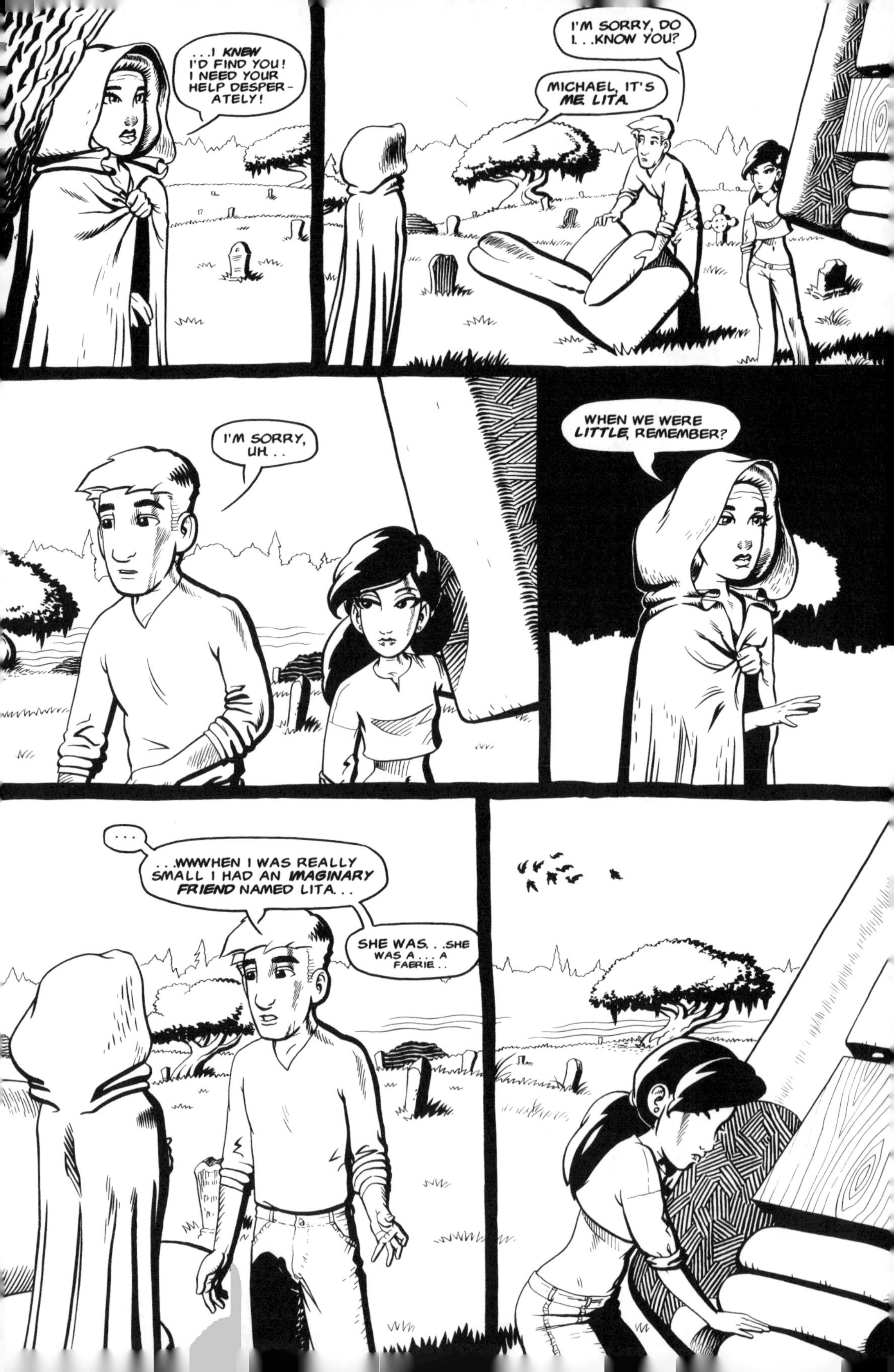
...I KNEW I'D FIND YOU! I NEED YOUR HELP DESPER-ATELY!
I'M SORRY, DO I...KNOW YOU?
MICHAEL, IT'S ME. LITA.
I'M SORRY, UH...
WHEN WE WERE LITTLE, REMEMBER?
...
...WWWHEN I WAS REALLY SMALL I HAD AN IMAGINARY FRIEND NAMED LITA...
SHE WAS...SHE WAS A... A FAERIE..

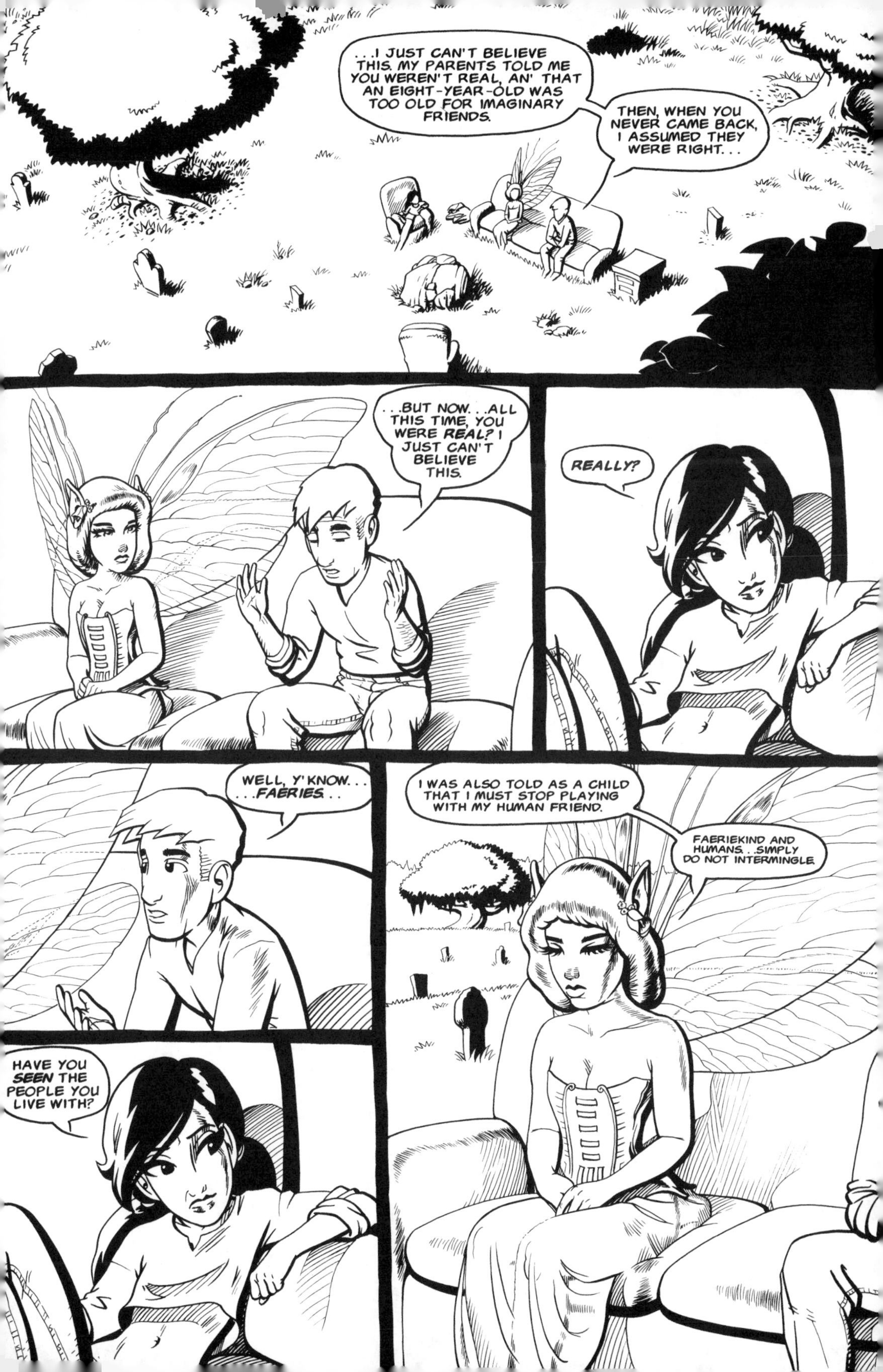

...I JUST CAN'T BELIEVE THIS. MY PARENTS TOLD ME YOU WEREN'T REAL, AN' THAT AN EIGHT-YEAR-OLD WAS TOO OLD FOR IMAGINARY FRIENDS.
THEN, WHEN YOU NEVER CAME BACK, I ASSUMED THEY WERE RIGHT...
...BUT NOW...ALL THIS TIME, YOU WERE REAL? I JUST CAN'T BELIEVE THIS.
REALLY?
WELL, Y'KNOW... ...FAERIES...
I WAS ALSO TOLD AS A CHILD THAT I MUST STOP PLAYING WITH MY HUMAN FRIEND.
FAERIEKIND AND HUMANS...SIMPLY DO NOT INTERMINGLE.
HAVE YOU SEEN THE PEOPLE YOU LIVE WITH?

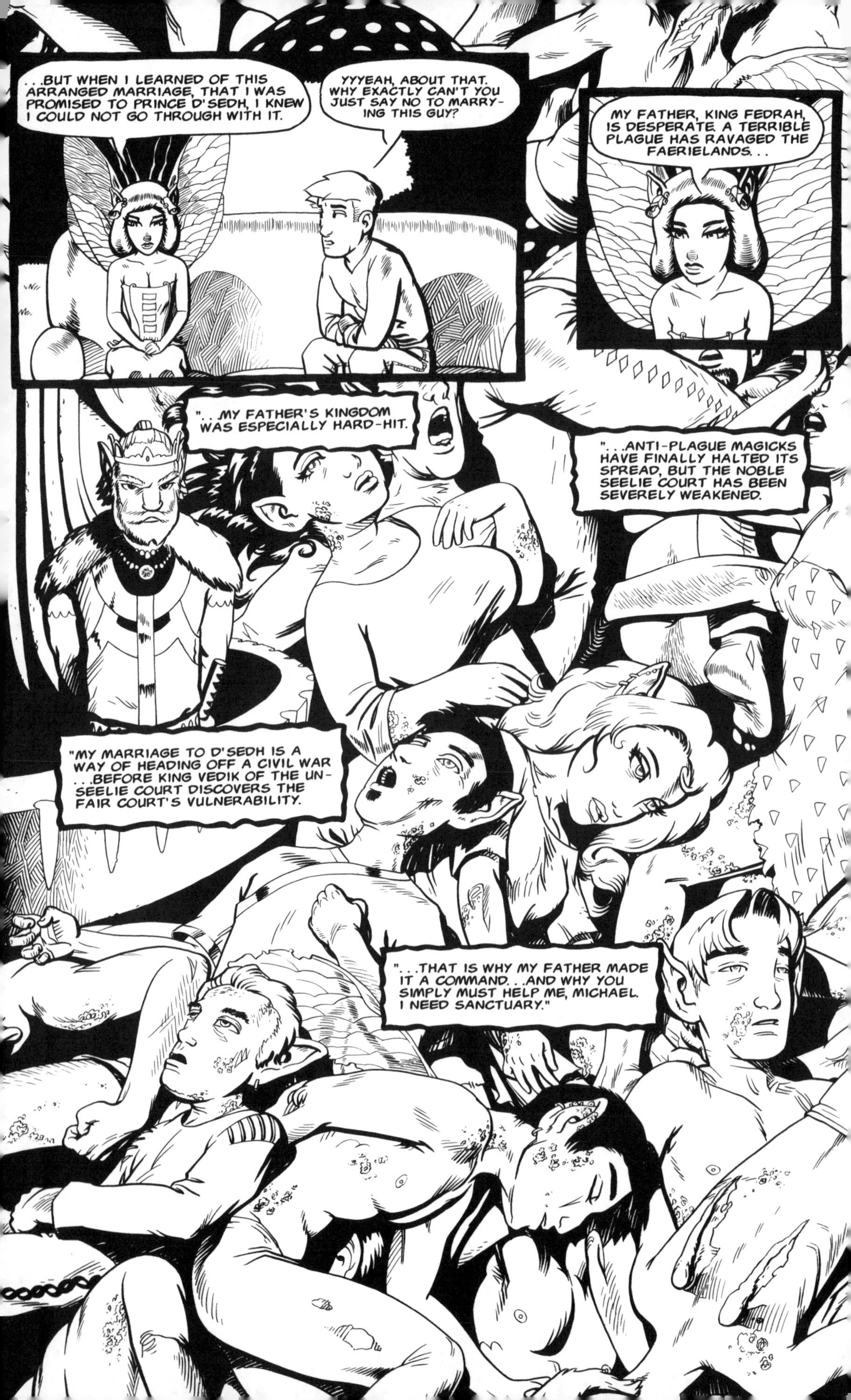
. . .BUT WHEN I LEARNED OF THIS ARRANGED MARRIAGE, THAT I WAS PROMISED TO PRINCE D'SEDH, I KNEW I COULD NOT GO THROUGH WITH IT.
YYYEAH, ABOUT THAT. WHY EXACTLY CAN'T YOU JUST SAY NO TO MARRYING THIS GUY?
MY FATHER, KING FEDRAH, IS DESPERATE. A TERRIBLE PLAGUE HAS RAVAGED THE FAERIELANDS. . .
". . .MY FATHER'S KINGDOM WAS ESPECIALLY HARD-HIT.
". . .ANTI-PLAGUE MAGICKS HAVE FINALLY HALTED ITS SPREAD, BUT THE NOBLE SEELIE COURT HAS BEEN SEVERELY WEAKENED.
"MY MARRIAGE TO D'SEDH IS A WAY OF HEADING OFF A CIVIL WAR . . .BEFORE KING VEDIK OF THE UNSEELIE COURT DISCOVERS THE FAIR COURT'S VULNERABILITY.
". . .THAT IS WHY MY FATHER MADE IT A COMMAND. . .AND WHY YOU SIMPLY MUST HELP ME, MICHAEL. I NEED SANCTUARY."

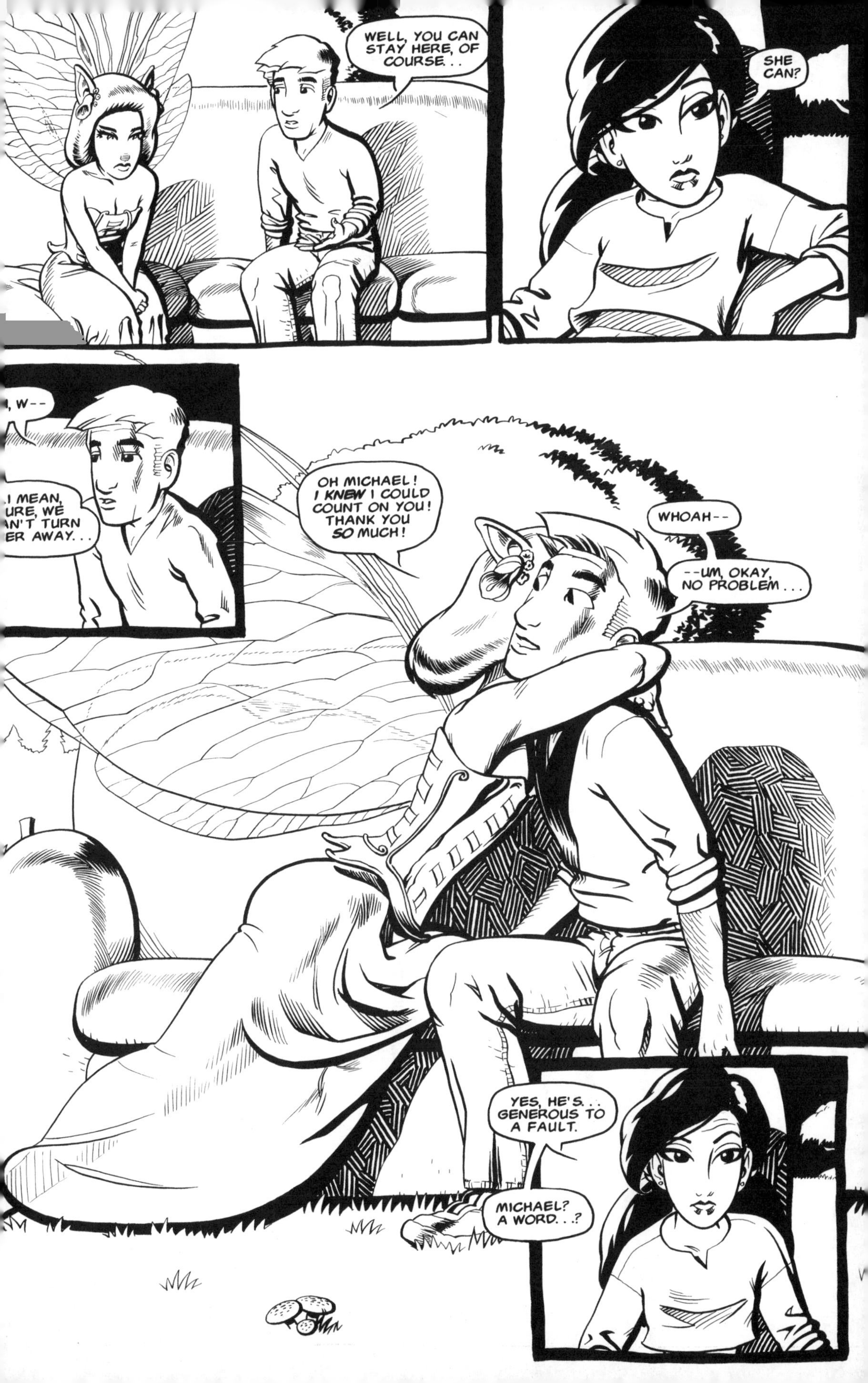

WELL, YOU CAN STAY HERE, OF COURSE. . .
SHE CAN?
, W--
.I MEAN, URE, WE AN'T TURN ER AWAY. . .
OH MICHAEL! I *KNEW* I COULD COUNT ON YOU! THANK YOU *SO* MUCH!
WHOAH--
--UM, OKAY, NO PROBLEM. . .
YES, HE'S. . . GENEROUS TO A FAULT.
MICHAEL? A WORD. . .?

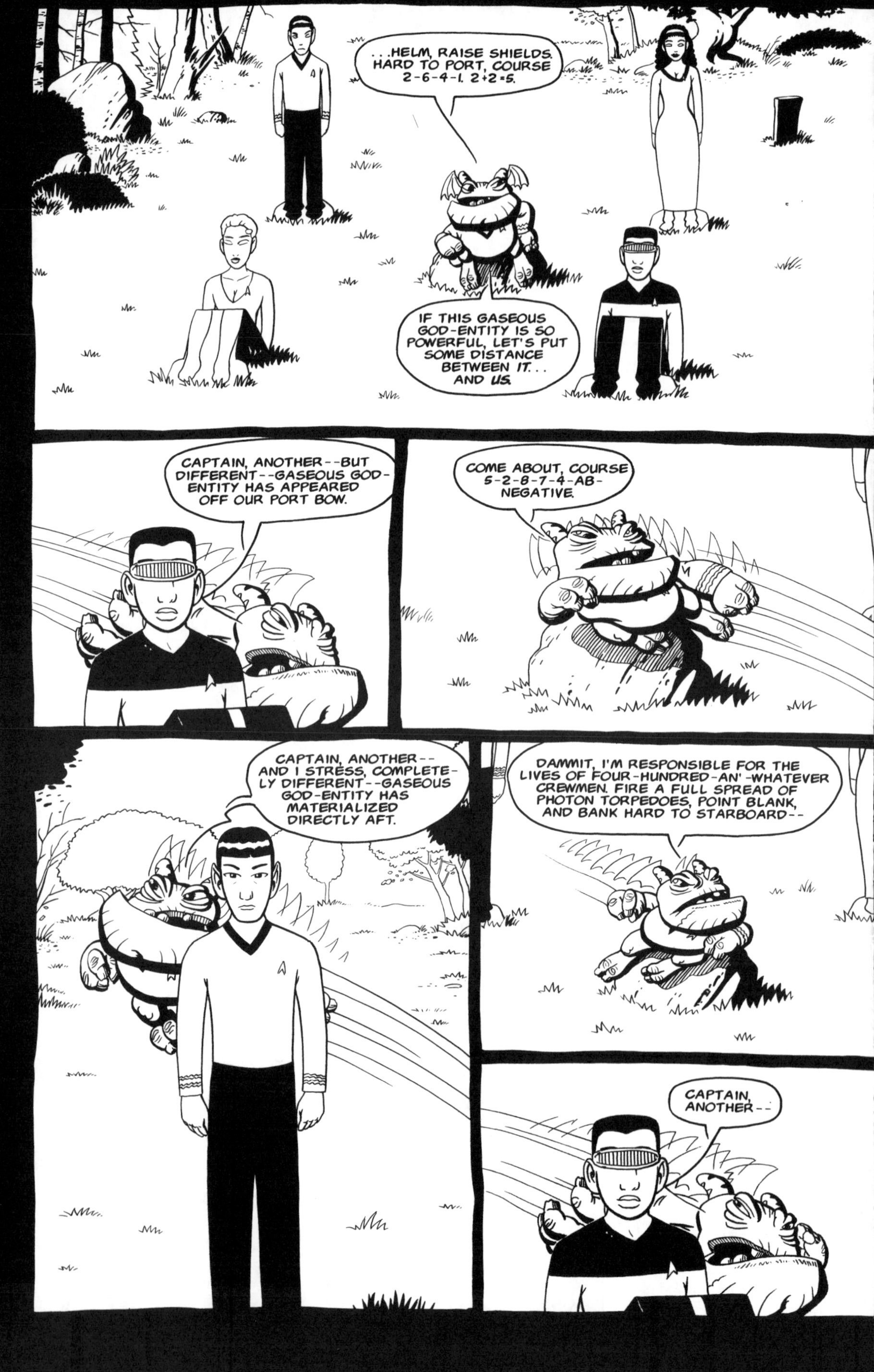
. . .HELM, RAISE SHIELDS. HARD TO PORT, COURSE 2-6-4-1. 2+2=5.
IF THIS GASEOUS GOD-ENTITY IS SO POWERFUL, LET'S PUT SOME DISTANCE BETWEEN IT. . . AND US.
CAPTAIN, ANOTHER--BUT DIFFERENT--GASEOUS GOD-ENTITY HAS APPEARED OFF OUR PORT BOW.
COME ABOUT, COURSE 5-2-8-7-4-AB-NEGATIVE.
CAPTAIN, ANOTHER--AND I STRESS, COMPLETELY DIFFERENT--GASEOUS GOD-ENTITY HAS MATERIALIZED DIRECTLY AFT.
DAMMIT, I'M RESPONSIBLE FOR THE LIVES OF FOUR-HUNDRED-AN'-WHATEVER CREWMEN. FIRE A FULL SPREAD OF PHOTON TORPEDOES, POINT BLANK, AND BANK HARD TO STARBOARD--
CAPTAIN, ANOTHER--

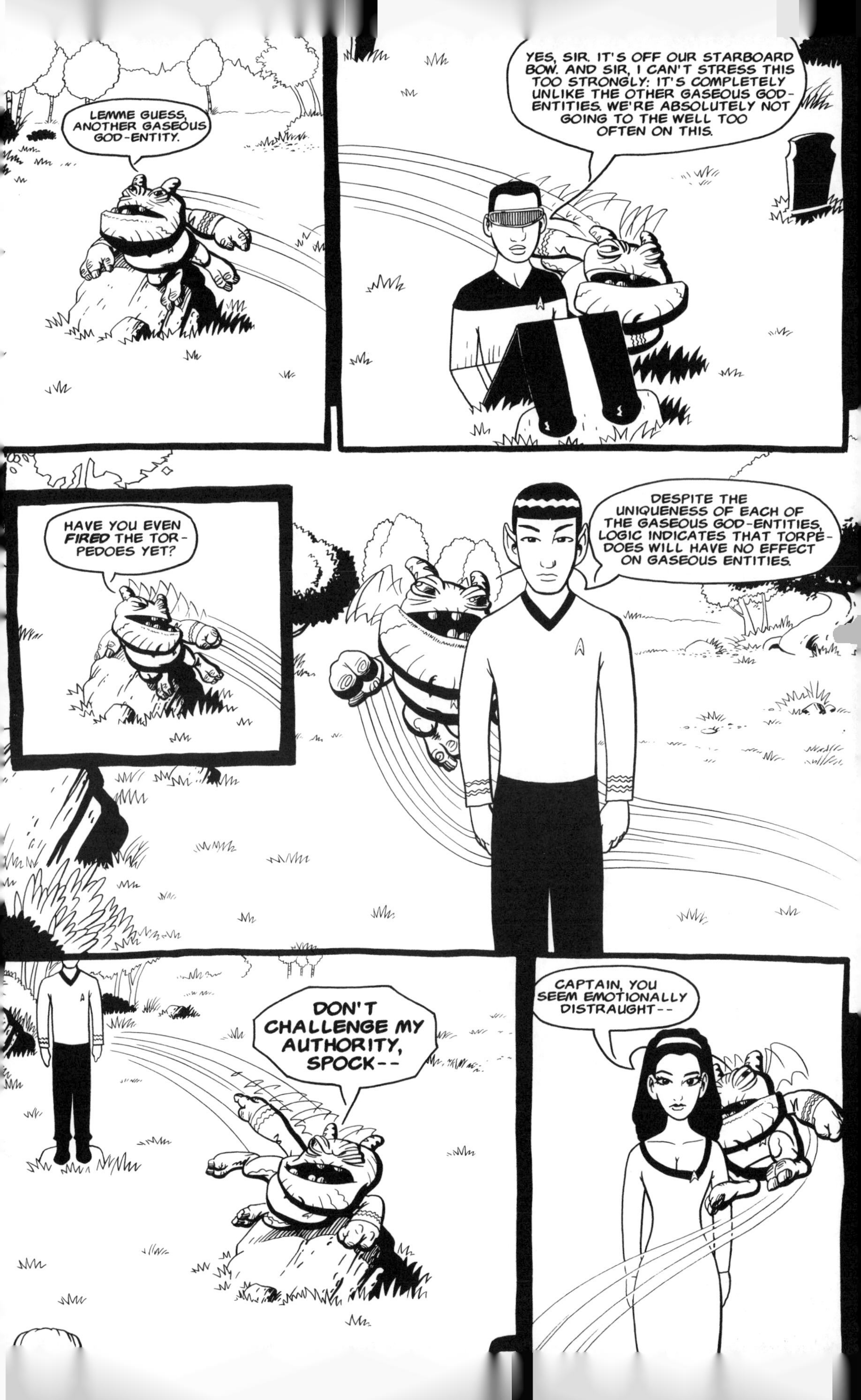

LEMME GUESS, ANOTHER GASEOUS GOD-ENTITY.
YES, SIR. IT'S OFF OUR STARBOARD BOW. AND SIR, I CAN'T STRESS THIS TOO STRONGLY: IT'S COMPLETELY UNLIKE THE OTHER GASEOUS GOD-ENTITIES. WE'RE ABSOLUTELY NOT GOING TO THE WELL TOO OFTEN ON THIS.
HAVE YOU EVEN FIRED THE TORPEDOES YET?
DESPITE THE UNIQUENESS OF EACH OF THE GASEOUS GOD-ENTITIES, LOGIC INDICATES THAT TORPEDOES WILL HAVE NO EFFECT ON GASEOUS ENTITIES.
DON'T CHALLENGE MY AUTHORITY, SPOCK--
CAPTAIN, YOU SEEM EMOTIONALLY DISTRAUGHT--

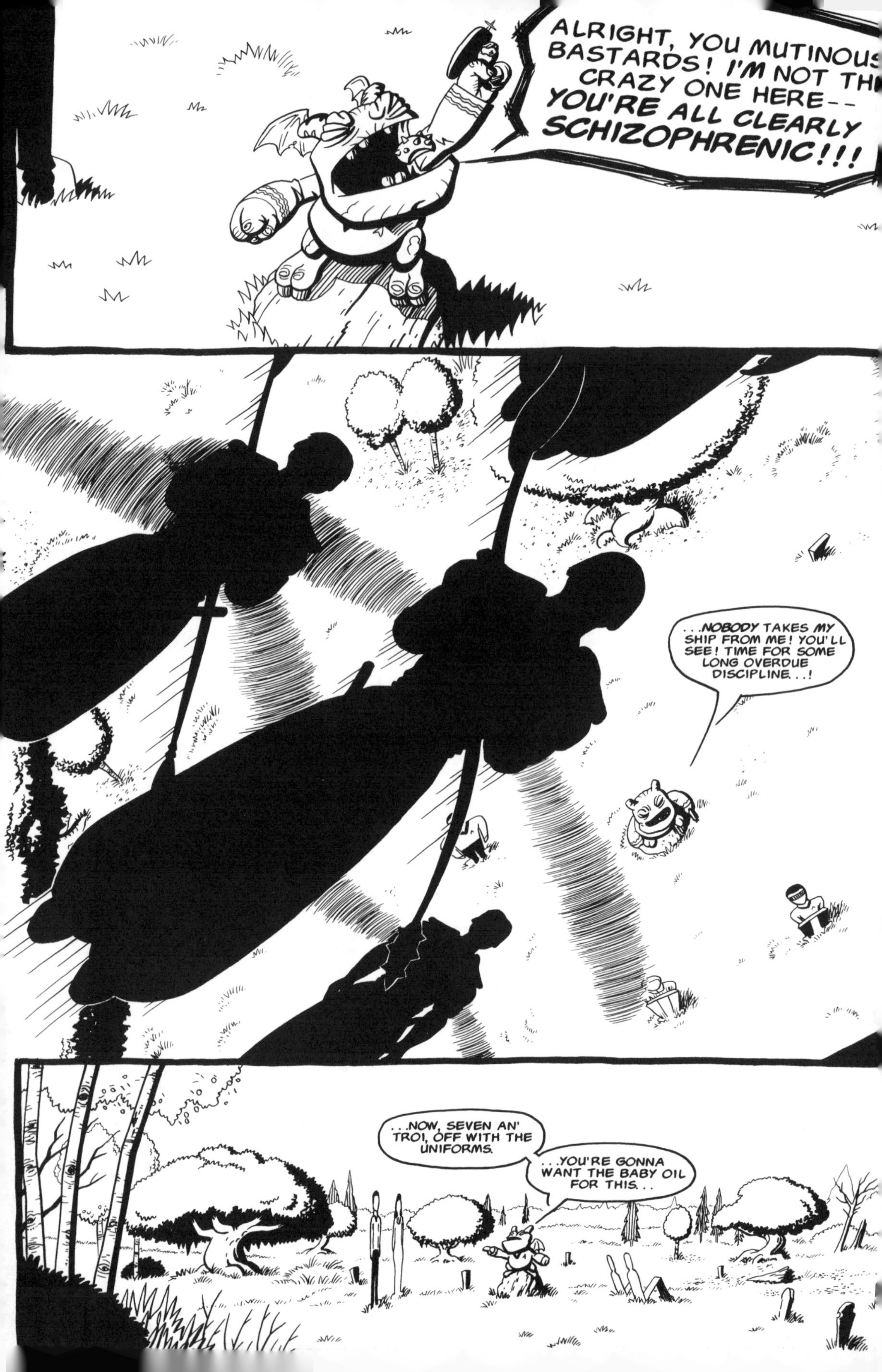
ALRIGHT, YOU MUTINOUS BASTARDS! I'M NOT TH CRAZY ONE HERE-- YOU'RE ALL CLEARLY SCHIZOPHRENIC!!!
...NOBODY TAKES MY SHIP FROM ME! YOU'LL SEE! TIME FOR SOME LONG OVERDUE DISCIPLINE...!
...NOW, SEVEN AN' TROI, OFF WITH THE UNIFORMS.
...YOU'RE GONNA WANT THE BABY OIL FOR THIS..

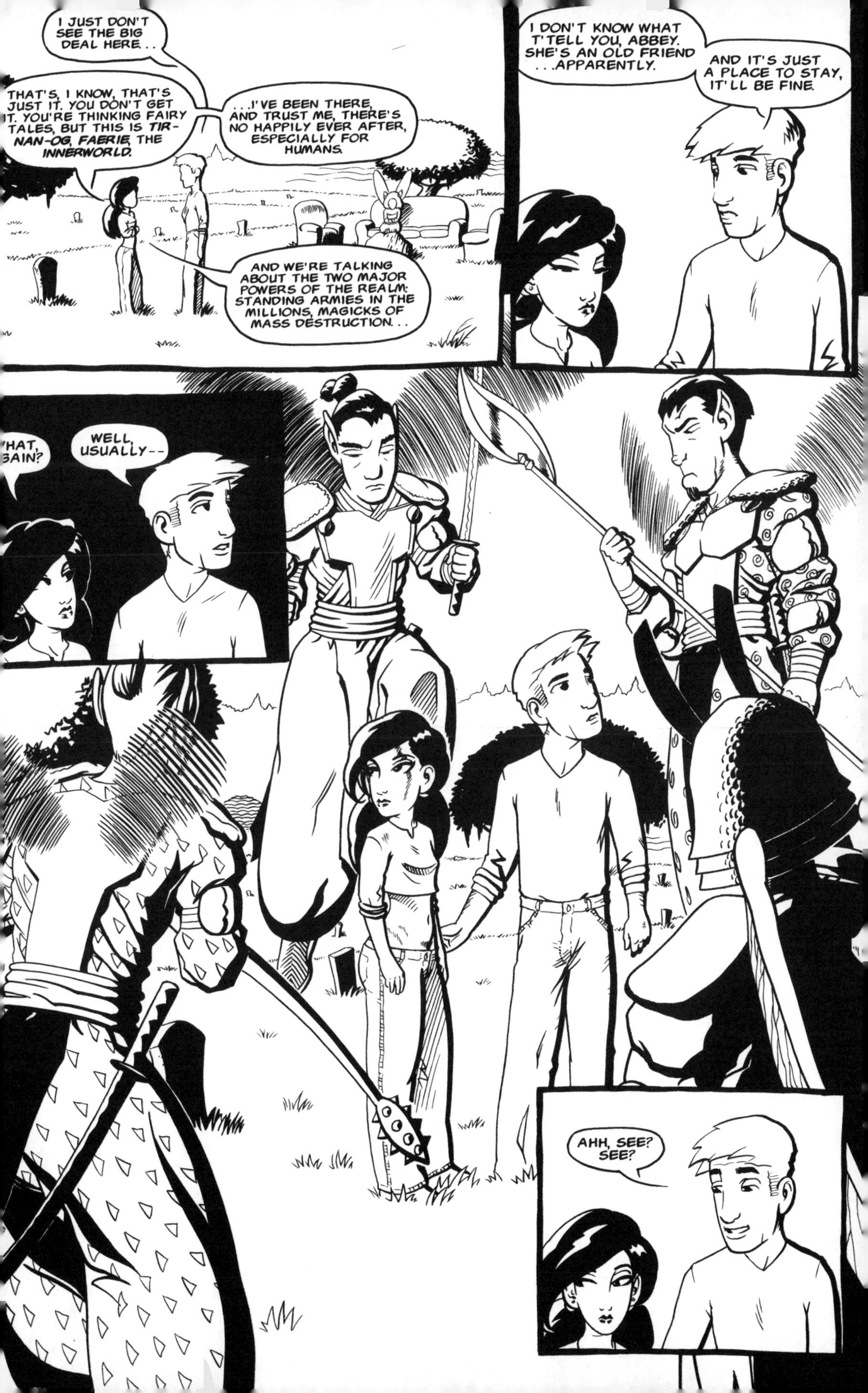

I JUST DON'T SEE THE BIG DEAL HERE . .
THAT'S, I KNOW, THAT'S JUST IT. YOU DON'T GET IT. YOU'RE THINKING FAIRY TALES, BUT THIS IS *TIR-NAN-OG, FAERIE*, THE *INNERWORLD*.
. . .I'VE BEEN THERE, AND TRUST ME, THERE'S NO HAPPILY EVER AFTER, ESPECIALLY FOR HUMANS.
AND WE'RE TALKING ABOUT THE TWO MAJOR POWERS OF THE REALM: STANDING ARMIES IN THE MILLIONS, MAGICKS OF MASS DESTRUCTION. . .
I DON'T KNOW WHAT T'TELL YOU, ABBEY. SHE'S AN OLD FRIEND . . .APPARENTLY.
AND IT'S JUST A PLACE TO STAY, IT'LL BE FINE.
WELL, USUALLY--
AHH, SEE? SEE?

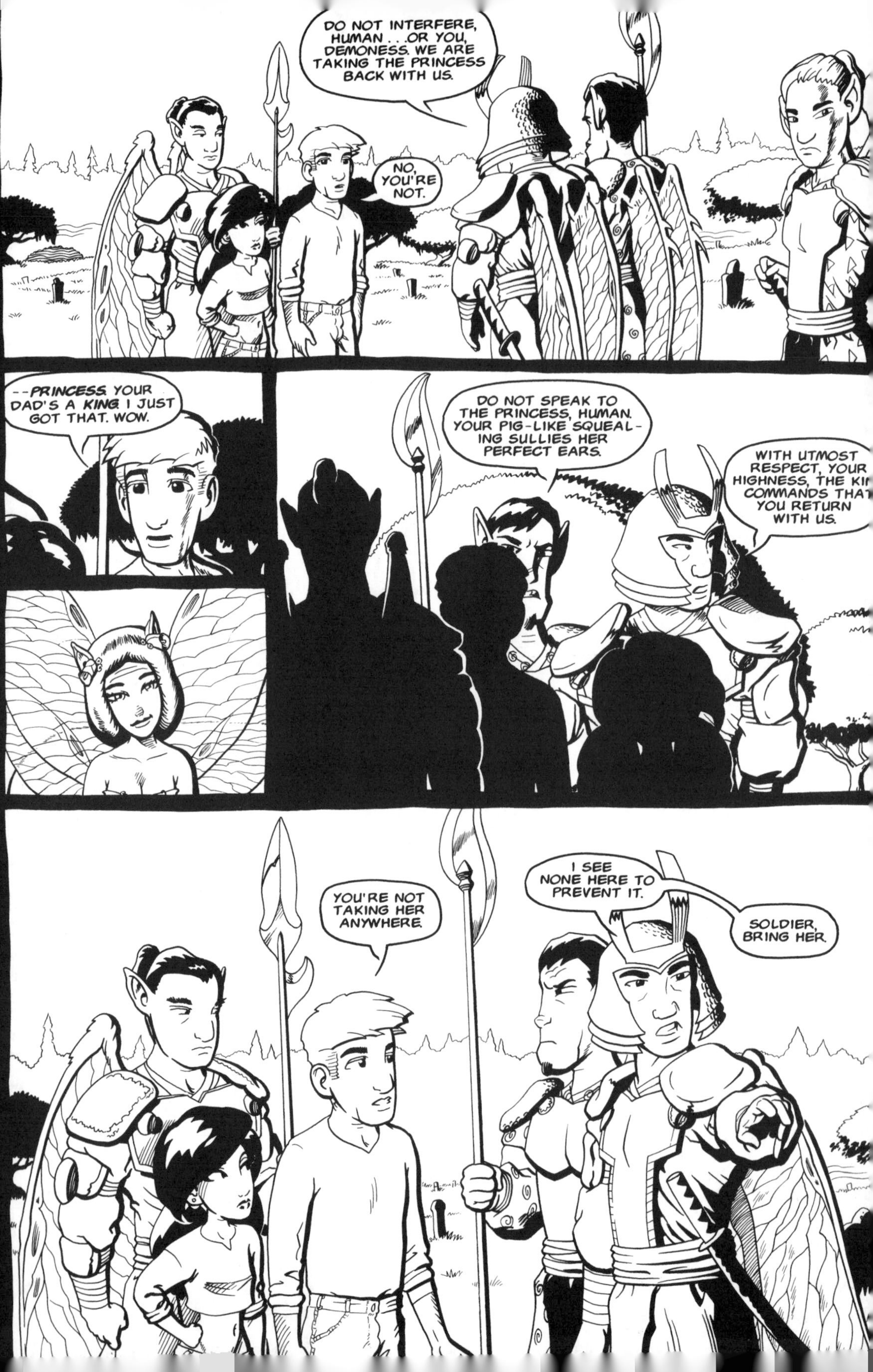
DO NOT INTERFERE, HUMAN . . . OR YOU, DEMONESS. WE ARE TAKING THE PRINCESS BACK WITH US.
NO, YOU'RE NOT.
--PRINCESS. YOUR DAD'S A KING. I JUST GOT THAT. WOW.
DO NOT SPEAK TO THE PRINCESS, HUMAN. YOUR PIG-LIKE SQUEALING SULLIES HER PERFECT EARS.
WITH UTMOST RESPECT, YOUR HIGHNESS, THE KI COMMANDS THAT YOU RETURN WITH US.
YOU'RE NOT TAKING HER ANYWHERE.
I SEE NONE HERE TO PREVENT IT.
SOLDIER, BRING HER.

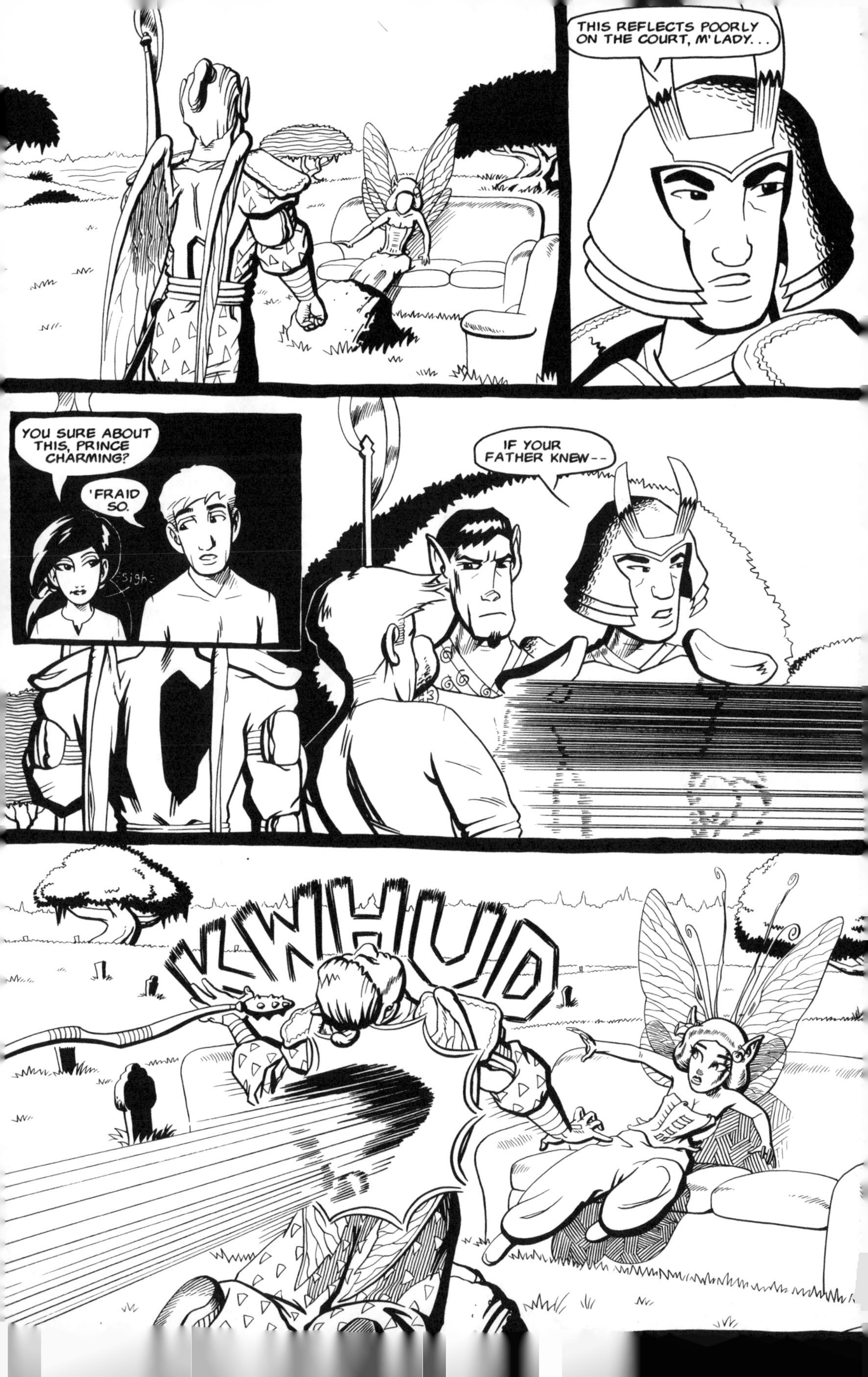
THIS REFLECTS POORLY ON THE COURT, M' LADY...
YOU SURE ABOUT THIS, PRINCE CHARMING?
'FRAID SO.
SIGH
IF YOUR FATHER KNEW--
KWHUD

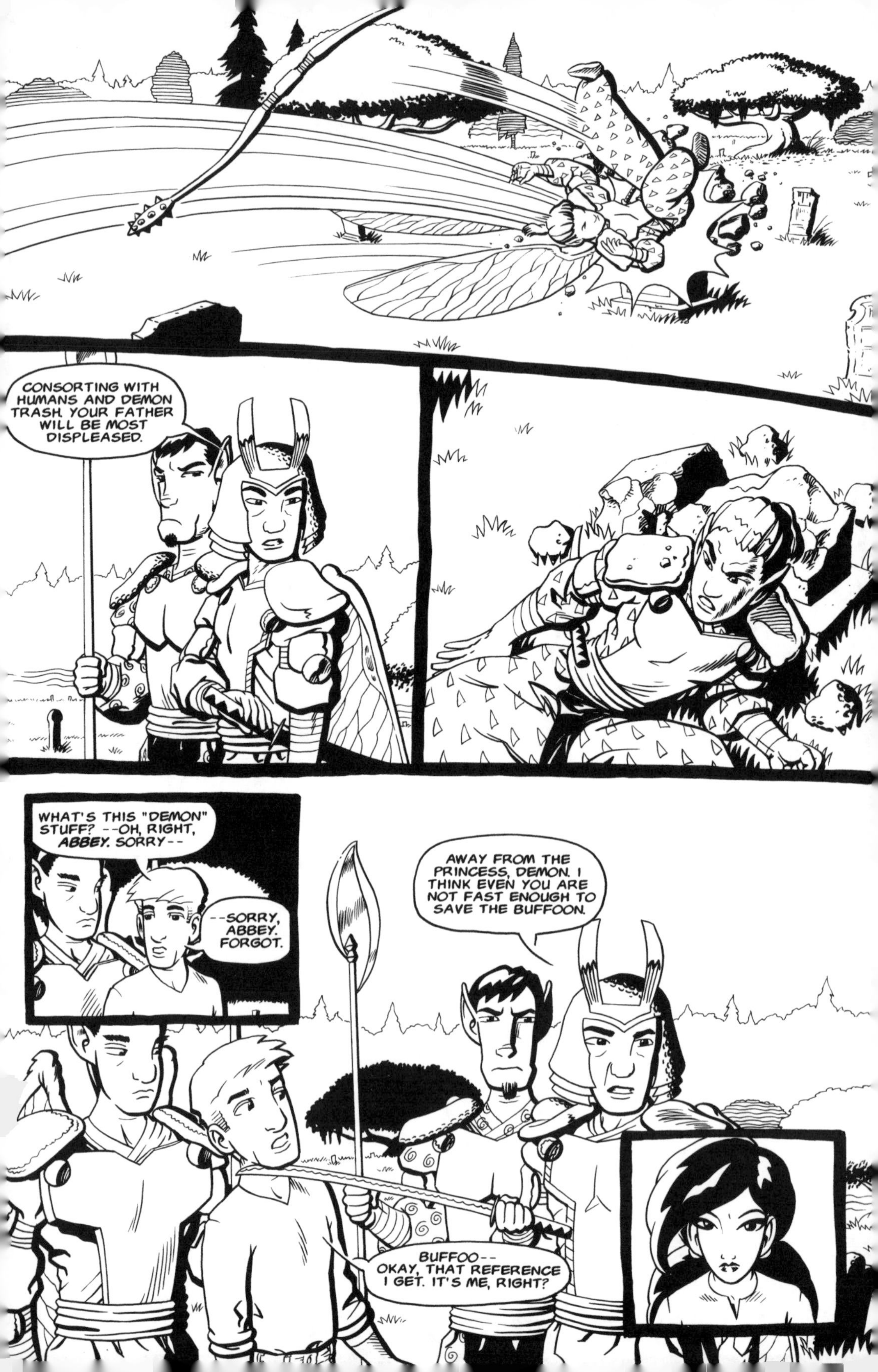
CONSORTING WITH HUMANS AND DEMON TRASH. YOUR FATHER WILL BE MOST DISPLEASED.
WHAT'S THIS "DEMON" STUFF? --OH, RIGHT, ABBEY. SORRY--
--SORRY, ABBEY. FORGOT.
AWAY FROM THE PRINCESS, DEMON. I THINK EVEN YOU ARE NOT FAST ENOUGH TO SAVE THE BUFFOON.
BUFFOO-- OKAY, THAT REFERENCE I GET. IT'S ME, RIGHT?

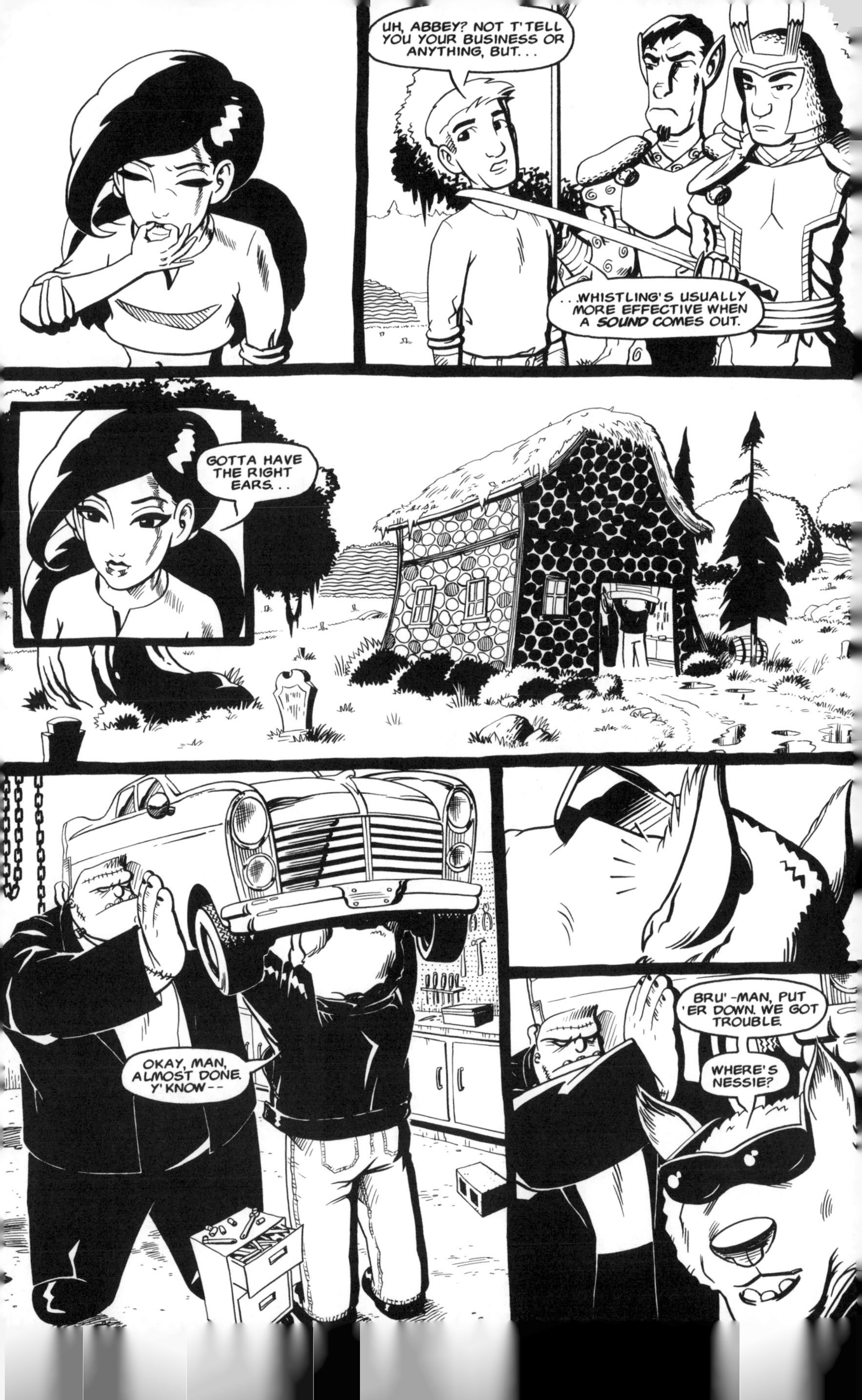
UH, ABBEY? NOT T'TELL YOU YOUR BUSINESS OR ANYTHING, BUT...
...WHISTLING'S USUALLY MORE EFFECTIVE WHEN A SOUND COMES OUT.
GOTTA HAVE THE RIGHT EARS...
OKAY, MAN, ALMOST DONE. Y'KNOW--
BRU'-MAN, PUT 'ER DOWN. WE GOT TROUBLE.
WHERE'S NESSIE?

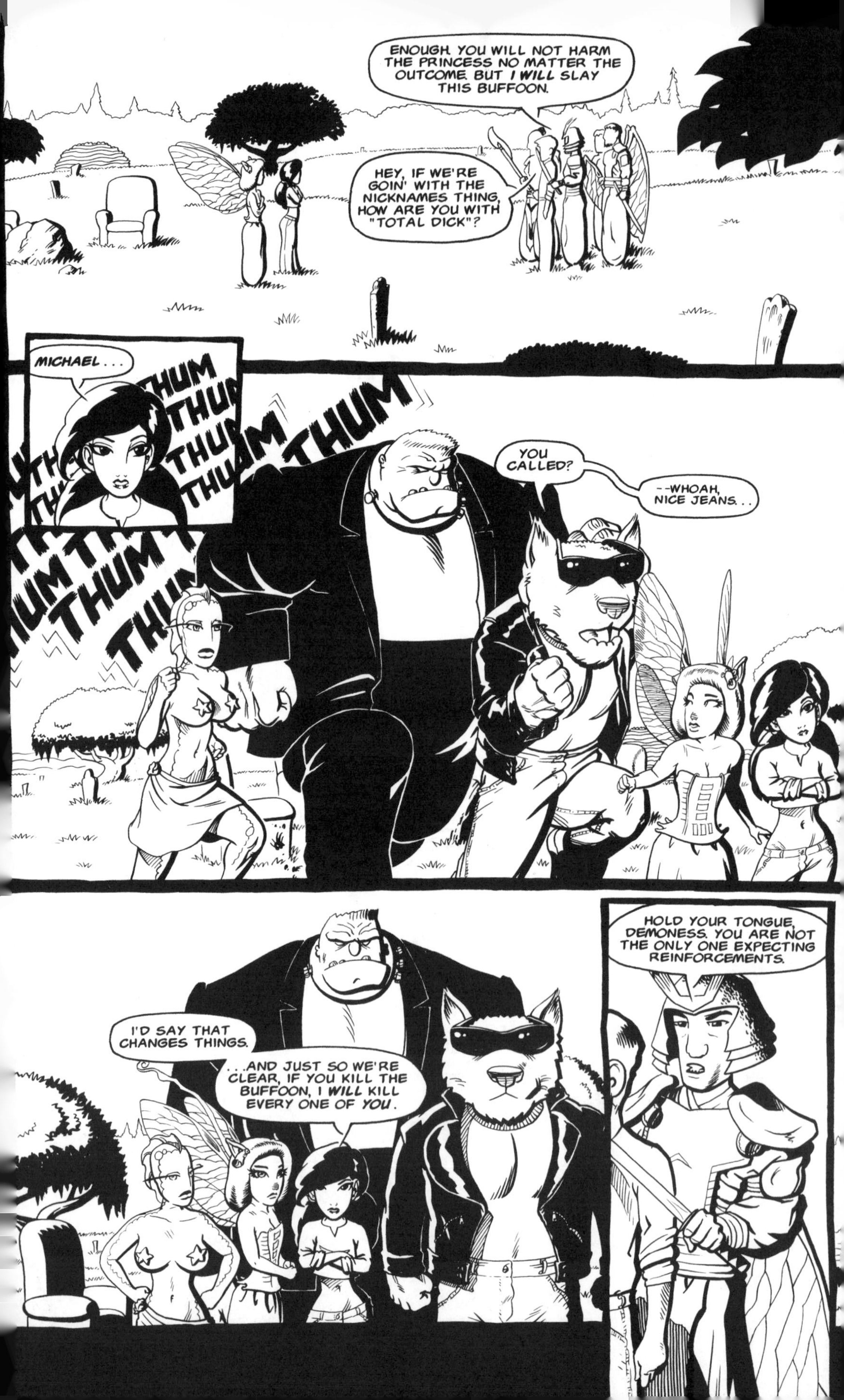

ENOUGH. YOU WILL NOT HARM THE PRINCESS NO MATTER THE OUTCOME. BUT I WILL SLAY THIS BUFFOON.
HEY, IF WE'RE GOIN' WITH THE NICKNAMES THING, HOW ARE YOU WITH "TOTAL DICK"?
MICHAEL . . .
THUM THUM THUM THUM THUM THUM THUM THUM
YOU CALLED?
--WHOAH, NICE JEANS . . .
HOLD YOUR TONGUE, DEMONESS. YOU ARE NOT THE ONLY ONE EXPECTING REINFORCEMENTS.
I'D SAY THAT CHANGES THINGS.
. . .AND JUST SO WE'RE CLEAR, IF YOU KILL THE BUFFOON, I WILL KILL EVERY ONE OF YOU.

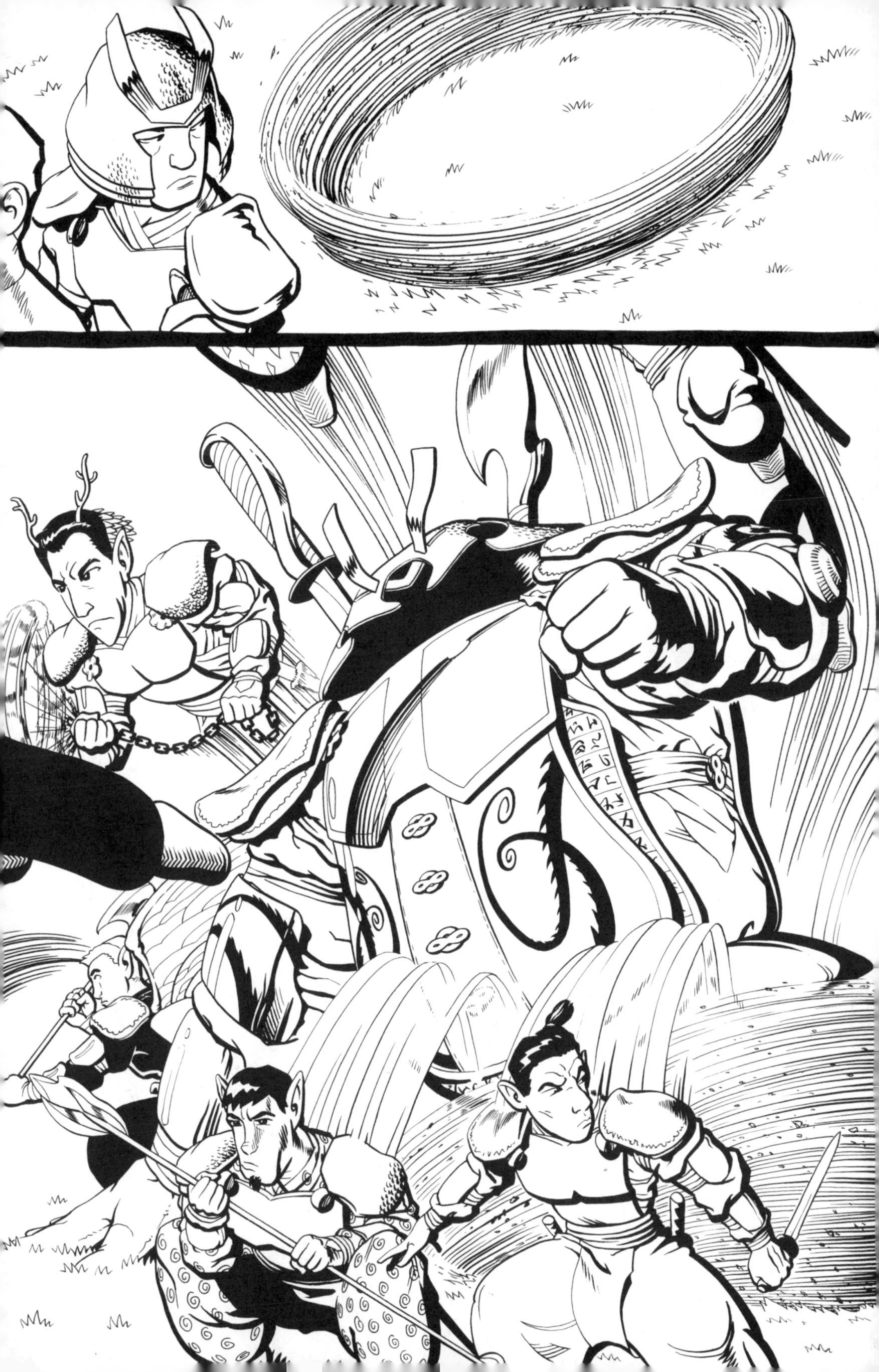

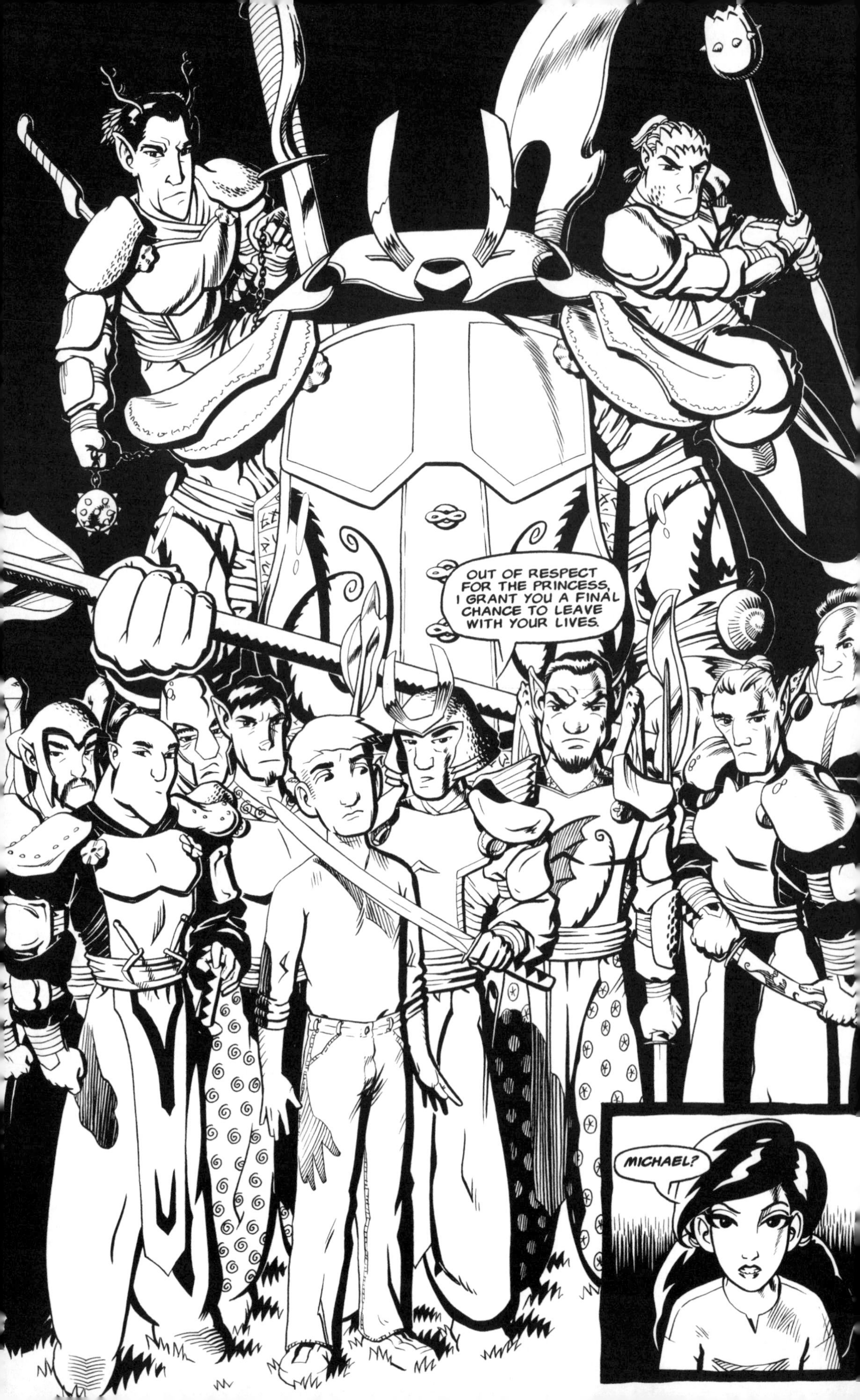
OUT OF RESPECT FOR THE PRINCESS, I GRANT YOU A FINAL CHANCE TO LEAVE WITH YOUR LIVES.
MICHAEL?

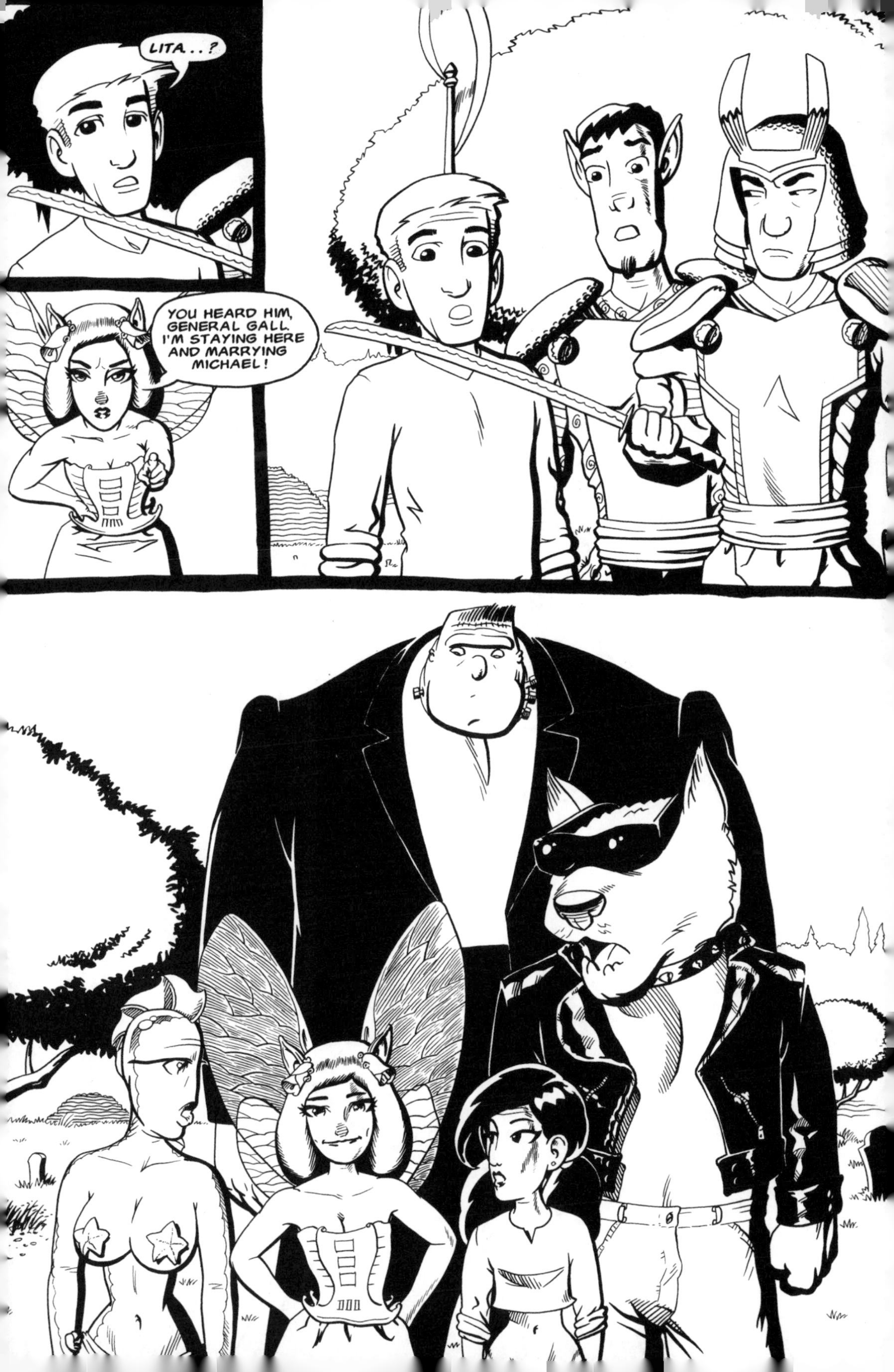
LITA...?
YOU HEARD HIM, GENERAL GALL. I'M STAYING HERE AND MARRYING MICHAEL!

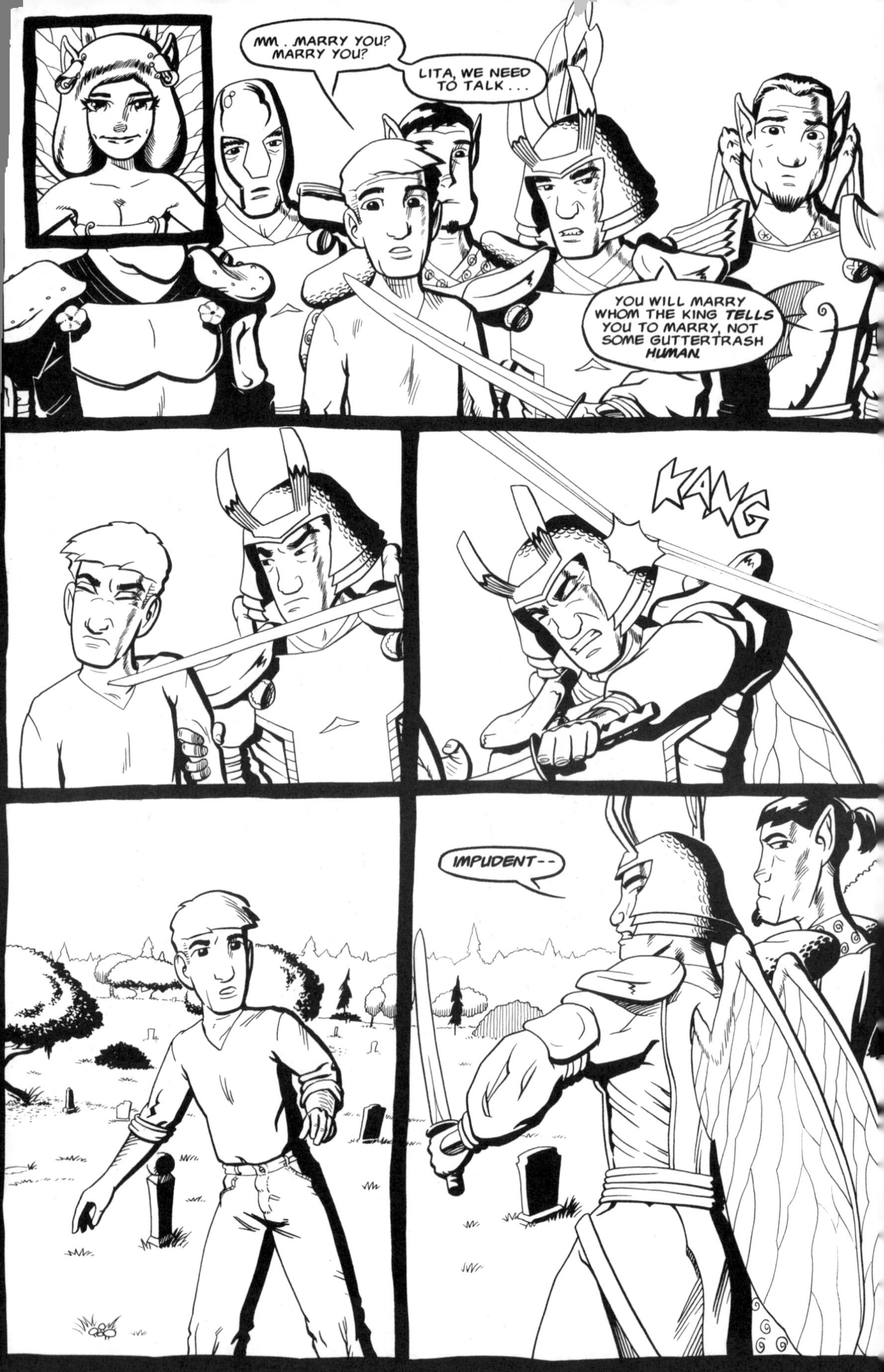
MM . MARRY YOU? MARRY YOU?
LITA, WE NEED TO TALK . . .
YOU WILL MARRY WHOM THE KING TELLS YOU TO MARRY, NOT SOME GUTTERTRASH HUMAN.
KANG
IMPUDENT--

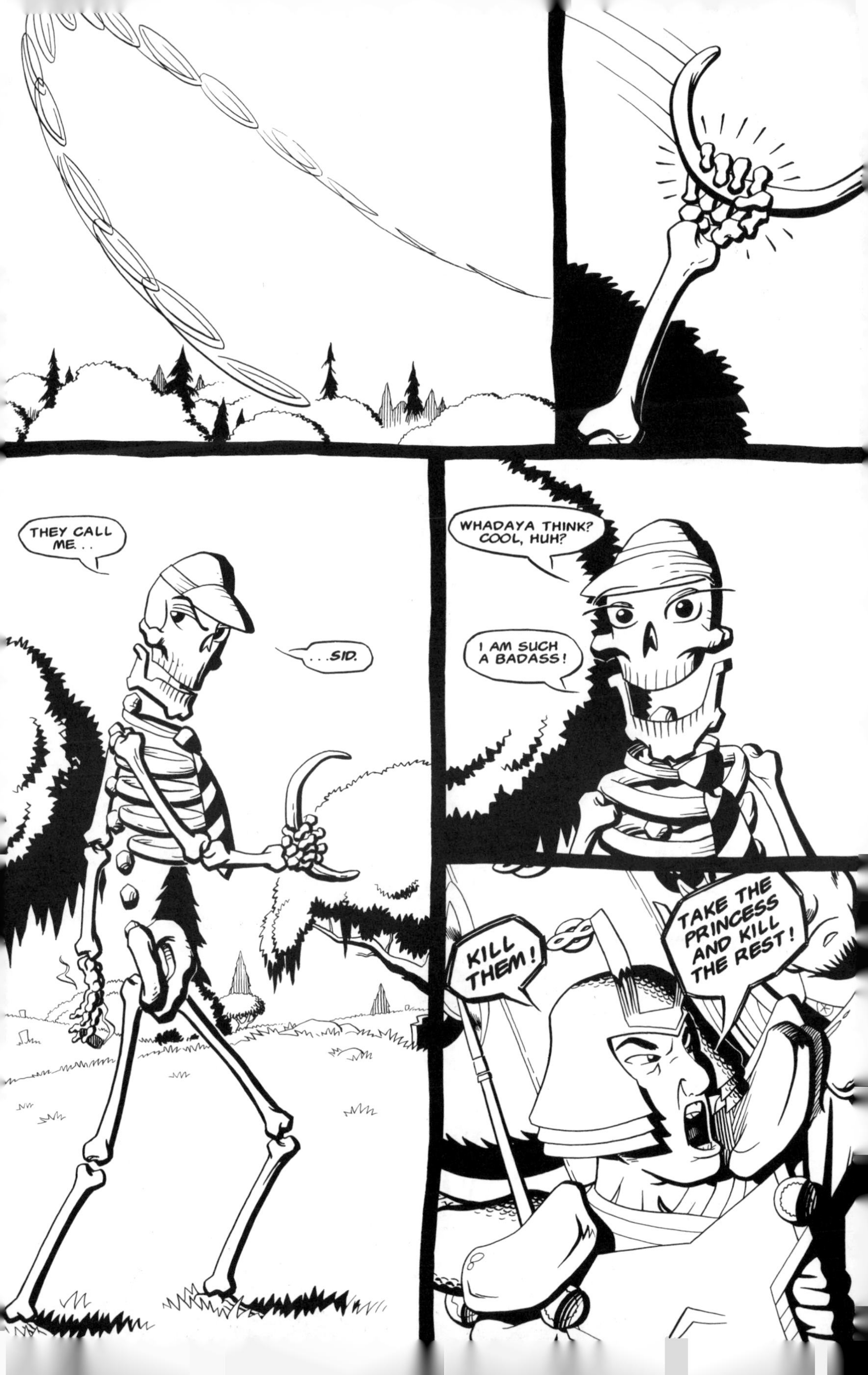
THEY CALL ME...
...SID.
WHADAYA THINK? COOL, HUH?
I AM SUCH A BADASS!
KILL THEM!
TAKE THE PRINCESS AND KILL THE REST!

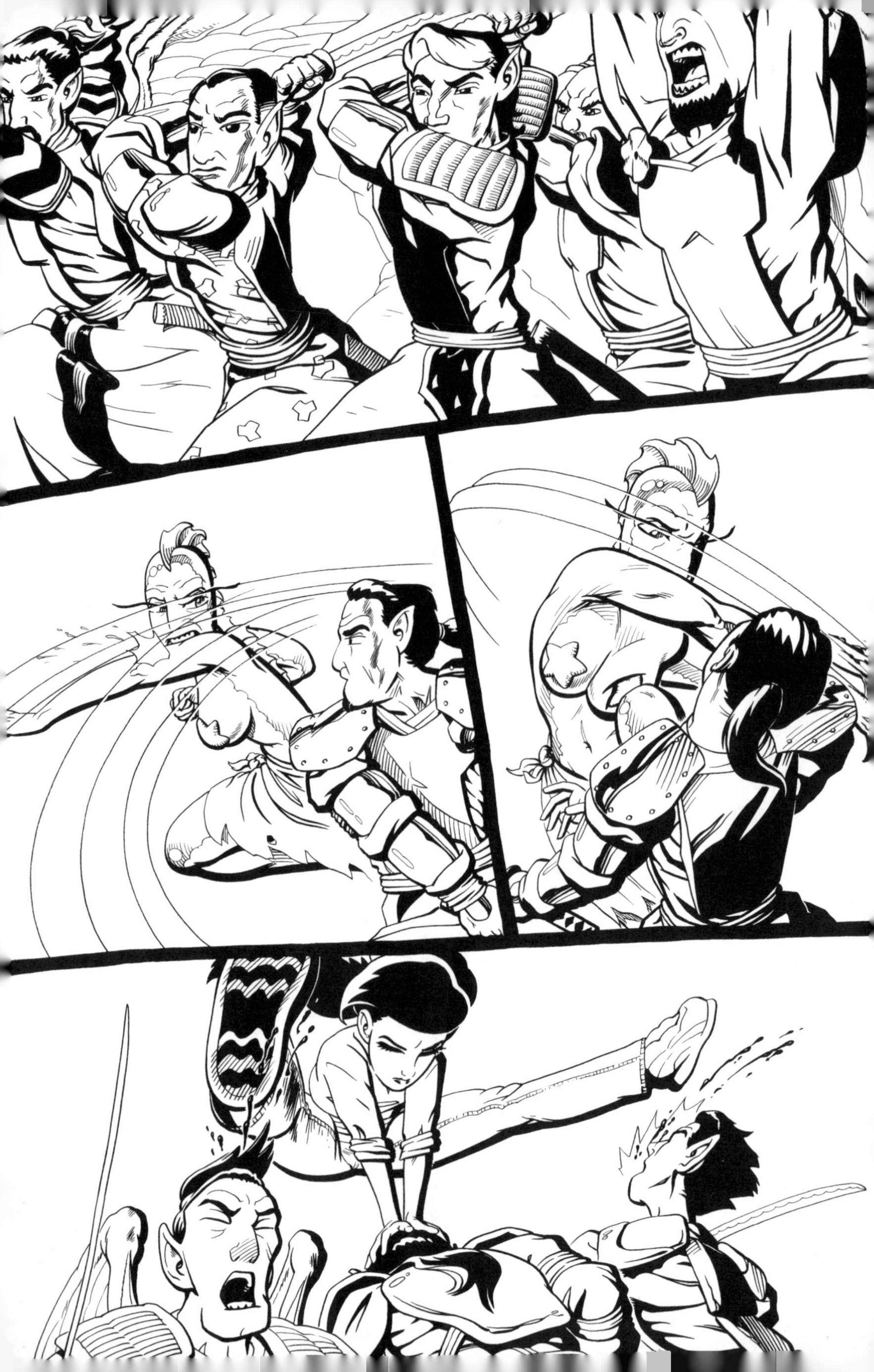

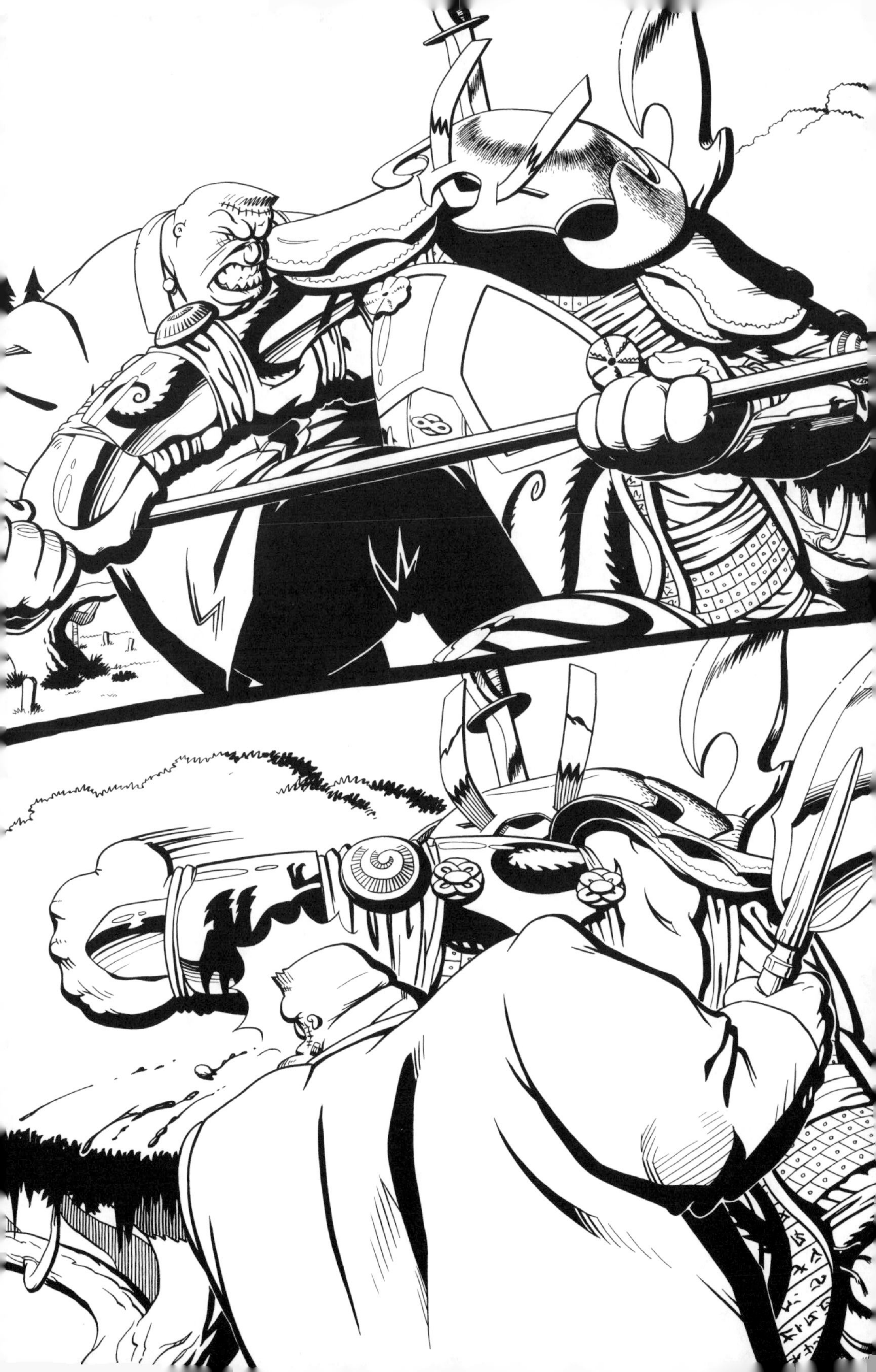

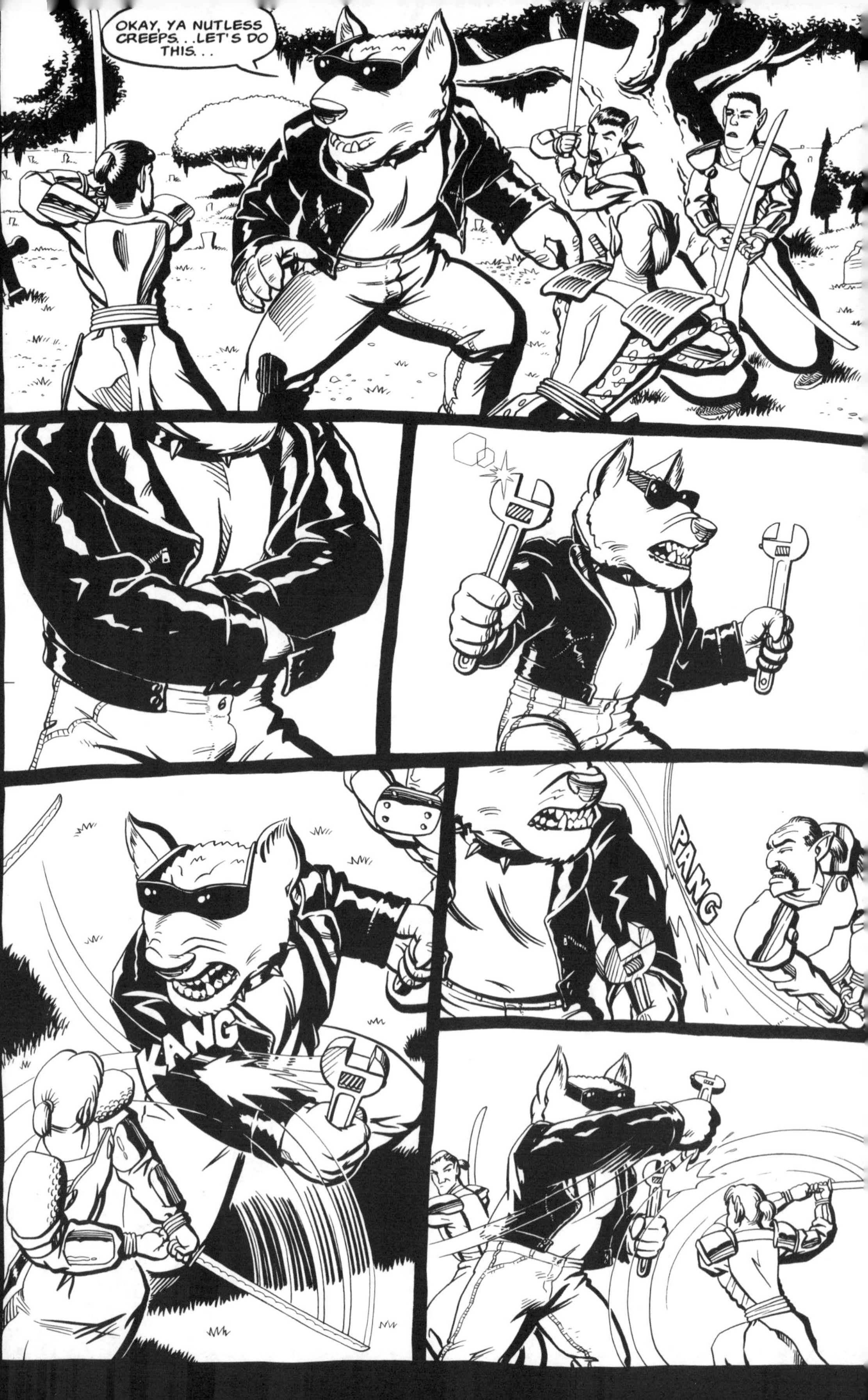
OKAY, YA NUTLESS CREEPS. . .LET'S DO THIS. . .
PANG
KANG

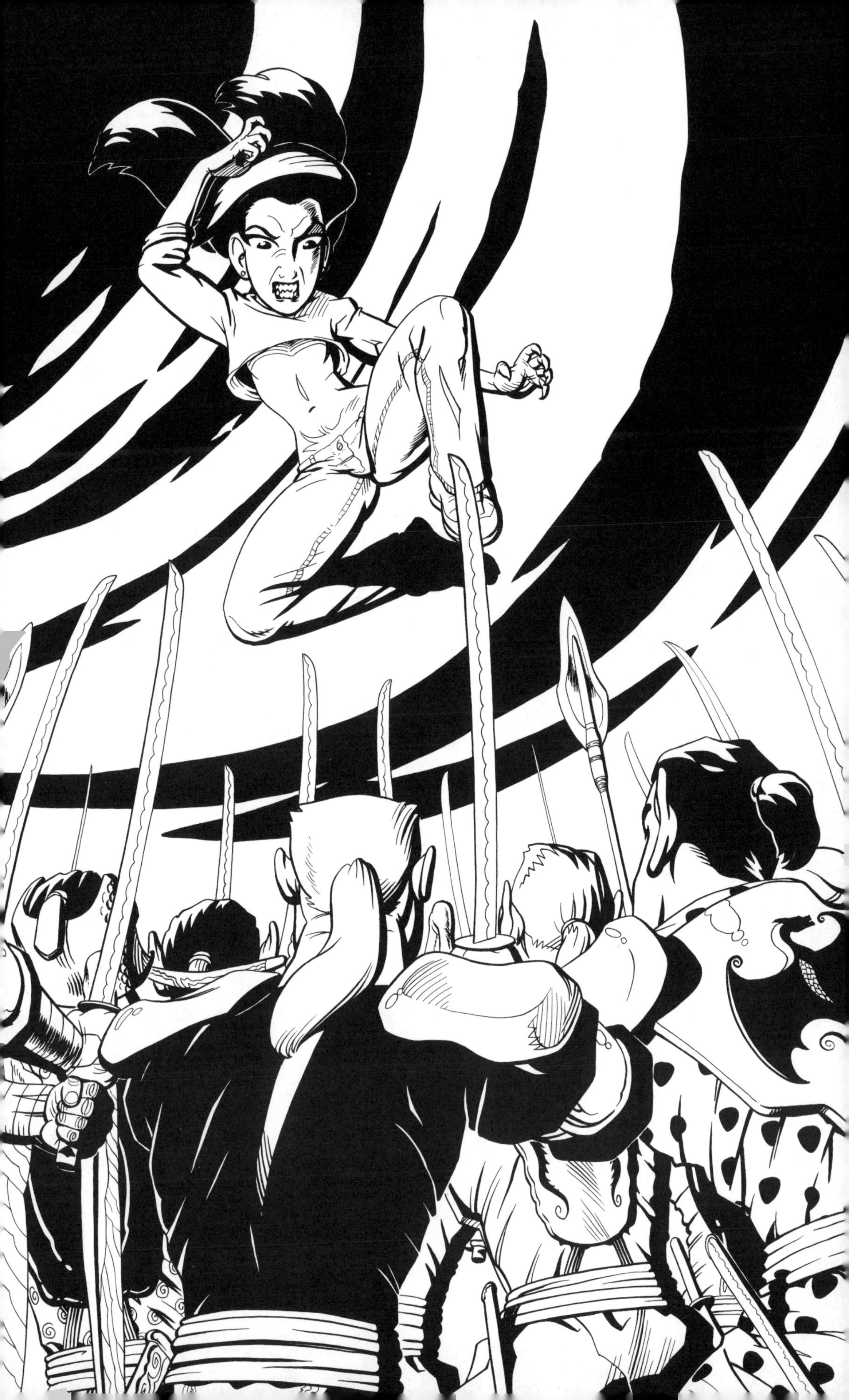

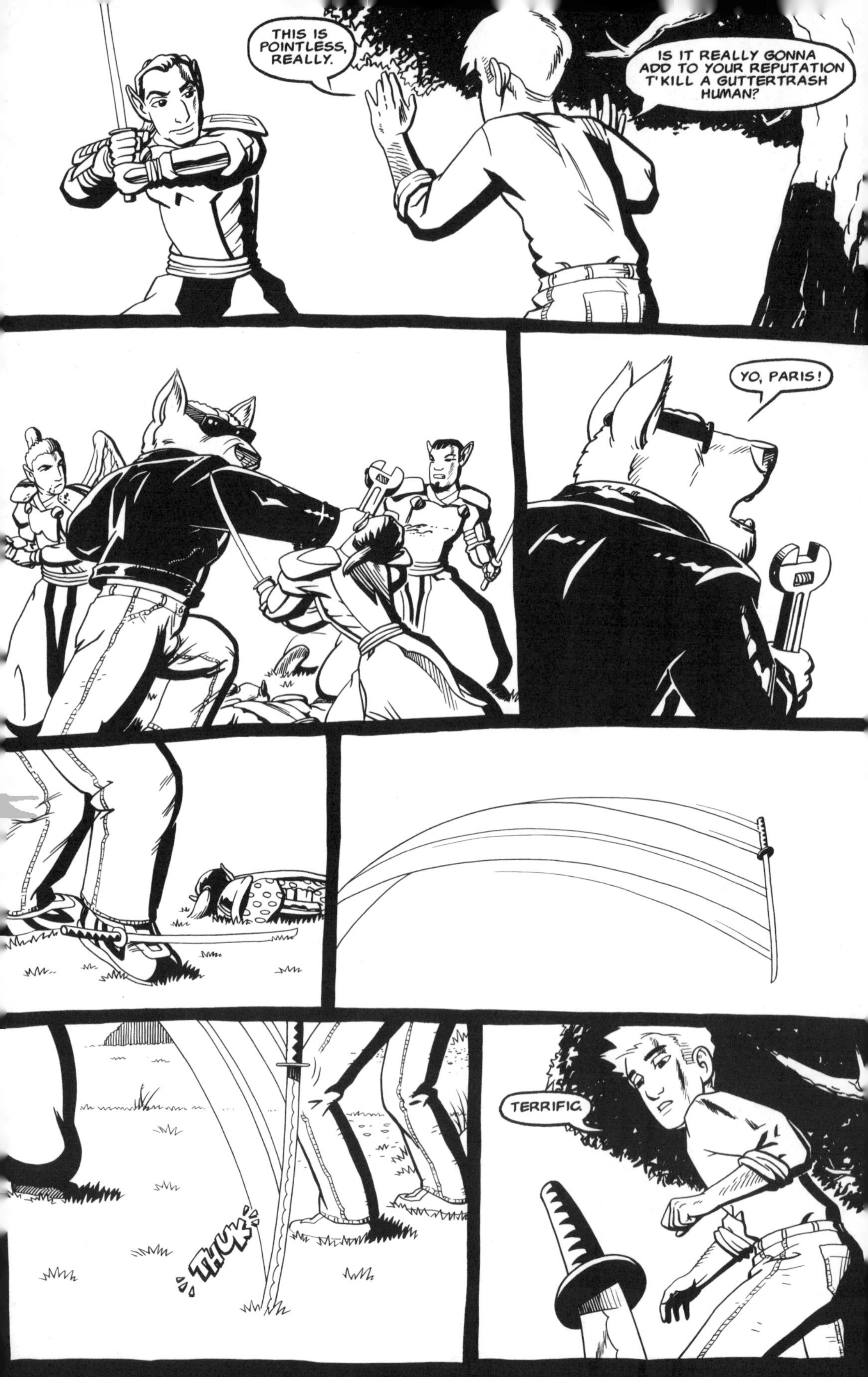
THIS IS POINTLESS, REALLY.
IS IT REALLY GONNA ADD TO YOUR REPUTATION T'KILL A GUTTERTRASH HUMAN?
YO, PARIS!
THUK
TERRIFIC.

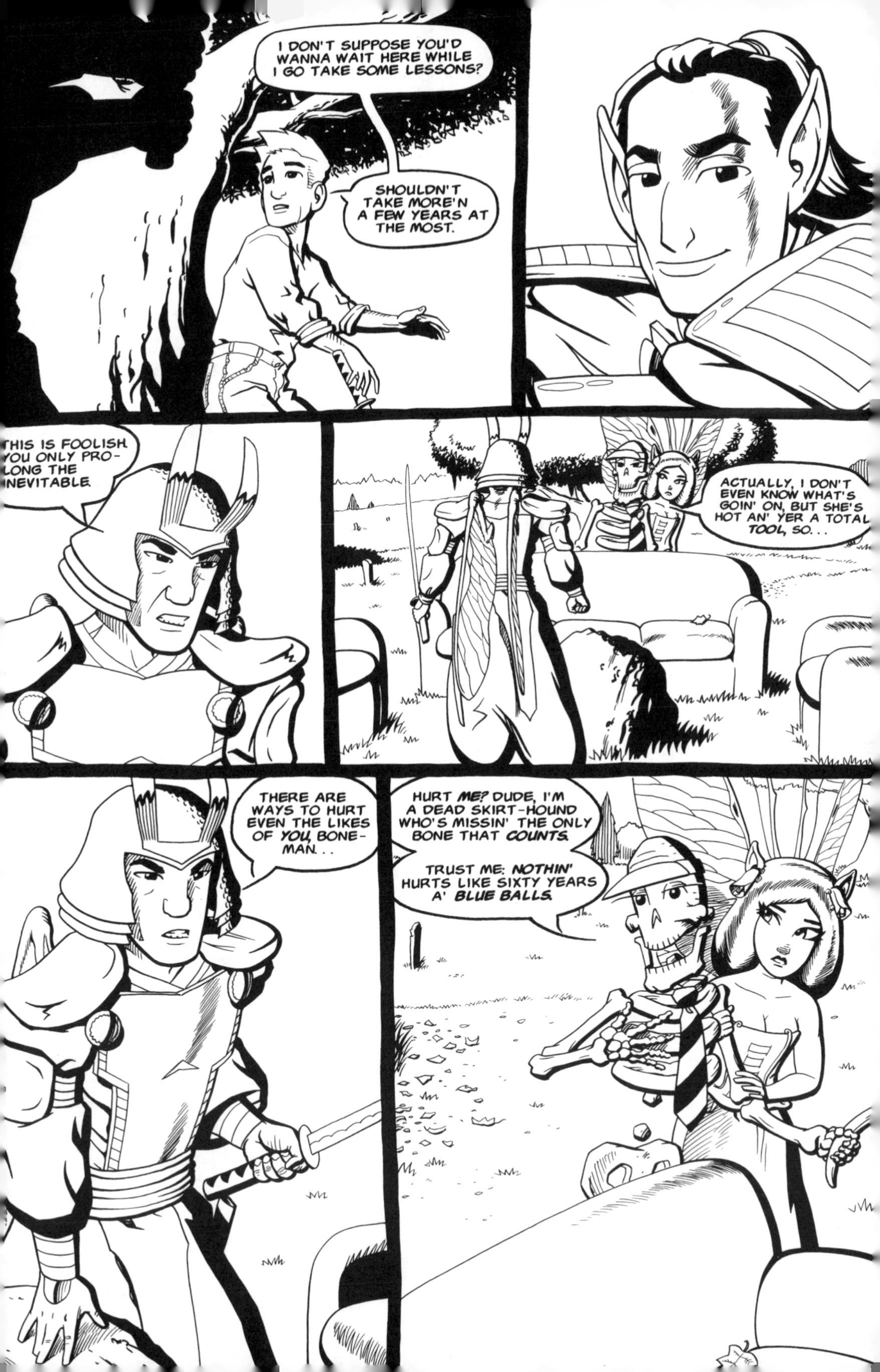
I DON'T SUPPOSE YOU'D WANNA WAIT HERE WHILE I GO TAKE SOME LESSONS?
SHOULDN'T TAKE MORE'N A FEW YEARS AT THE MOST.
THIS IS FOOLISH. YOU ONLY PRO-LONG THE INEVITABLE.
ACTUALLY, I DON'T EVEN KNOW WHAT'S GOIN' ON, BUT SHE'S HOT AN' YER A TOTAL TOOL, SO...
THERE ARE WAYS TO HURT EVEN THE LIKES OF YOU, BONE-MAN...
HURT ME? DUDE, I'M A DEAD SKIRT-HOUND WHO'S MISSIN' THE ONLY BONE THAT COUNTS.
TRUST ME: NOTHIN' HURTS LIKE SIXTY YEARS A' BLUE BALLS.

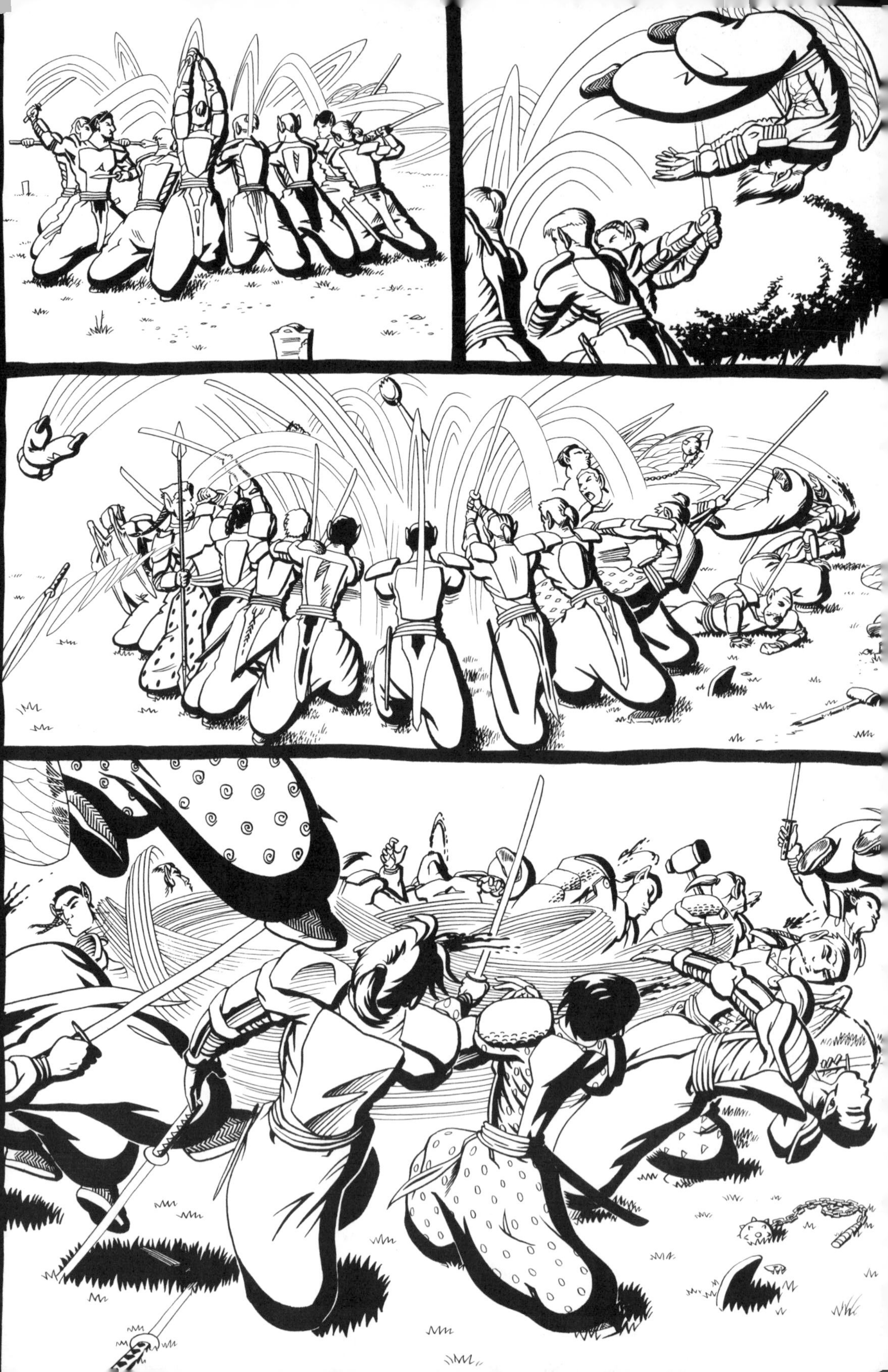

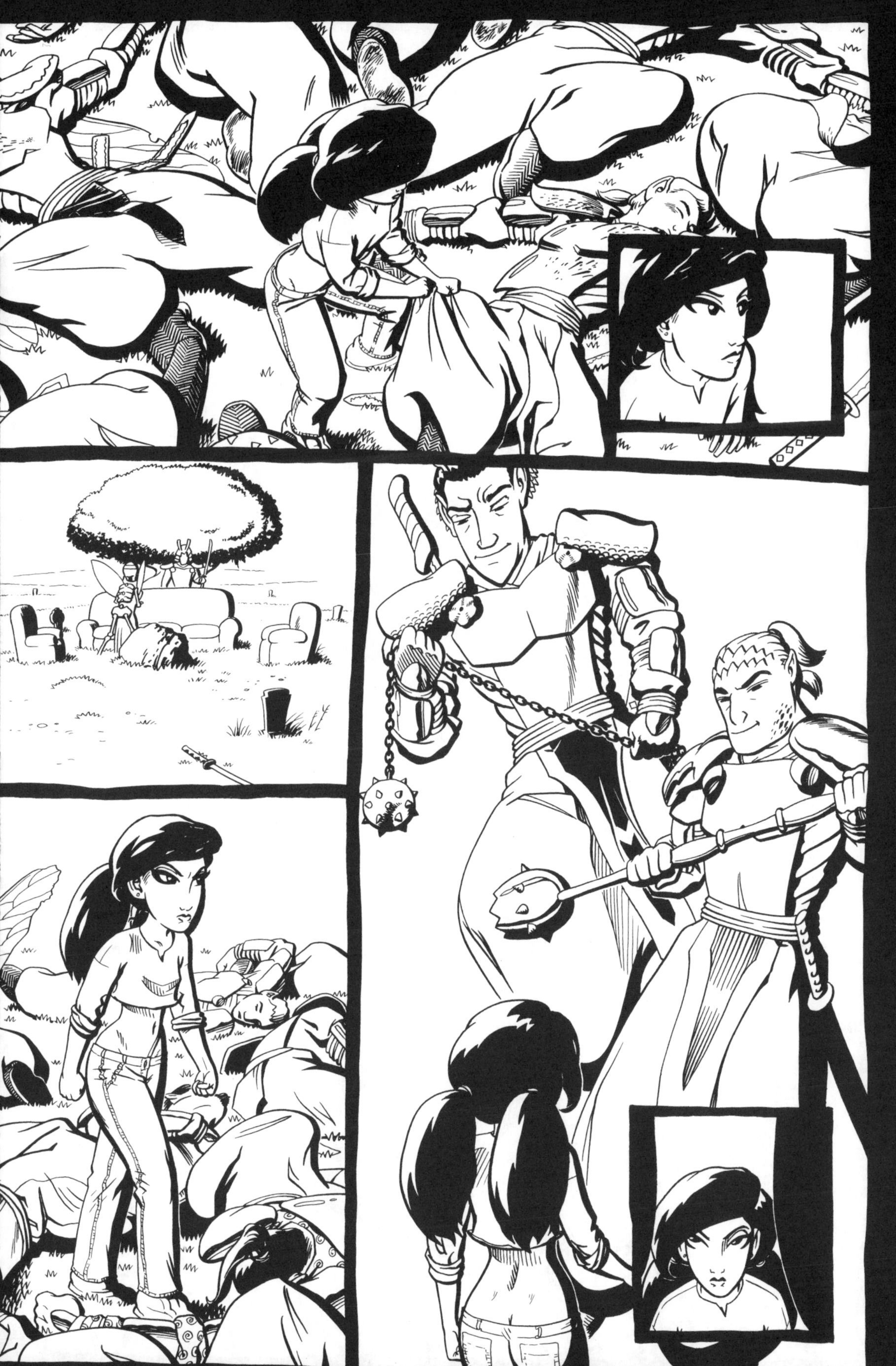

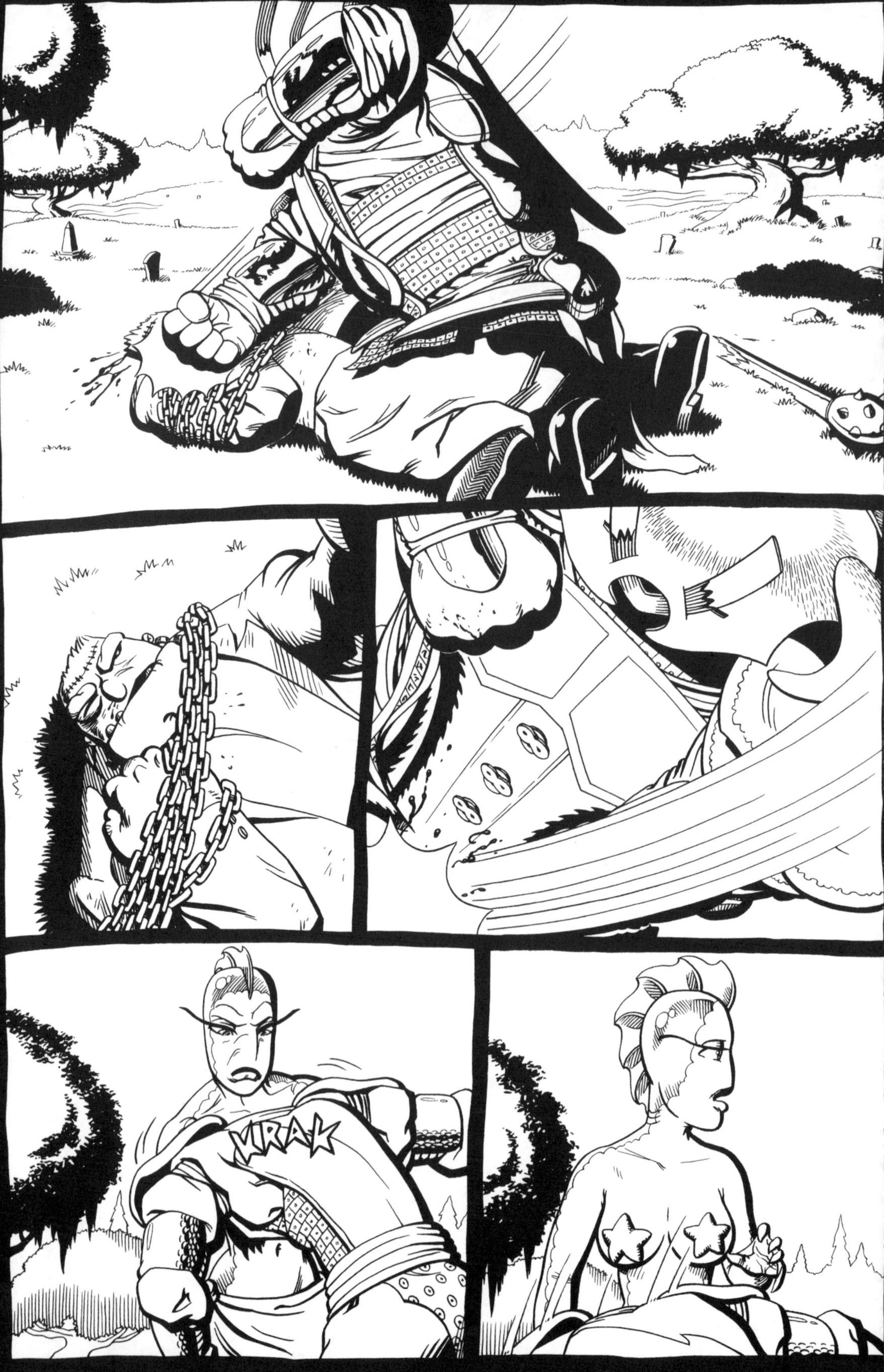
VRAK

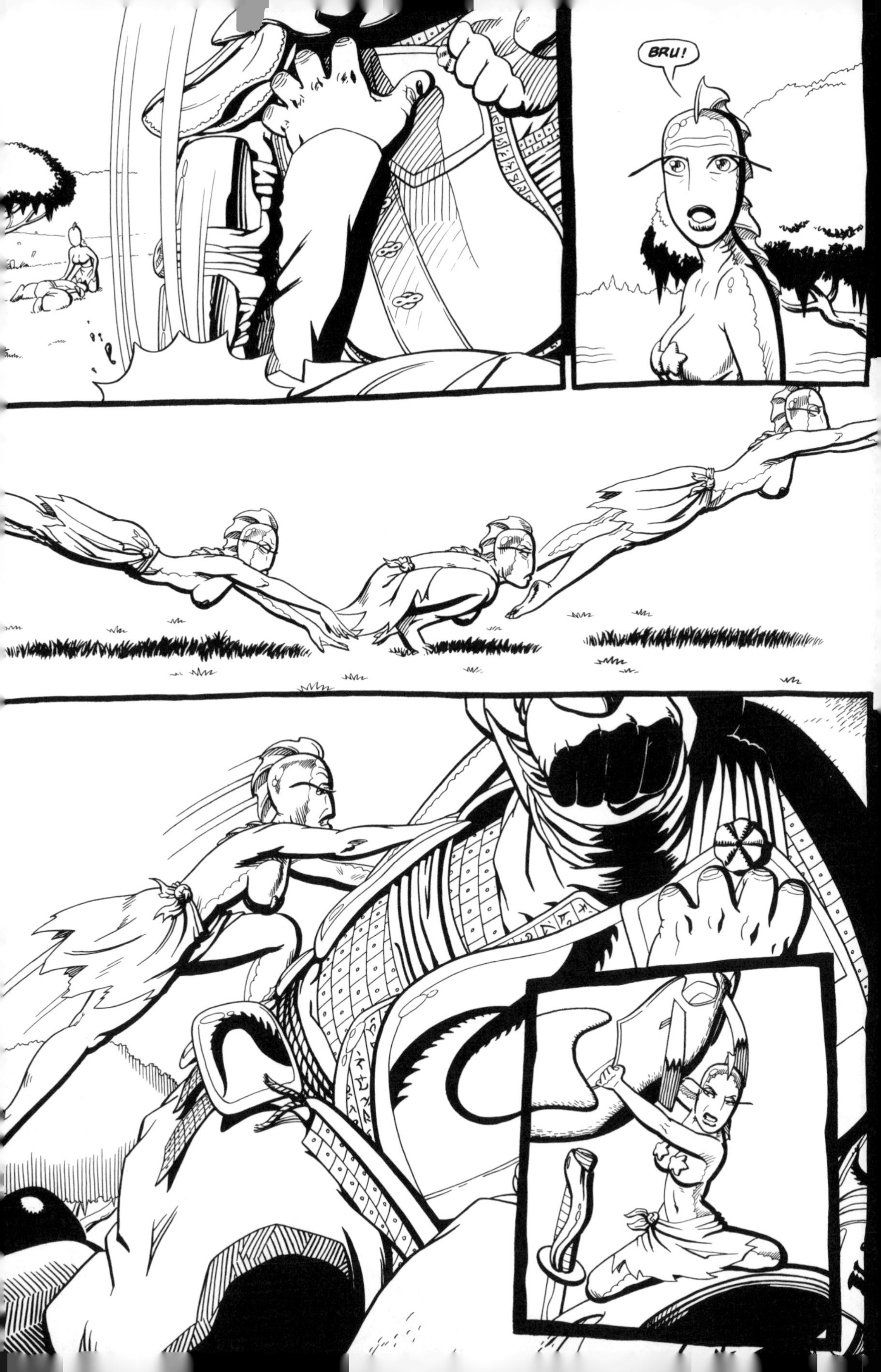
BRU!

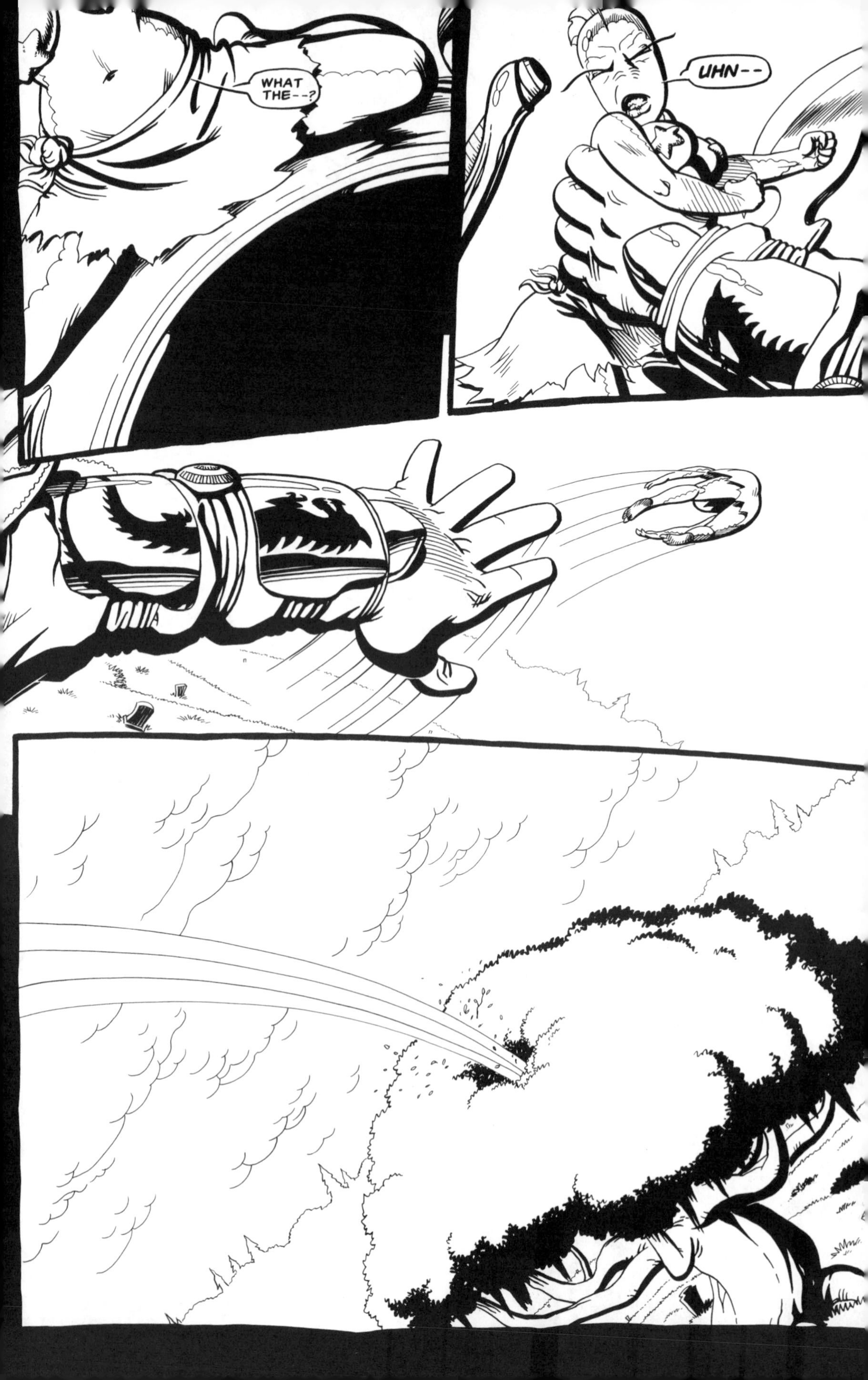
WHAT THE--?
UHN--

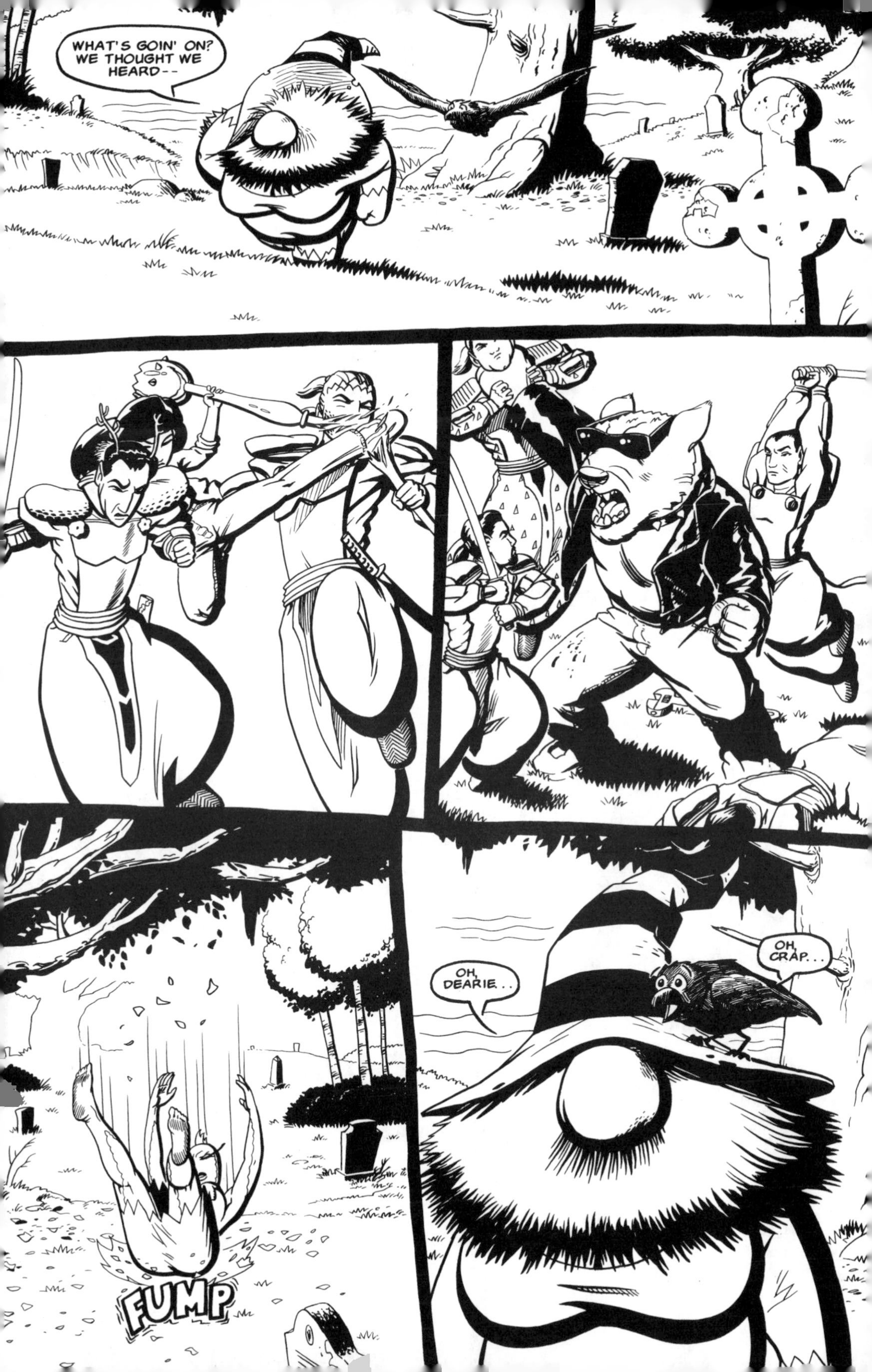
WHAT'S GOIN' ON? WE THOUGHT WE HEARD--
FUMP
OH, DEARIE..
OH, CRAP...

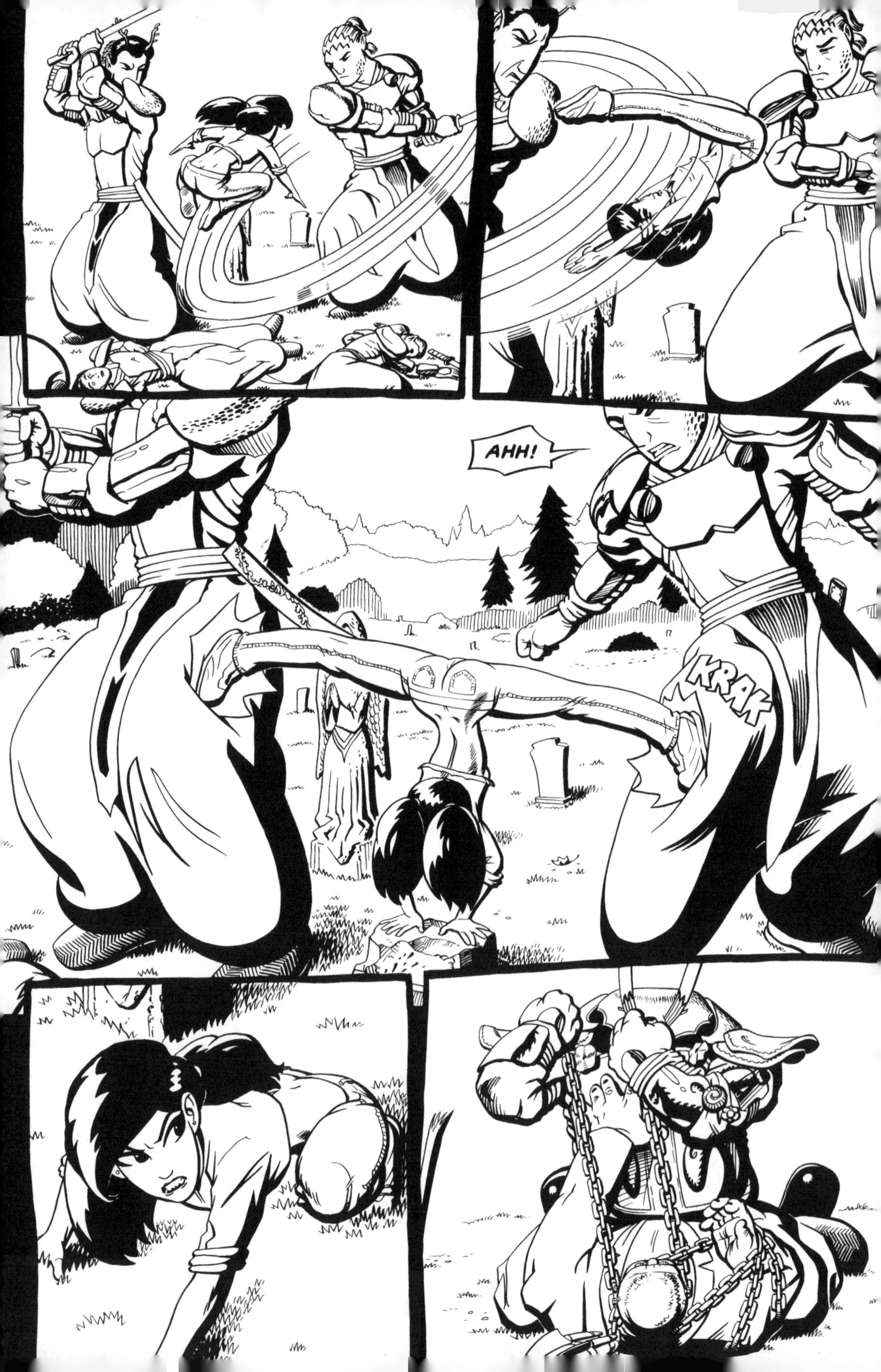
AHH!
KRAK

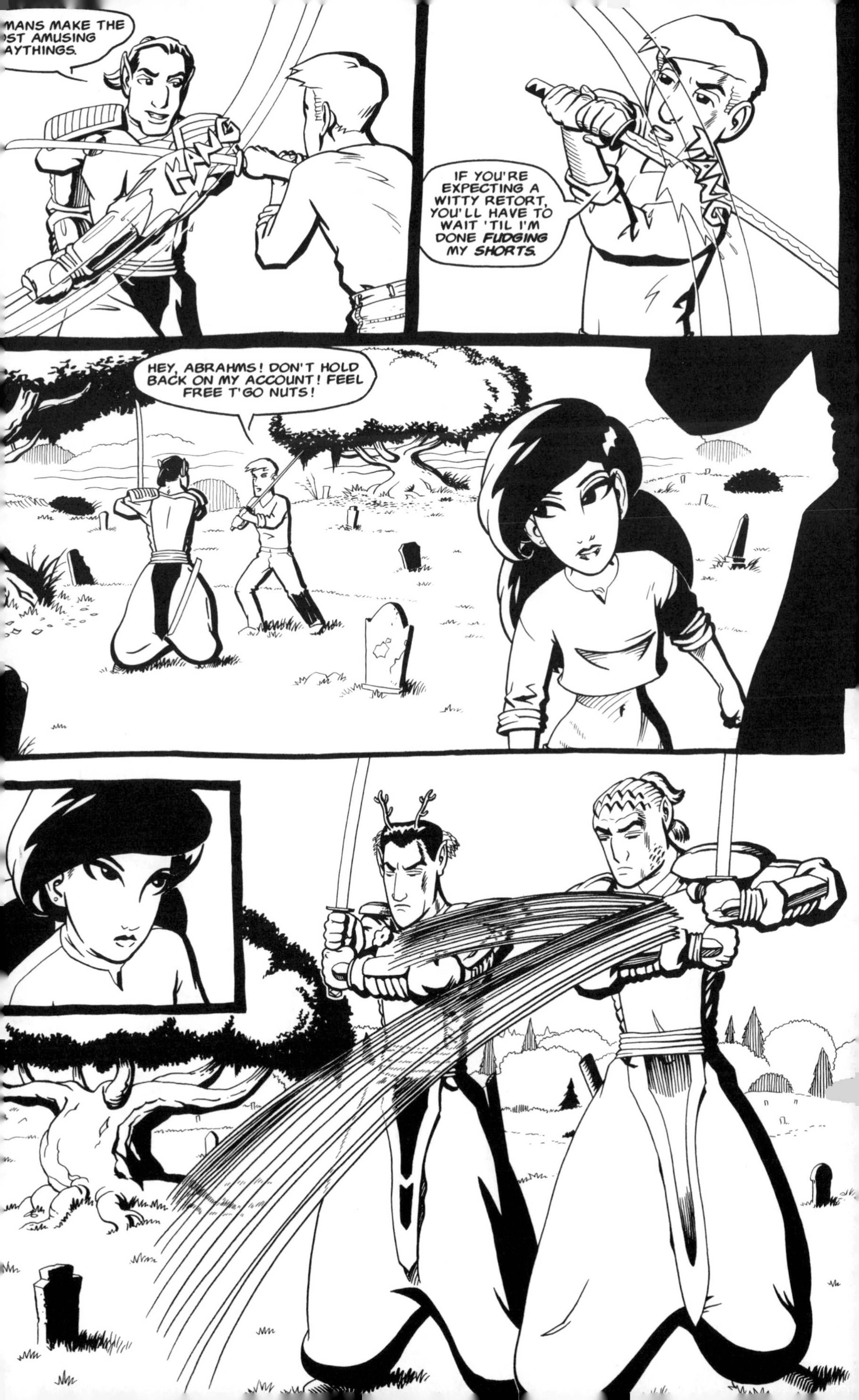

MANS MAKE THE
OST AMUSING
AYTHINGS.
IF YOU'RE EXPECTING A WITTY RETORT, YOU'LL HAVE TO WAIT 'TIL I'M DONE *FUDGING* MY *SHORTS.*
HEY, ABRAHMS! DON'T HOLD BACK ON MY ACCOUNT! FEEL FREE T'GO NUTS!

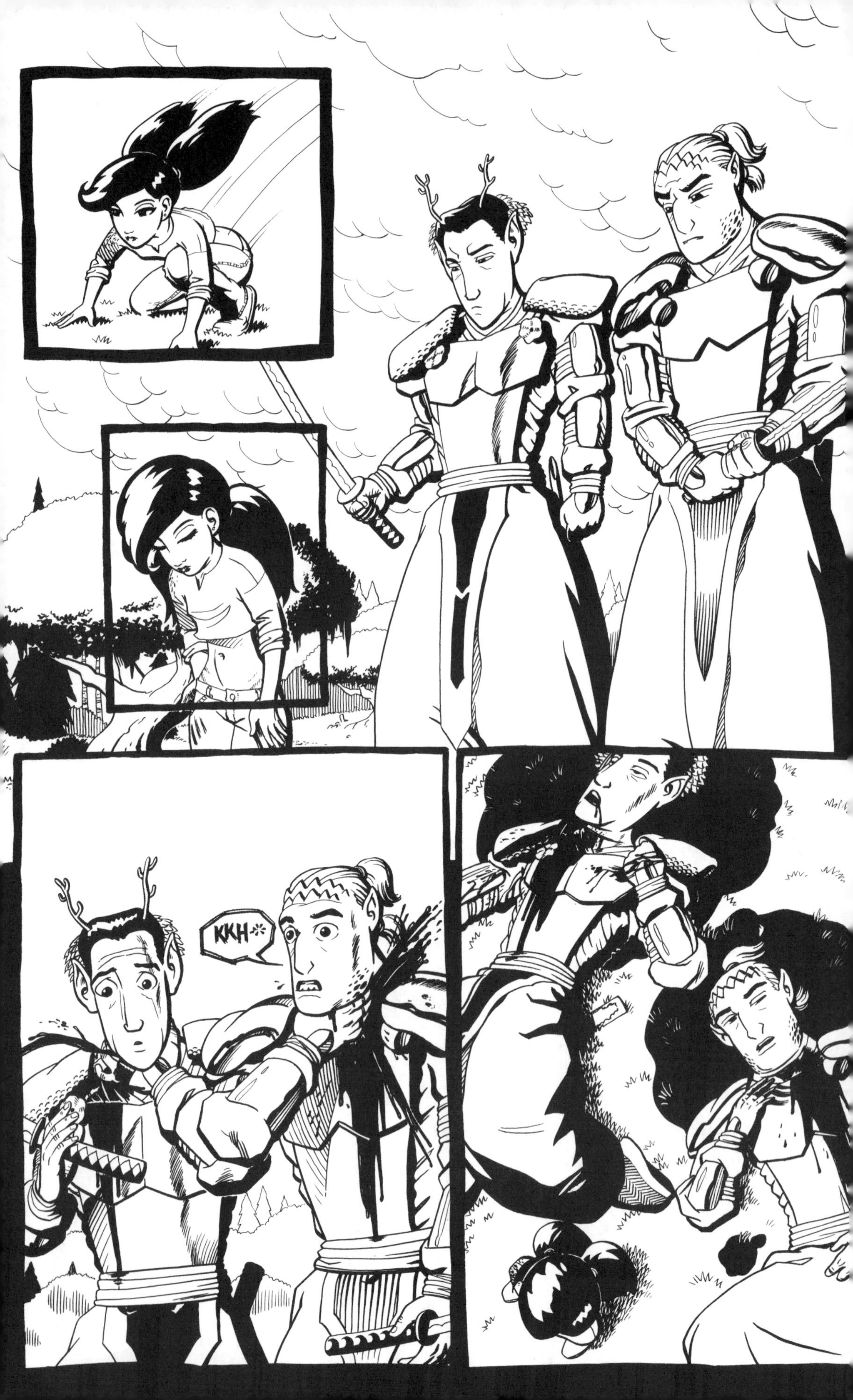
KKH-

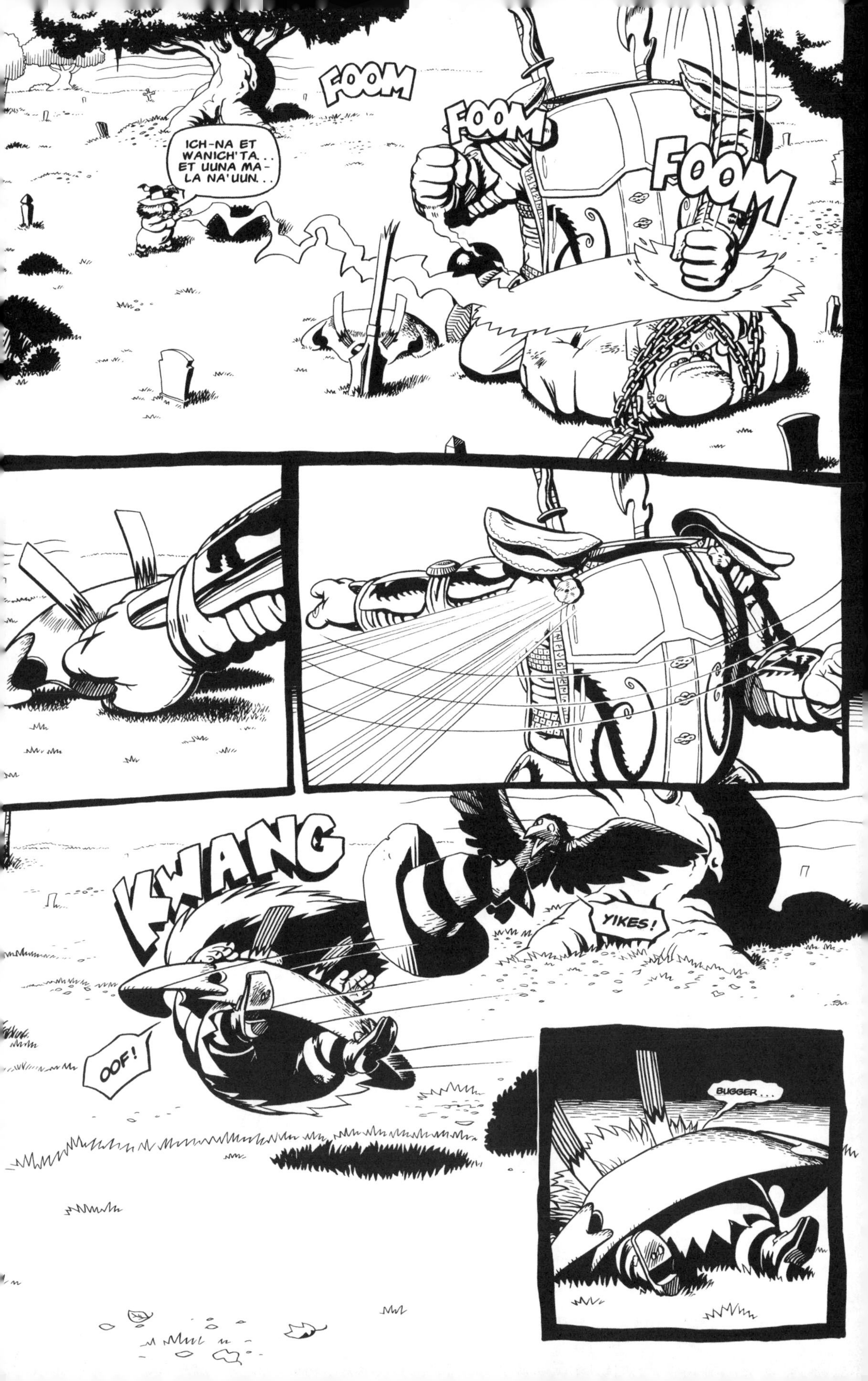
FOOM
FOOM
ICH-NA ET WANICH'TA... ET UUNA MA-LA NA'UUN...
FOOM
KWANG
YIKES!
OOF!
BUGGER...

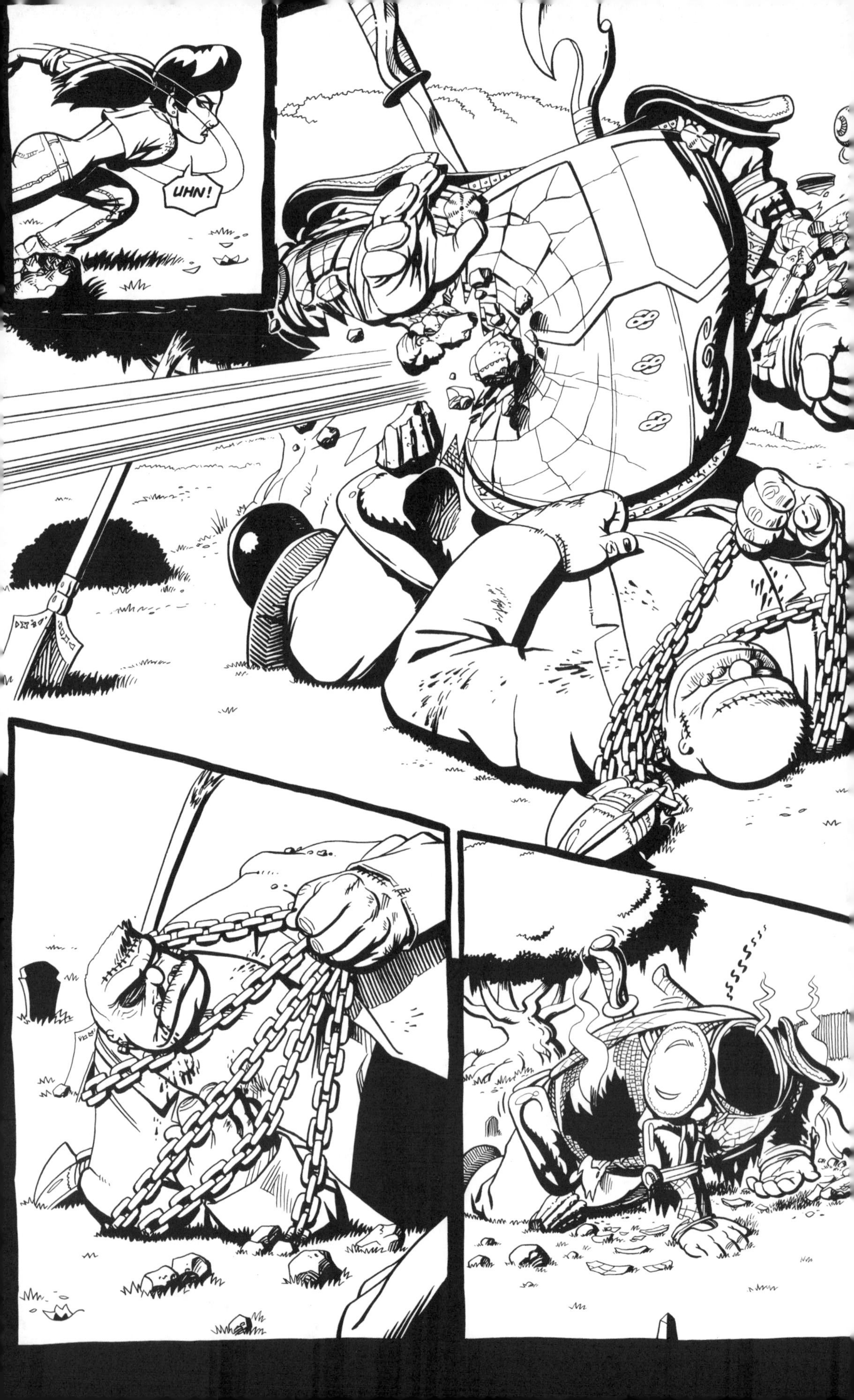
UHN!
SSSSSSS

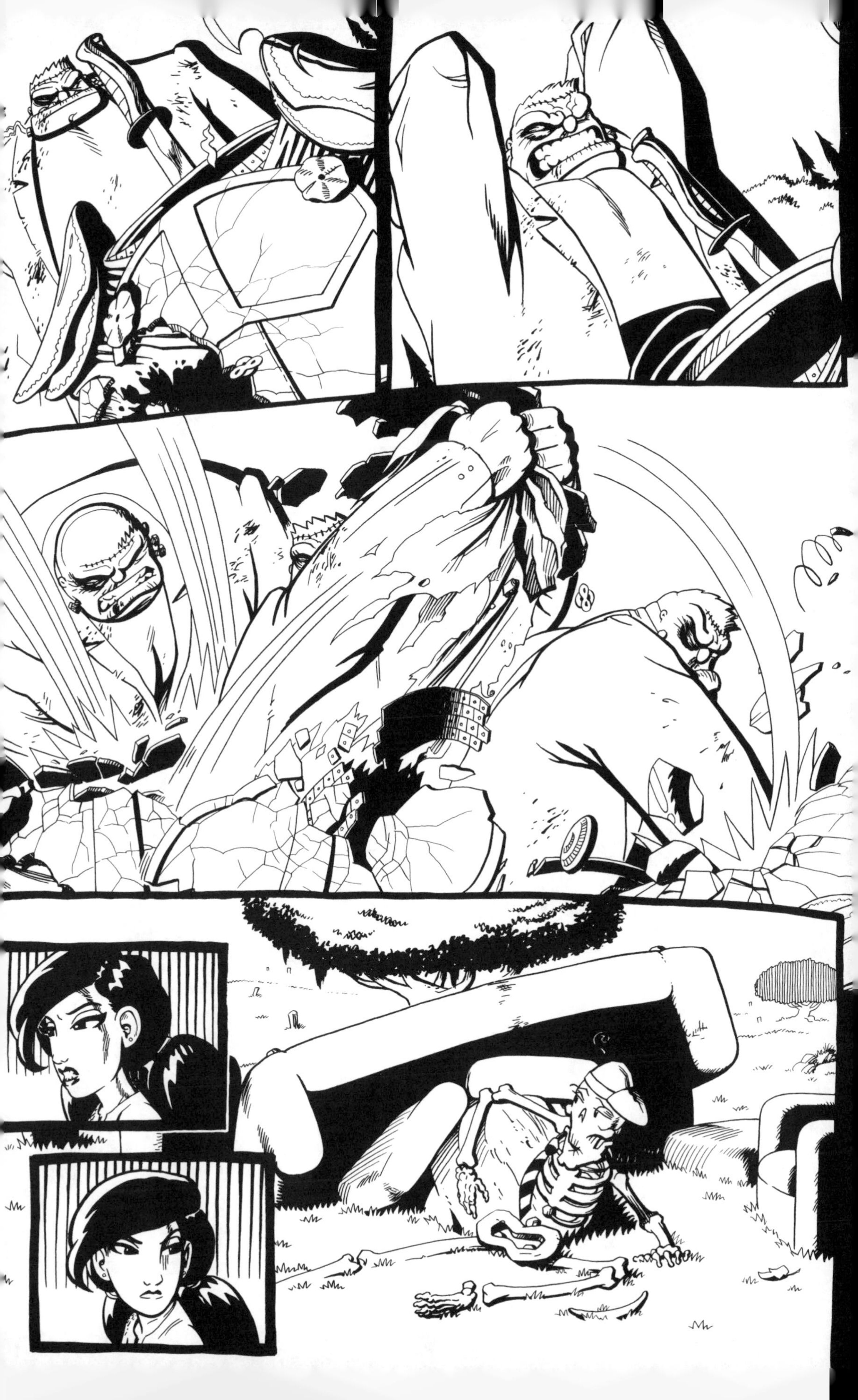

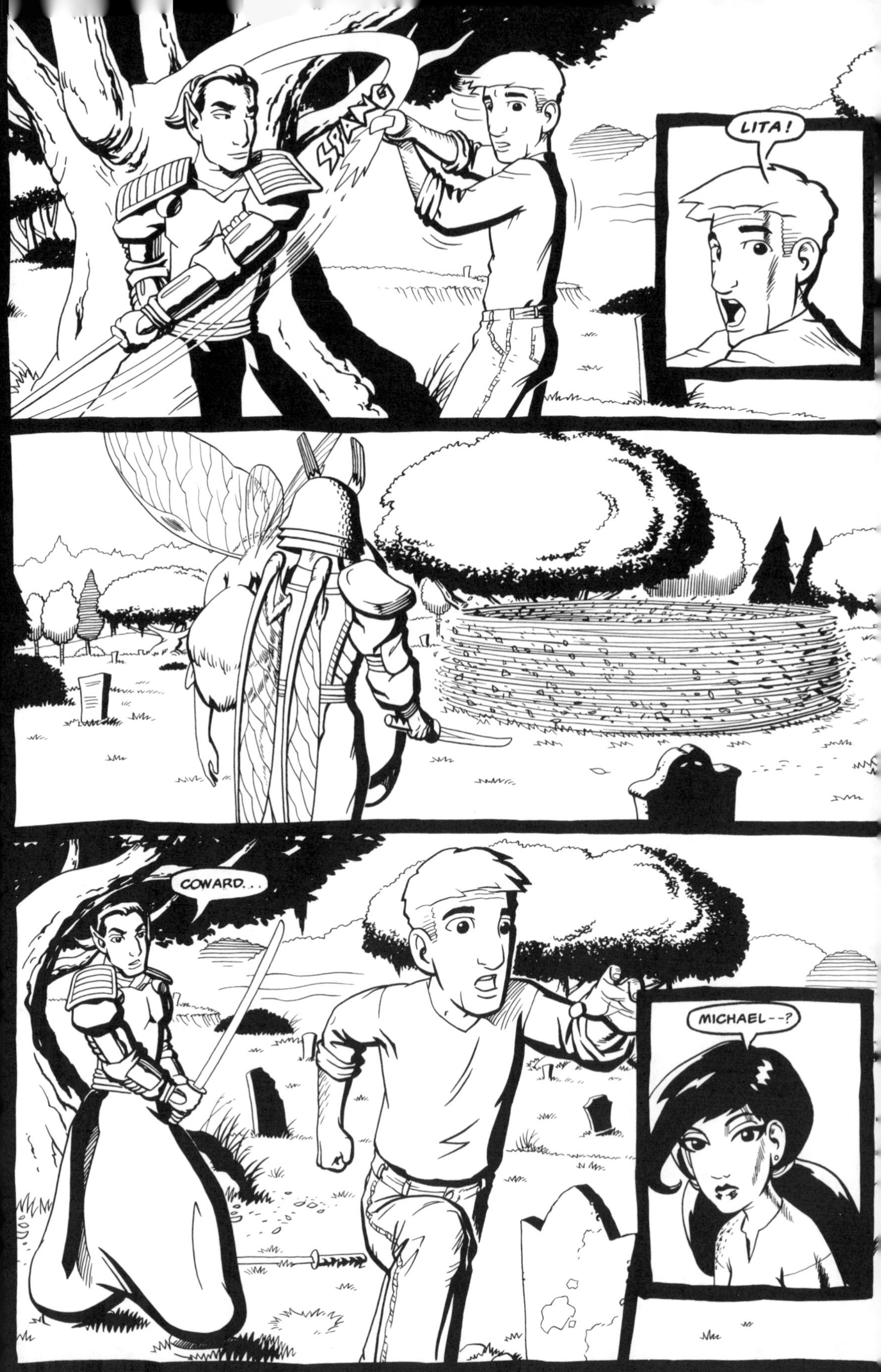
SPANG
LITA!
COWARD...
MICHAEL--?

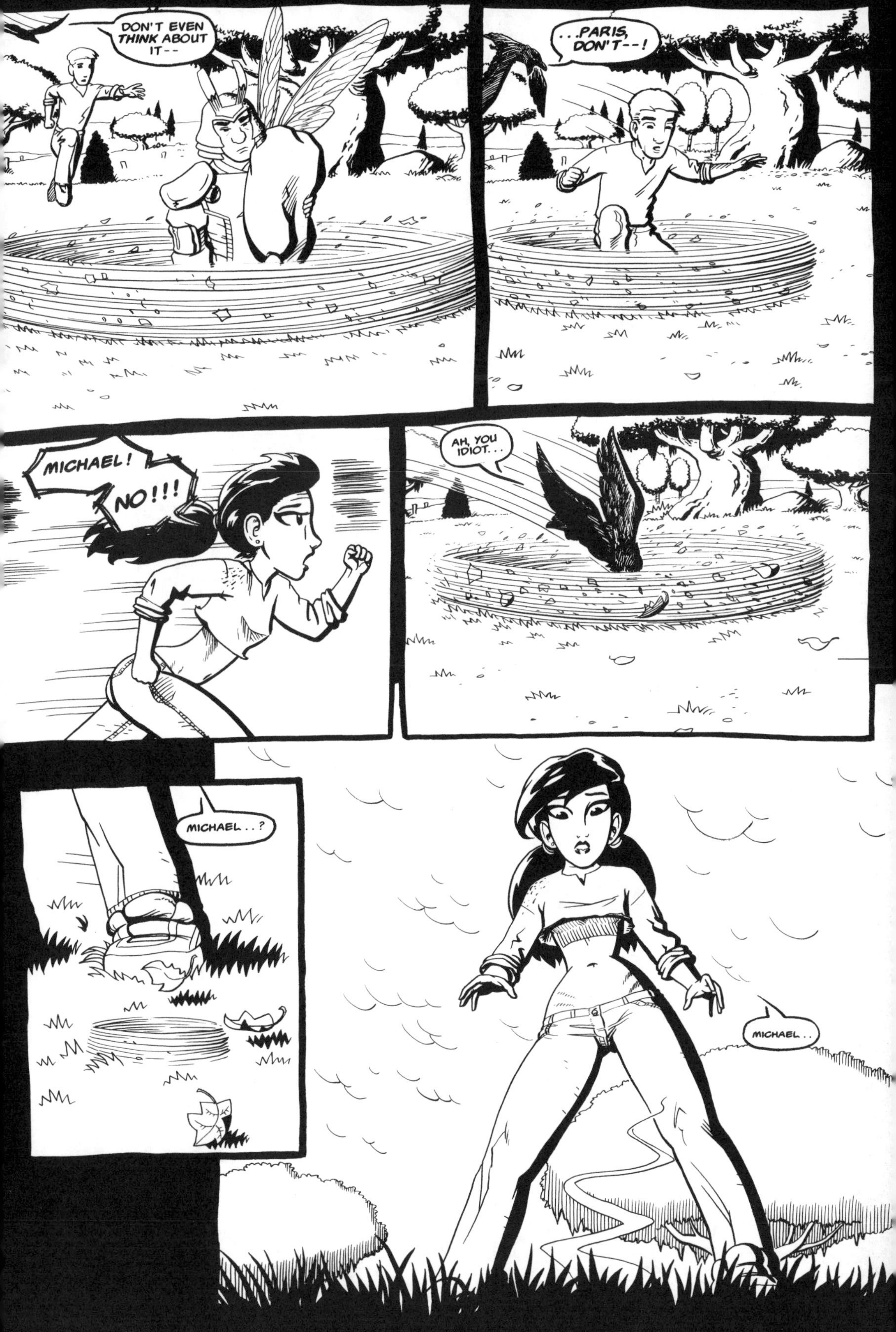
DON'T EVEN THINK ABOUT IT--
...PARIS, DON'T--!
MICHAEL!
NO!!!
AH, YOU IDIOT...
MICHAEL..?
MICHAEL..

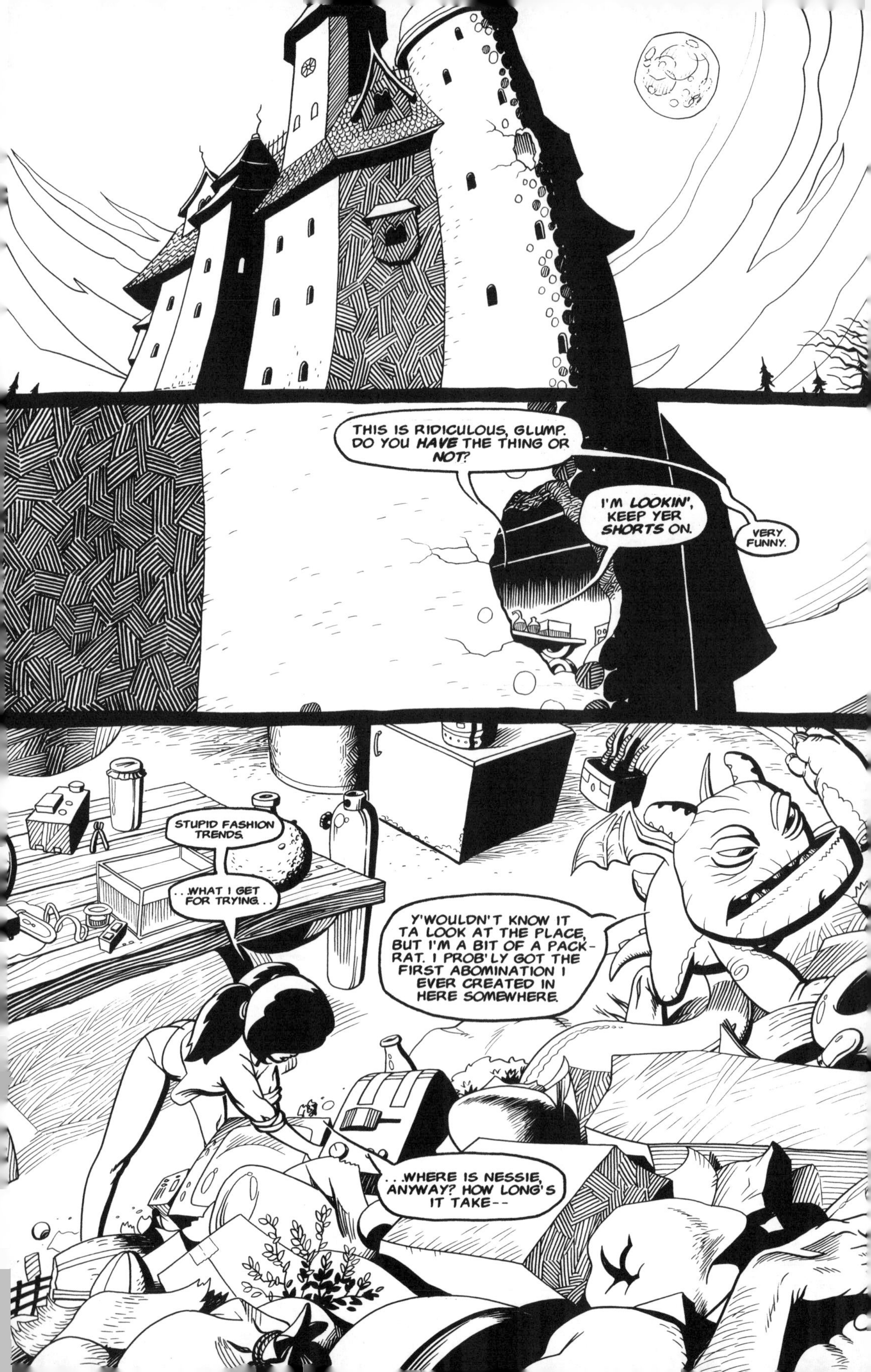

THIS IS RIDICULOUS, GLUMP. DO YOU HAVE THE THING OR NOT?
I'M LOOKIN', KEEP YER SHORTS ON.
VERY FUNNY.
STUPID FASHION TRENDS.
...WHAT I GET FOR TRYING...
Y'WOULDN'T KNOW IT TA LOOK AT THE PLACE, BUT I'M A BIT OF A PACK-RAT. I PROB'LY GOT THE FIRST ABOMINATION I EVER CREATED IN HERE SOMEWHERE.
...WHERE IS NESSIE, ANYWAY? HOW LONG'S IT TAKE--

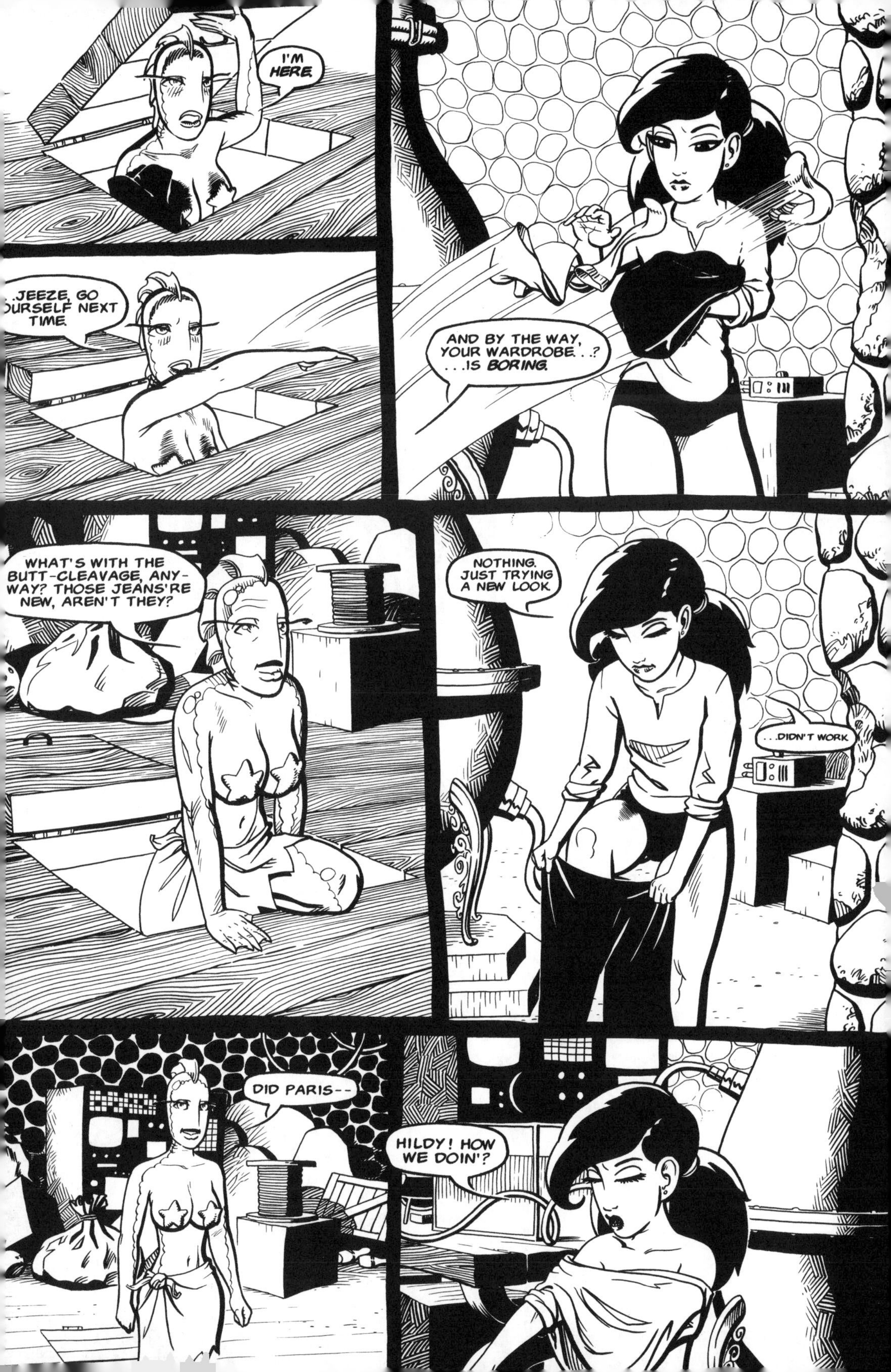
I'M HERE.
..JEEZE, GO OURSELF NEXT TIME.
AND BY THE WAY, YOUR WARDROBE. . .? . . .IS BORING.
WHAT'S WITH THE BUTT-CLEAVAGE, ANY-WAY? THOSE JEANS'RE NEW, AREN'T THEY?
NOTHING. JUST TRYING A NEW LOOK.
. . .DIDN'T WORK
DID PARIS--
HILDY! HOW WE DOIN'?

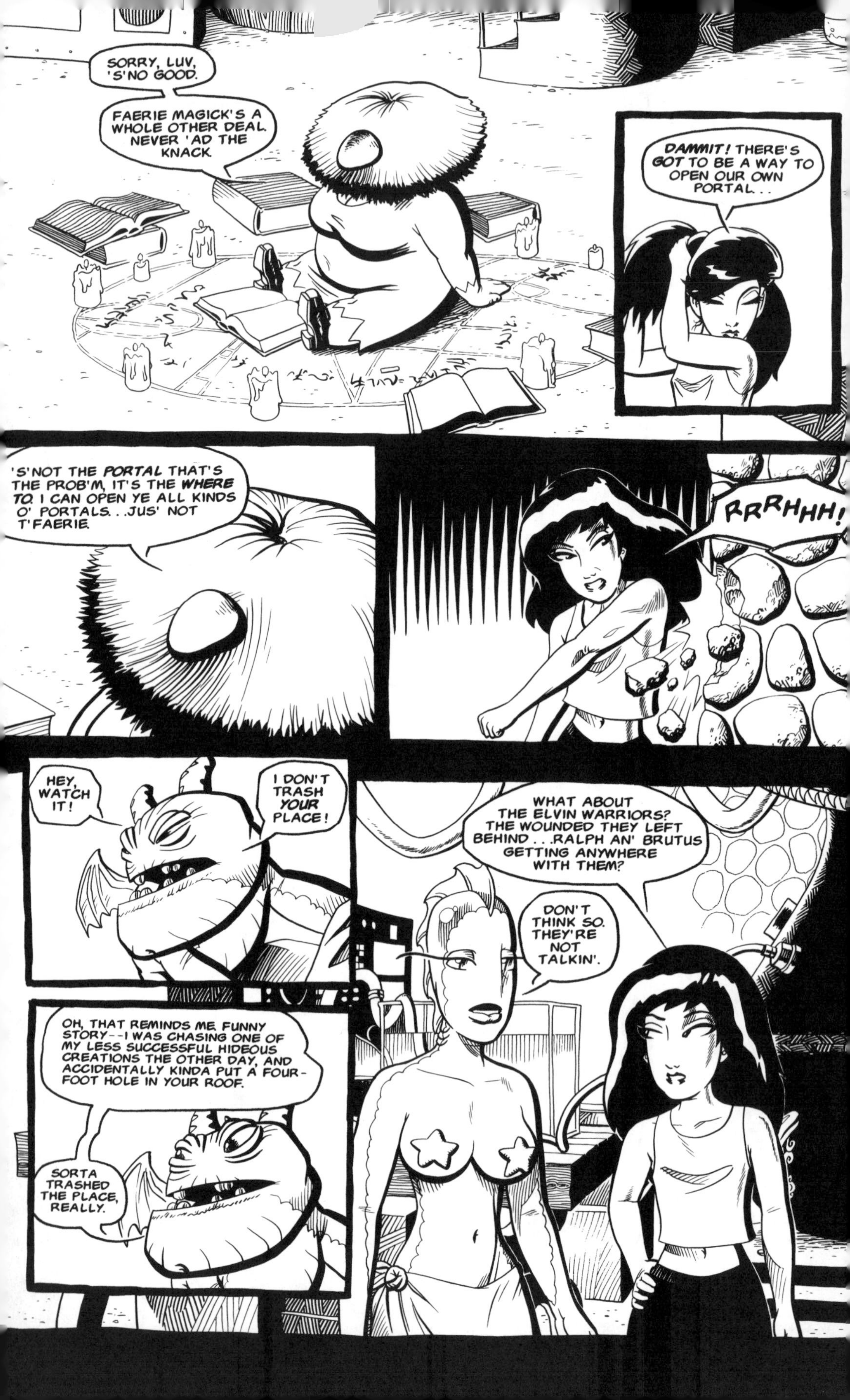
SORRY, LUV, 'S'NO GOOD.
FAERIE MAGICK'S A WHOLE OTHER DEAL. NEVER 'AD THE KNACK.
DAMMIT! THERE'S GOT TO BE A WAY TO OPEN OUR OWN PORTAL . . .
'S'NOT THE PORTAL THAT'S THE PROB'M, IT'S THE WHERE TO. I CAN OPEN YE ALL KINDS O' PORTALS. . .JUS' NOT T'FAERIE.
RRRHHH!
HEY, WATCH IT!
I DON'T TRASH YOUR PLACE!
OH, THAT REMINDS ME. FUNNY STORY--I WAS CHASING ONE OF MY LESS SUCCESSFUL HIDEOUS CREATIONS THE OTHER DAY, AND ACCIDENTALLY KINDA PUT A FOUR-FOOT HOLE IN YOUR ROOF.
SORTA TRASHED THE PLACE, REALLY.
WHAT ABOUT THE ELVIN WARRIORS? THE WOUNDED THEY LEFT BEHIND . . .RALPH AN' BRUTUS GETTING ANYWHERE WITH THEM?
DON'T THINK SO. THEY'RE NOT TALKIN'.

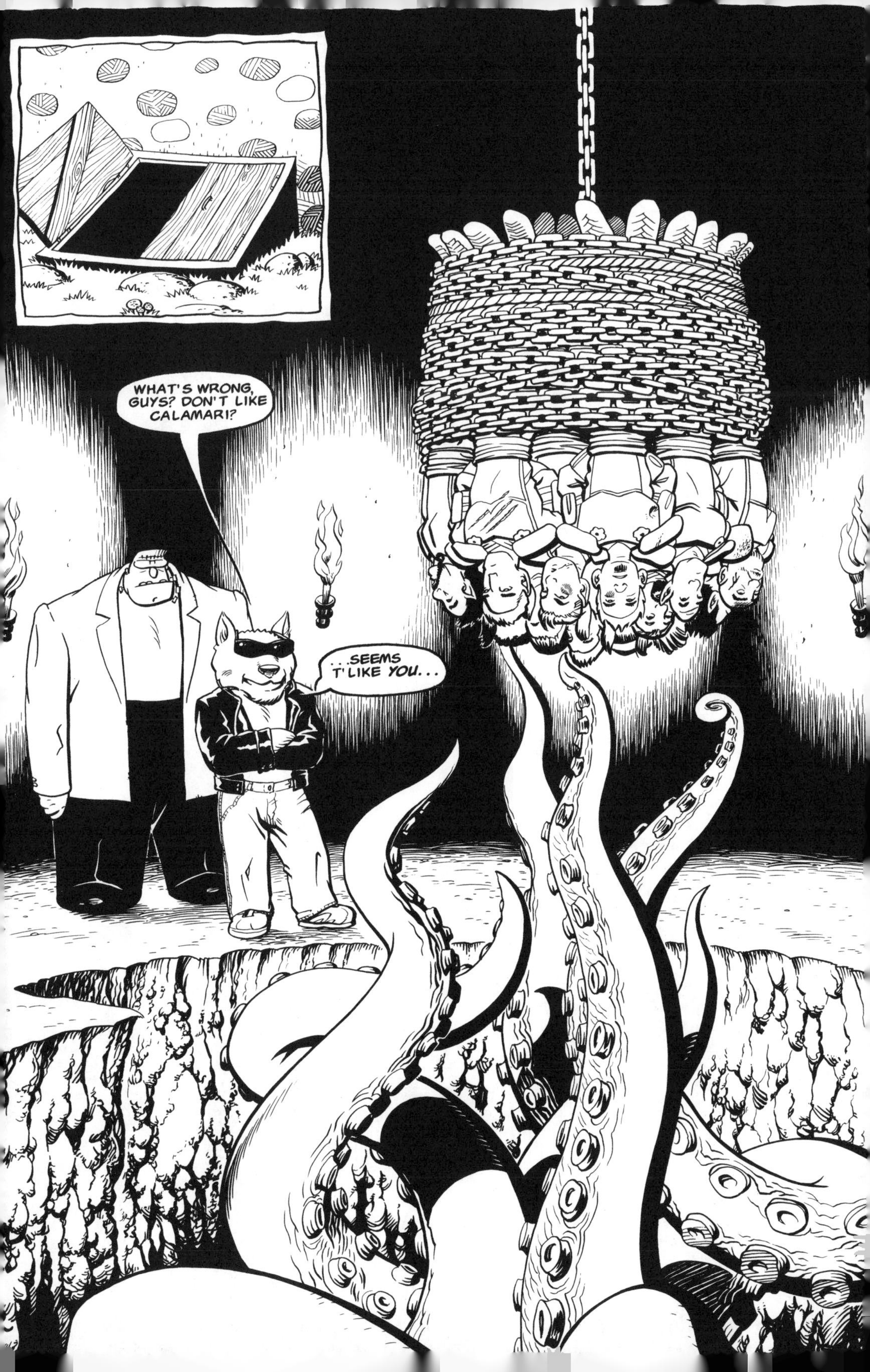
WHAT'S WRONG, GUYS? DON'T LIKE CALAMARI?
...SEEMS T'LIKE YOU...

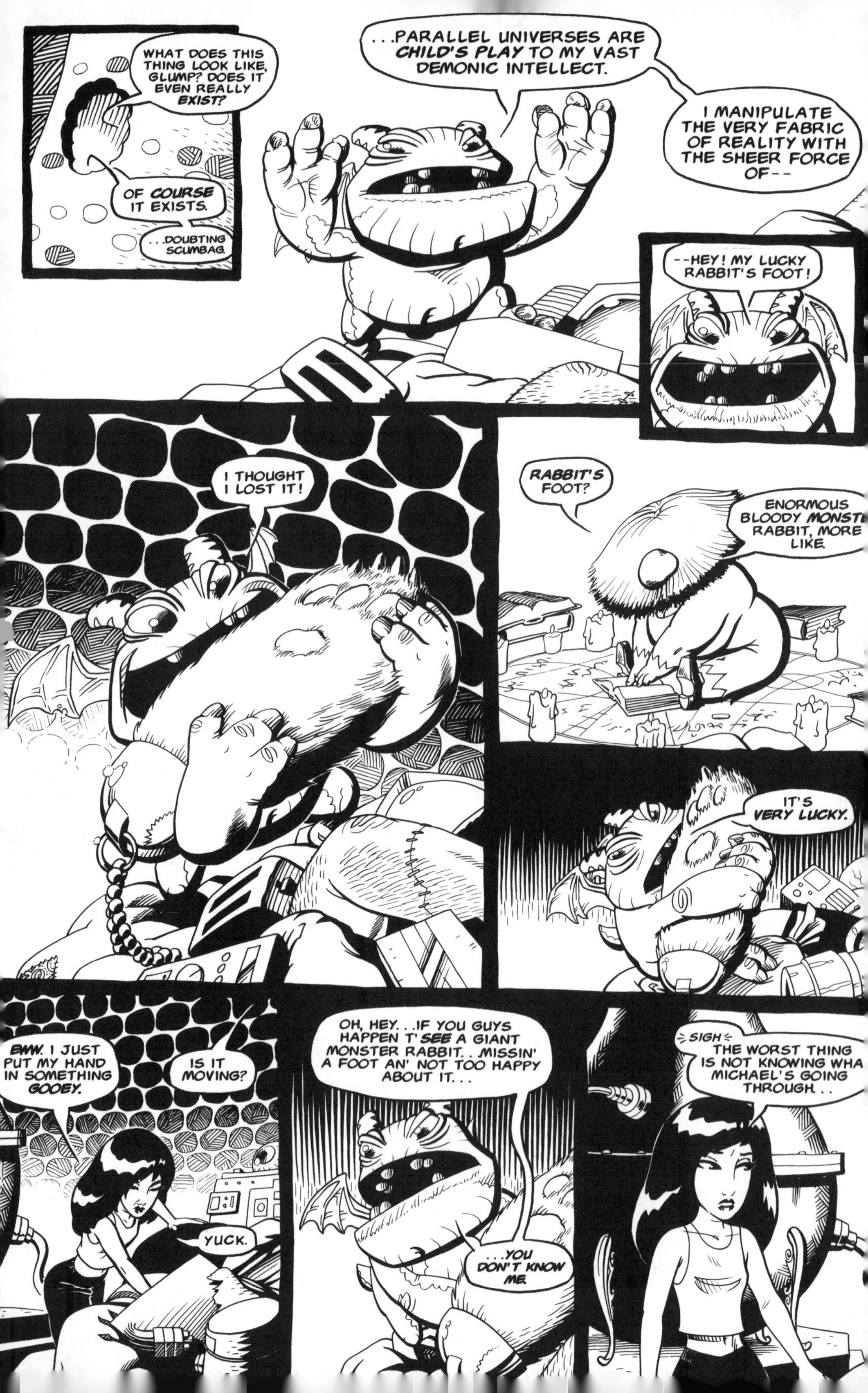
WHAT DOES THIS THING LOOK LIKE, GLUMP? DOES IT EVEN REALLY EXIST?
OF COURSE IT EXISTS.
...DOUBTING SCUMBAG.
...PARALLEL UNIVERSES ARE CHILD'S PLAY TO MY VAST DEMONIC INTELLECT.
I MANIPULATE THE VERY FABRIC OF REALITY WITH THE SHEER FORCE OF--
--HEY! MY LUCKY RABBIT'S FOOT!
I THOUGHT I LOST IT!
RABBIT'S FOOT?
ENORMOUS BLOODY MONST RABBIT, MORE LIKE.
IT'S VERY LUCKY.
EWW. I JUST PUT MY HAND IN SOMETHING GOOEY.
IS IT MOVING?
YUCK.
OH, HEY...IF YOU GUYS HAPPEN T' SEE A GIANT MONSTER RABBIT.. MISSIN' A FOOT AN' NOT TOO HAPPY ABOUT IT...
...YOU DON'T KNOW ME.
SIGH
THE WORST THING IS NOT KNOWING WHA MICHAEL'S GOING THROUGH..

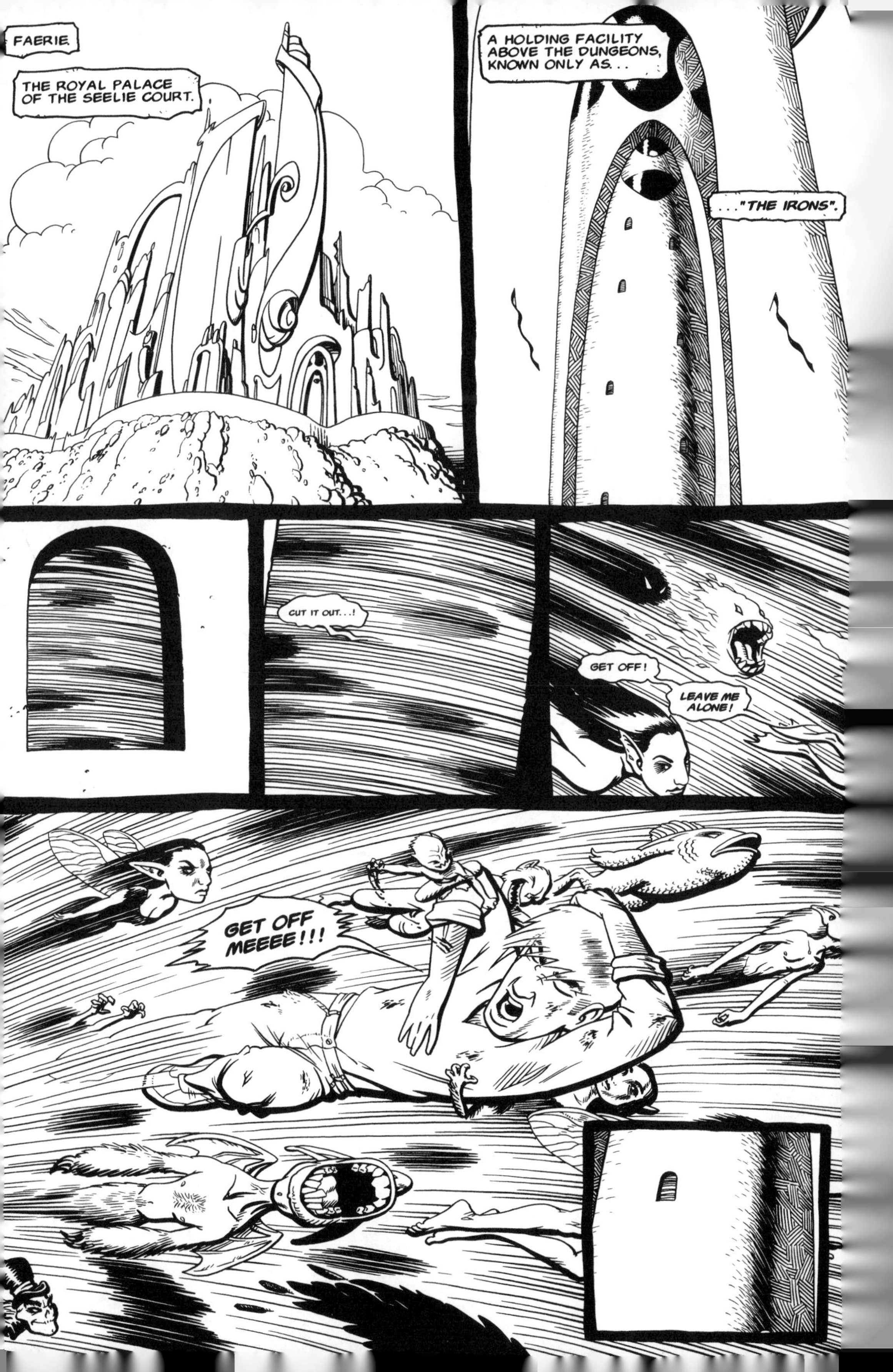
FAERIE.
THE ROYAL PALACE OF THE SEELIE COURT.
A HOLDING FACILITY ABOVE THE DUNGEONS, KNOWN ONLY AS...
..."THE IRONS".
CUT IT OUT...!
GET OFF!
LEAVE ME ALONE!
GET OFF MEEEE!!!

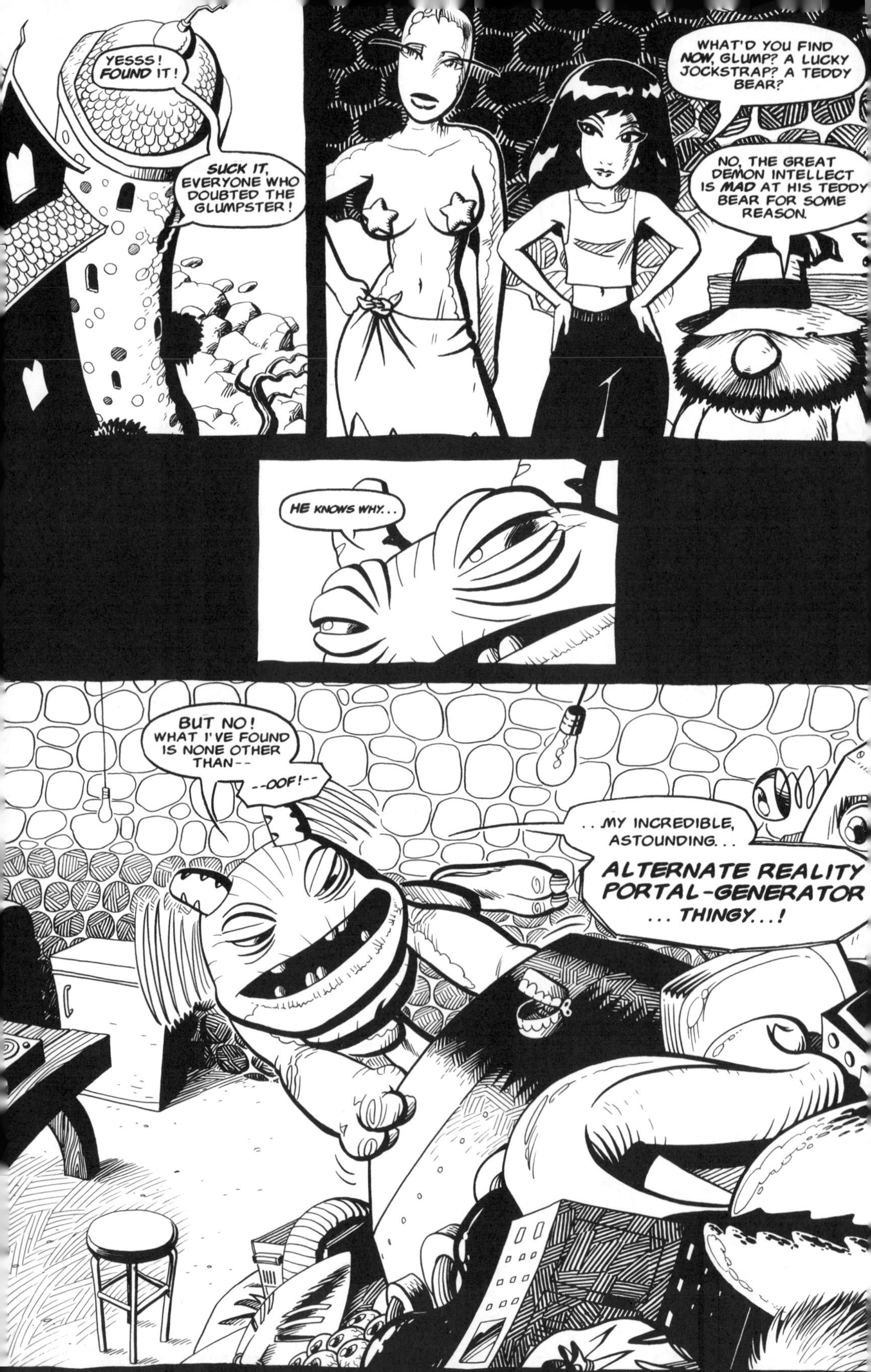
YESSS! FOUND IT!
SUCK IT, EVERYONE WHO DOUBTED THE GLUMPSTER!
WHAT'D YOU FIND NOW, GLUMP? A LUCKY JOCKSTRAP? A TEDDY BEAR?
NO, THE GREAT DEMON INTELLECT IS MAD AT HIS TEDDY BEAR FOR SOME REASON.
HE KNOWS WHY...
BUT NO! WHAT I'VE FOUND IS NONE OTHER THAN--
--OOF!--
...MY INCREDIBLE, ASTOUNDING...
ALTERNATE REALITY PORTAL-GENERATOR ...THINGY...!

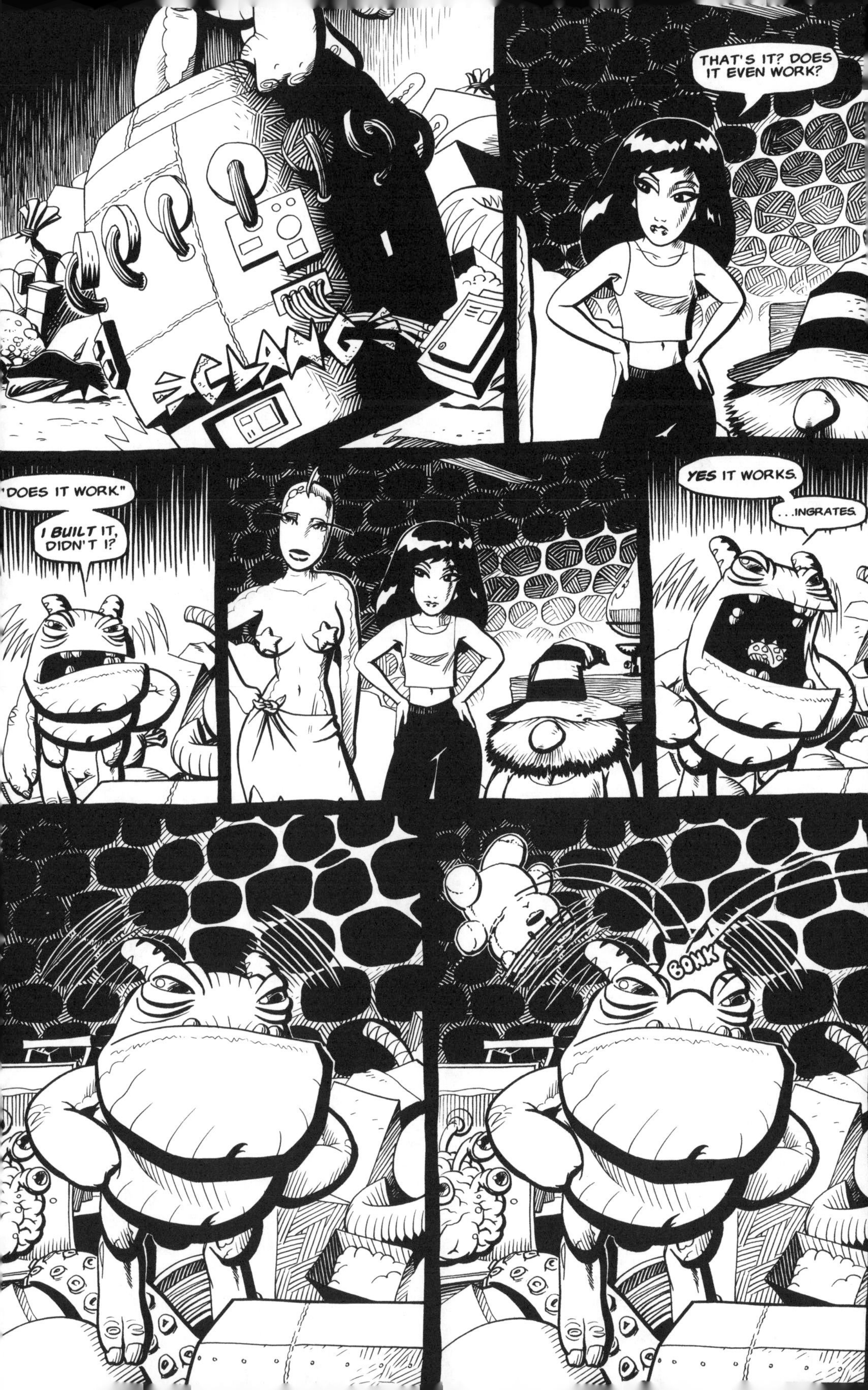
CLANG
THAT'S IT? DOES IT EVEN WORK?
"DOES IT WORK."
I BUILT IT, DIDN'T I?
YES IT WORKS.
...INGRATES.
BONK

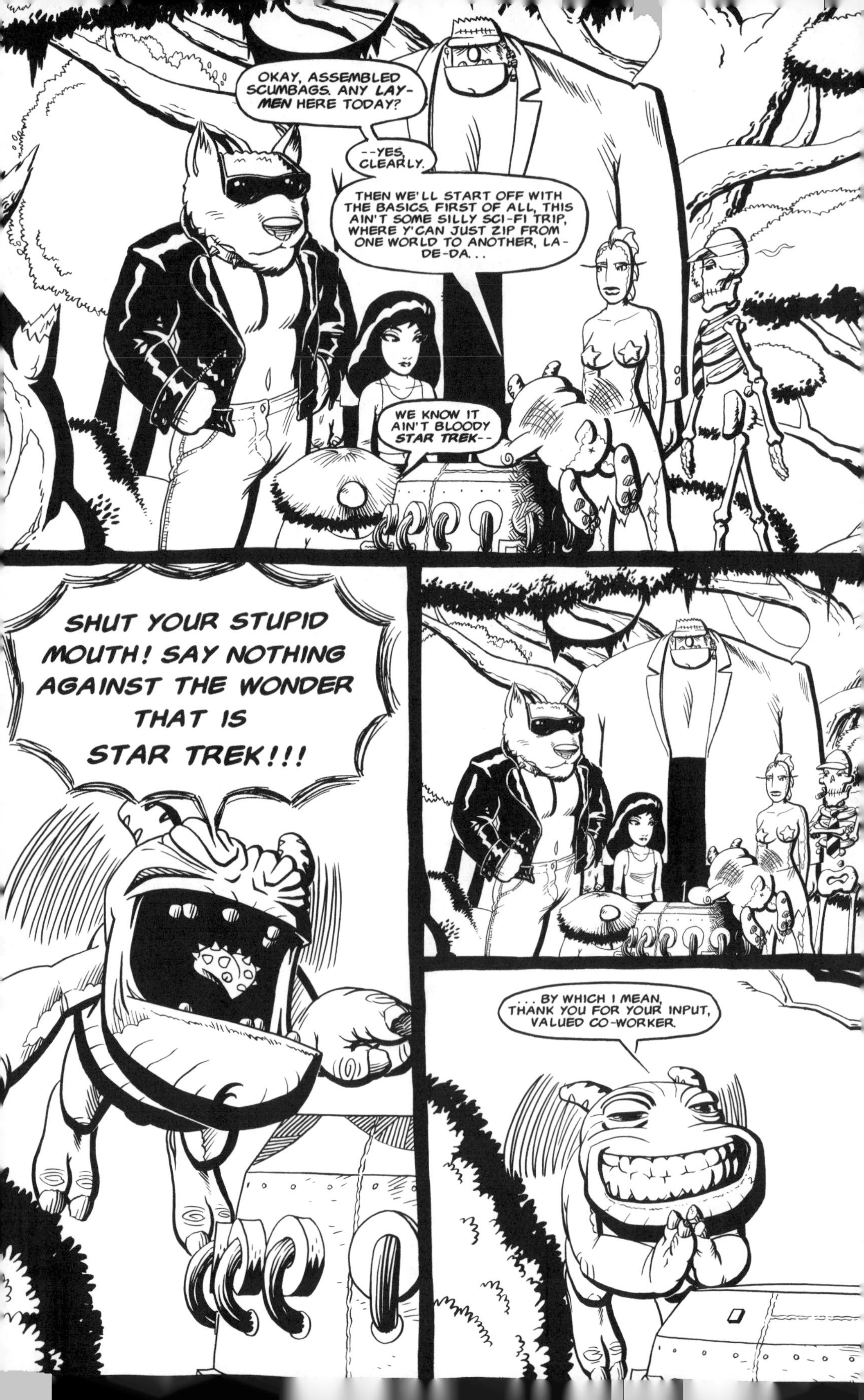
OKAY, ASSEMBLED SCUMBAGS. ANY LAYMEN HERE TODAY?
--YES, CLEARLY.
THEN WE'LL START OFF WITH THE BASICS. FIRST OF ALL, THIS AIN'T SOME SILLY SCI-FI TRIP, WHERE Y'CAN JUST ZIP FROM ONE WORLD TO ANOTHER, LA-DE-DA...
WE KNOW IT AIN'T BLOODY STAR TREK--
SHUT YOUR STUPID MOUTH! SAY NOTHING AGAINST THE WONDER THAT IS STAR TREK!!!
...BY WHICH I MEAN, THANK YOU FOR YOUR INPUT, VALUED CO-WORKER.

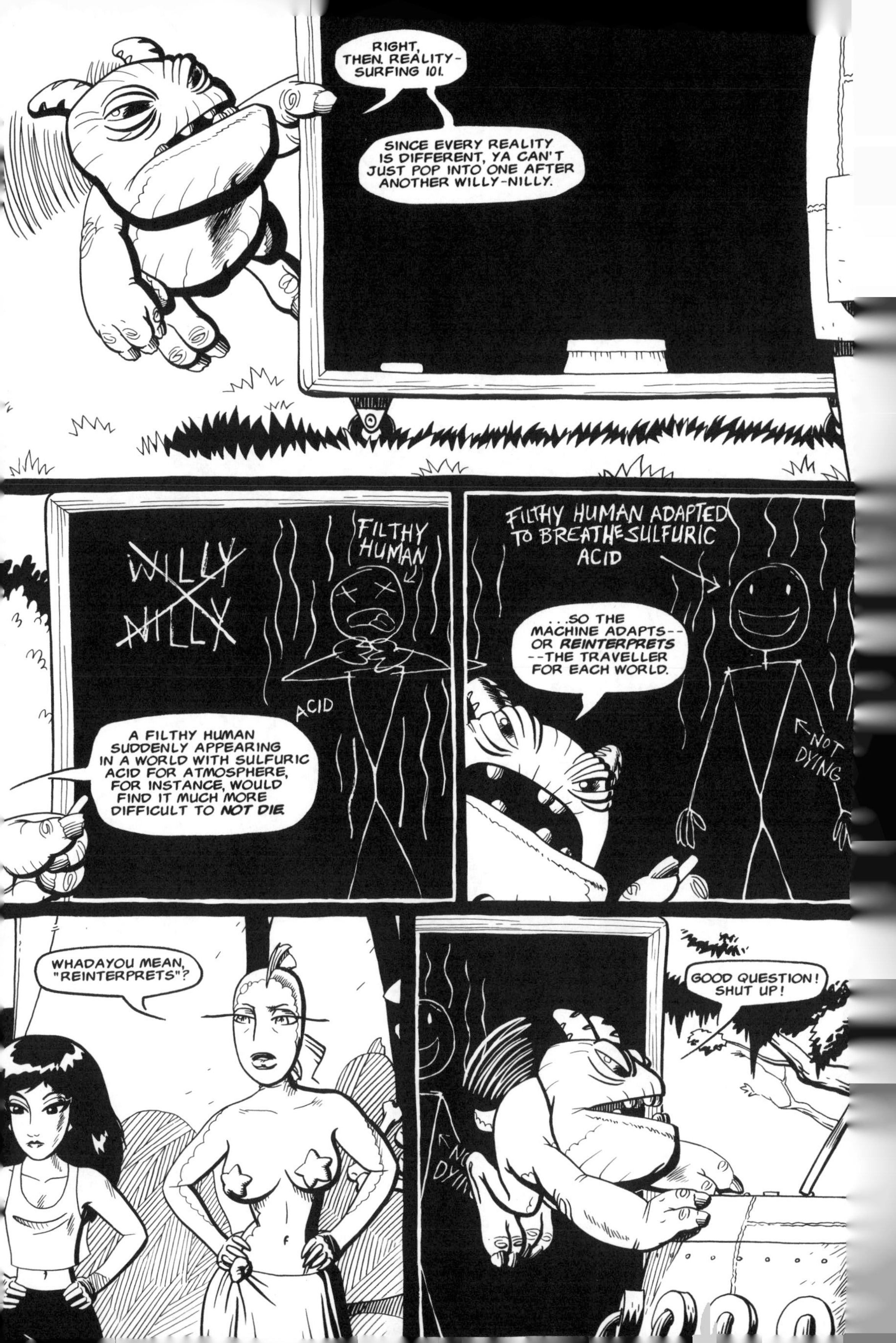
RIGHT, THEN. REALITY-SURFING 101.
SINCE EVERY REALITY IS DIFFERENT, YA CAN'T JUST POP INTO ONE AFTER ANOTHER WILLY-NILLY.
WILLY NILLY
FILTHY HUMAN
ACID
A FILTHY HUMAN SUDDENLY APPEARING IN A WORLD WITH SULFURIC ACID FOR ATMOSPHERE, FOR INSTANCE, WOULD FIND IT MUCH MORE DIFFICULT TO NOT DIE.
FILTHY HUMAN ADAPTED TO BREATHE SULFURIC ACID
...SO THE MACHINE ADAPTS--OR REINTERPRETS--THE TRAVELLER FOR EACH WORLD.
NOT DYING
WHADAYOU MEAN, "REINTERPRETS"?
GOOD QUESTION! SHUT UP!

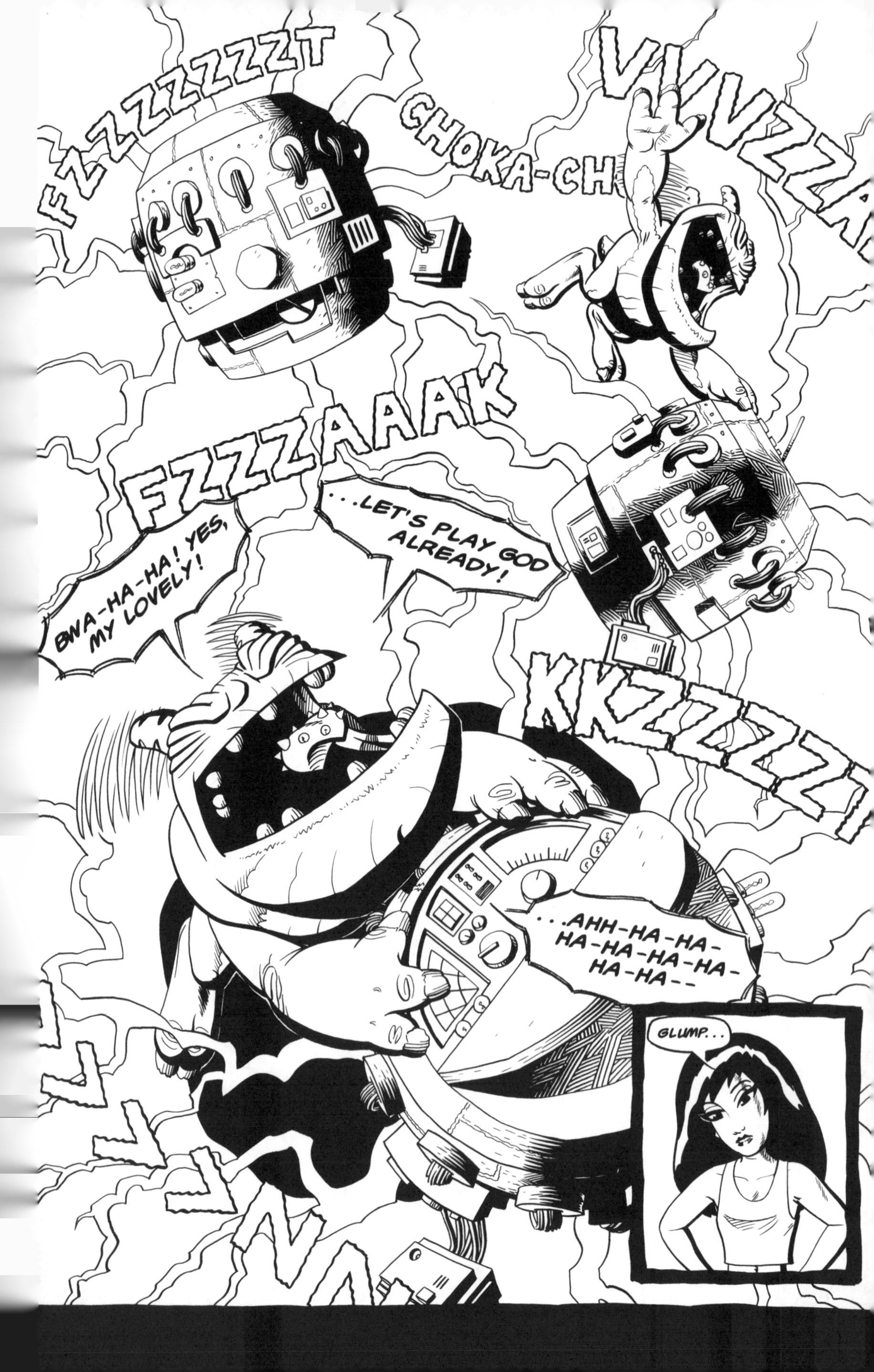
FZZZZZZZT
CHOKA-CH
VVVZZA
FZZZAAAK
...LET'S PLAY GOD ALREADY!
BWA-HA-HA! YES, MY LOVELY!
KKZZZZ
...AHH-HA-HA-HA-HA-HA-HA-HA-HA--
GLUMP...

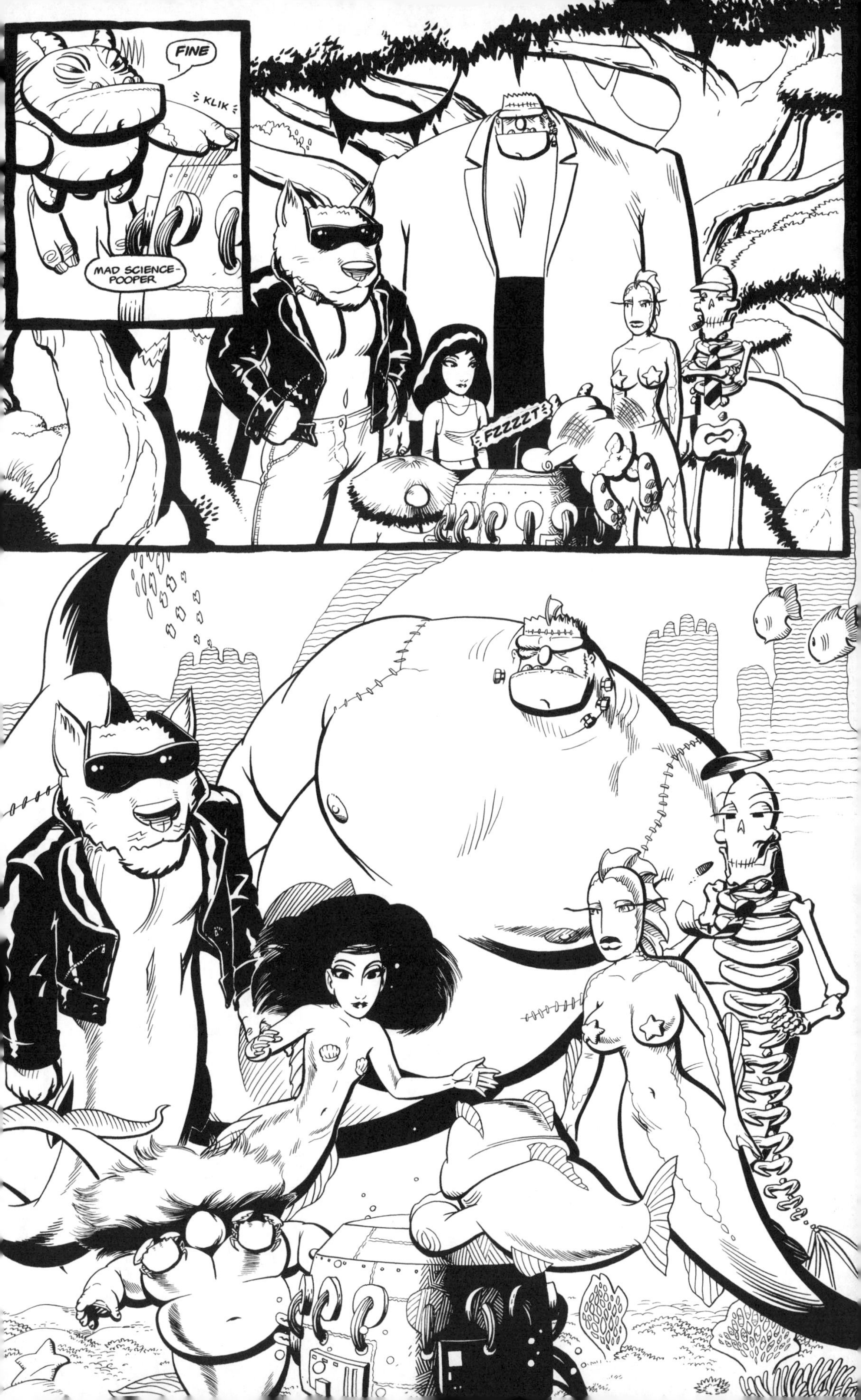

FINE
KLIK
MAD SCIENCE-POOPER
FZZZZZT

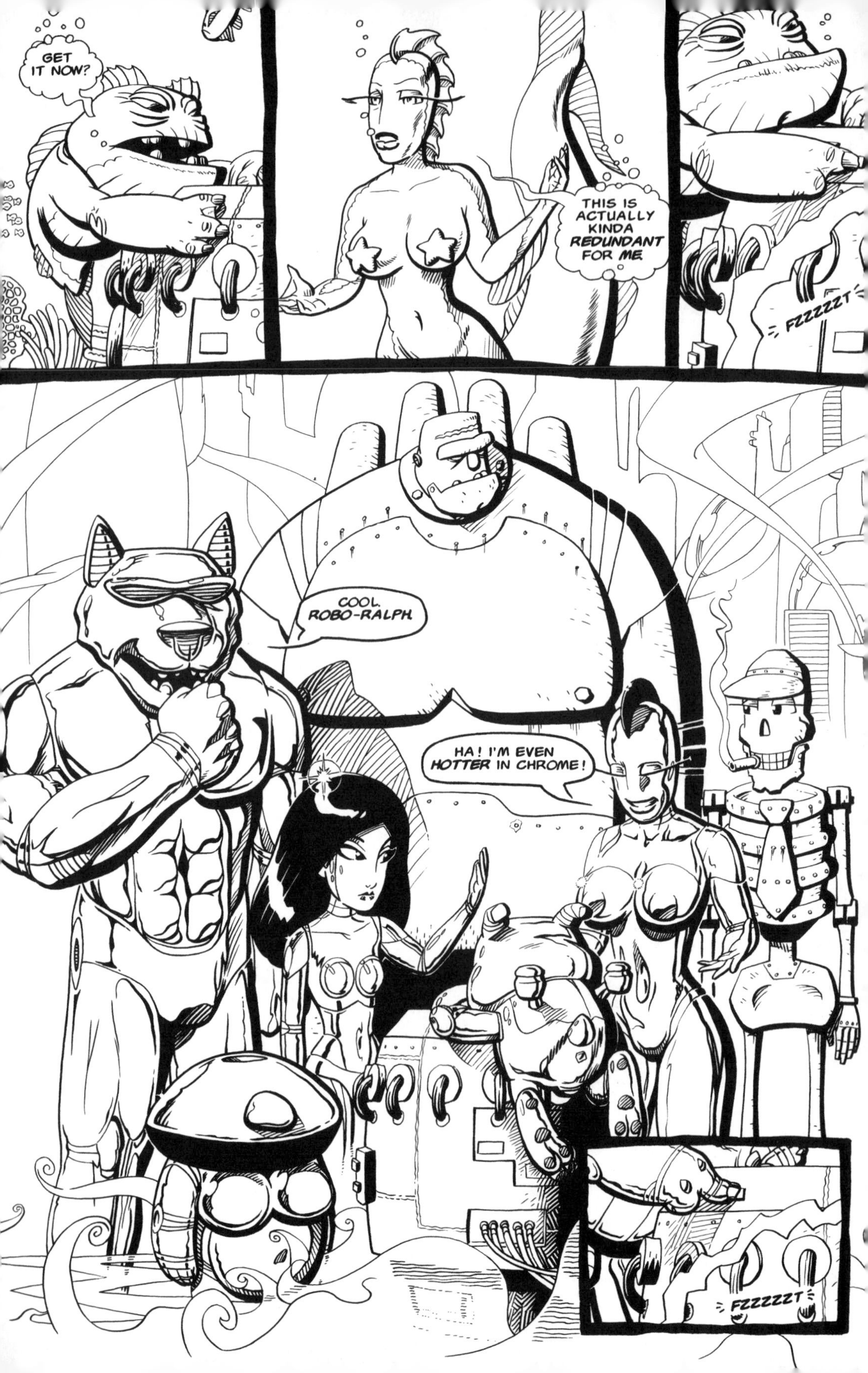

GET IT NOW?
THIS IS ACTUALLY KINDA REDUNDANT FOR ME.
FZZZZZT
COOL. ROBO-RALPH.
HA! I'M EVEN HOTTER IN CHROME!
FZZZZZT

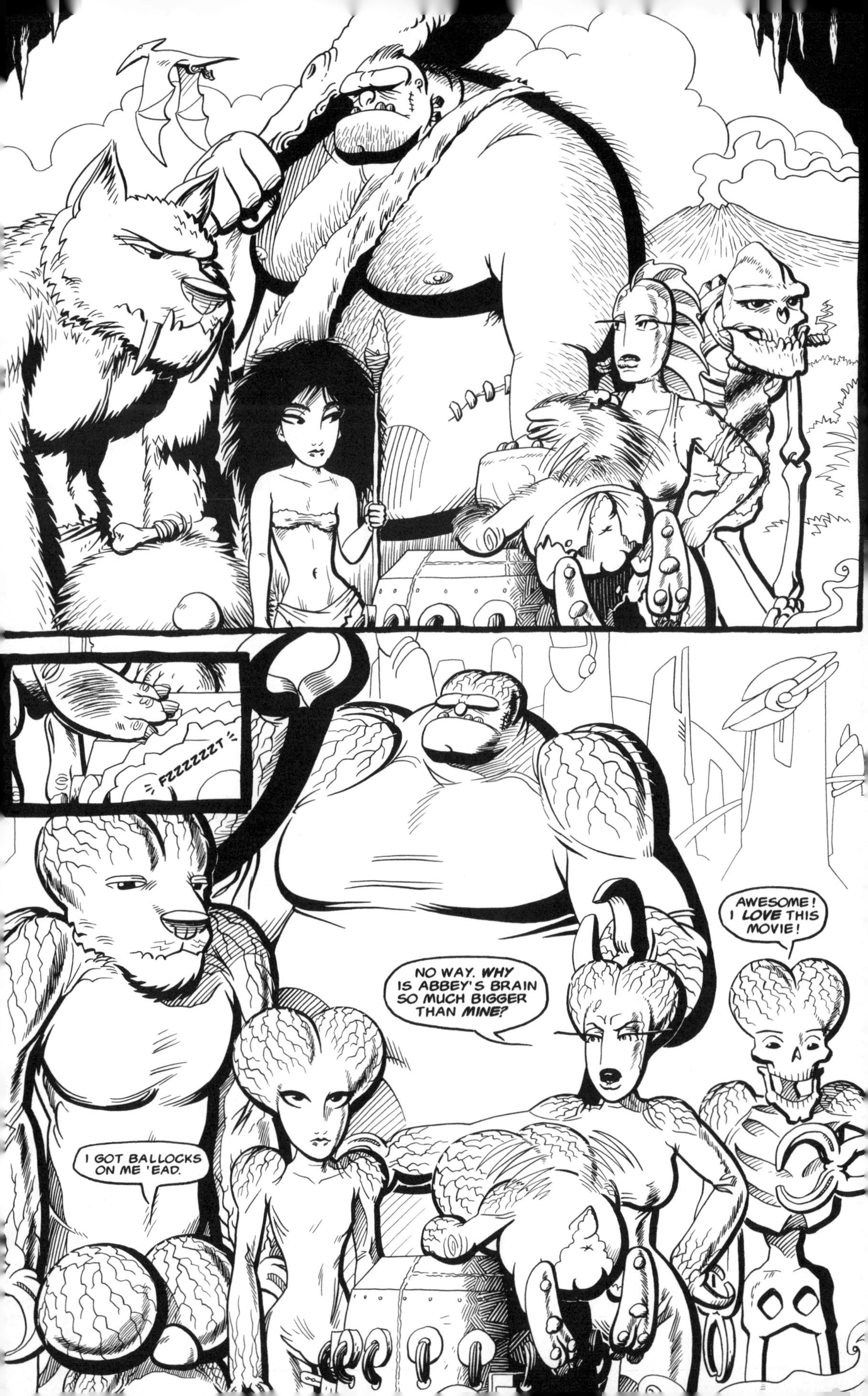
FZZZZZZT
I GOT BALLOCKS ON ME 'EAD.
NO WAY. WHY IS ABBEY'S BRAIN SO MUCH BIGGER THAN MINE?
AWESOME! I LOVE THIS MOVIE!

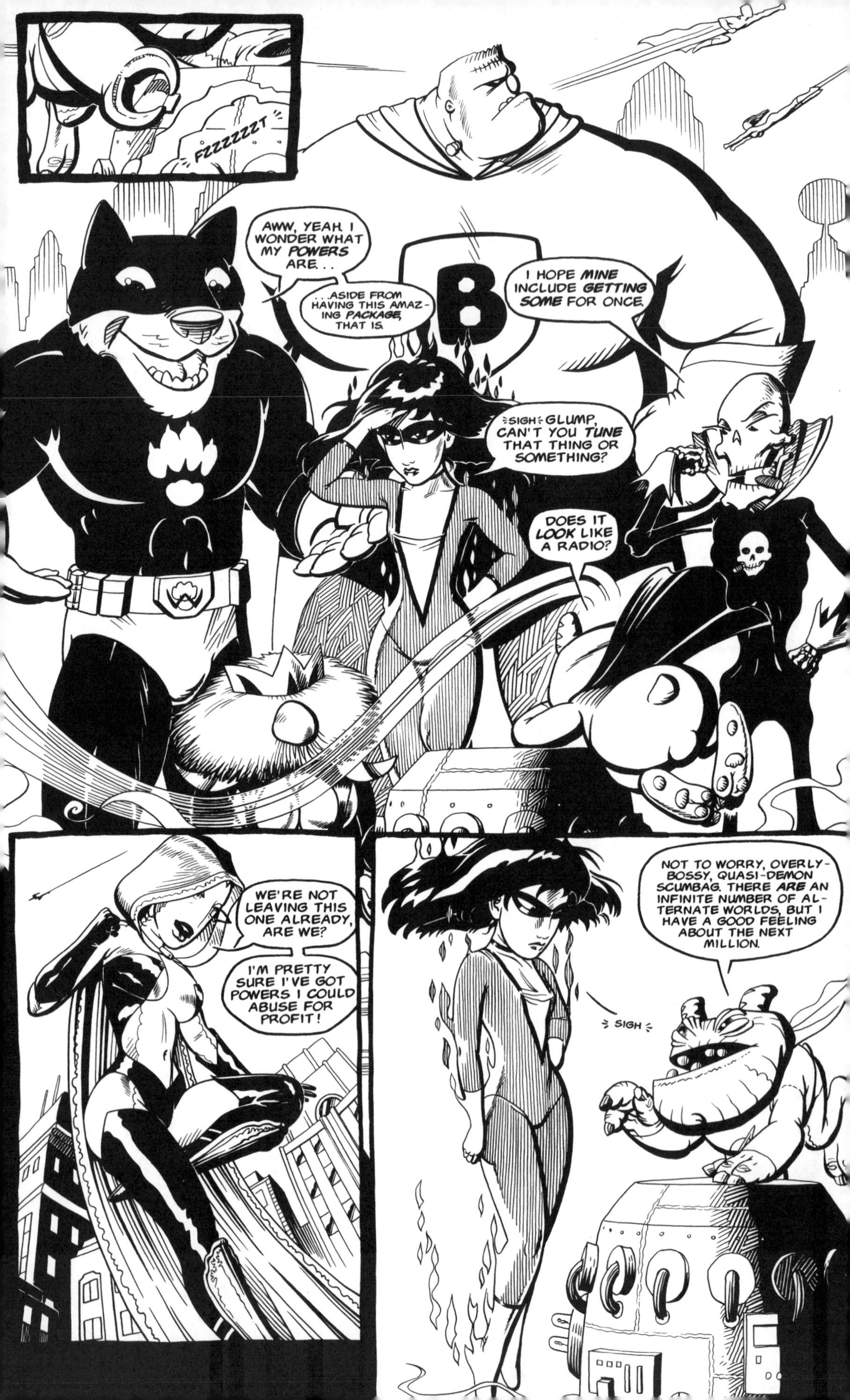
FZZZZZZZT
AWW, YEAH. I WONDER WHAT MY POWERS ARE...
...ASIDE FROM HAVING THIS AMAZING PACKAGE, THAT IS.
B
I HOPE MINE INCLUDE GETTING SOME FOR ONCE.
SIGH GLUMP, CAN'T YOU TUNE THAT THING OR SOMETHING?
DOES IT LOOK LIKE A RADIO?
WE'RE NOT LEAVING THIS ONE ALREADY, ARE WE?
I'M PRETTY SURE I'VE GOT POWERS I COULD ABUSE FOR PROFIT!
SIGH
NOT TO WORRY, OVERLY-BOSSY, QUASI-DEMON SCUMBAG. THERE ARE AN INFINITE NUMBER OF ALTERNATE WORLDS, BUT I HAVE A GOOD FEELING ABOUT THE NEXT MILLION.

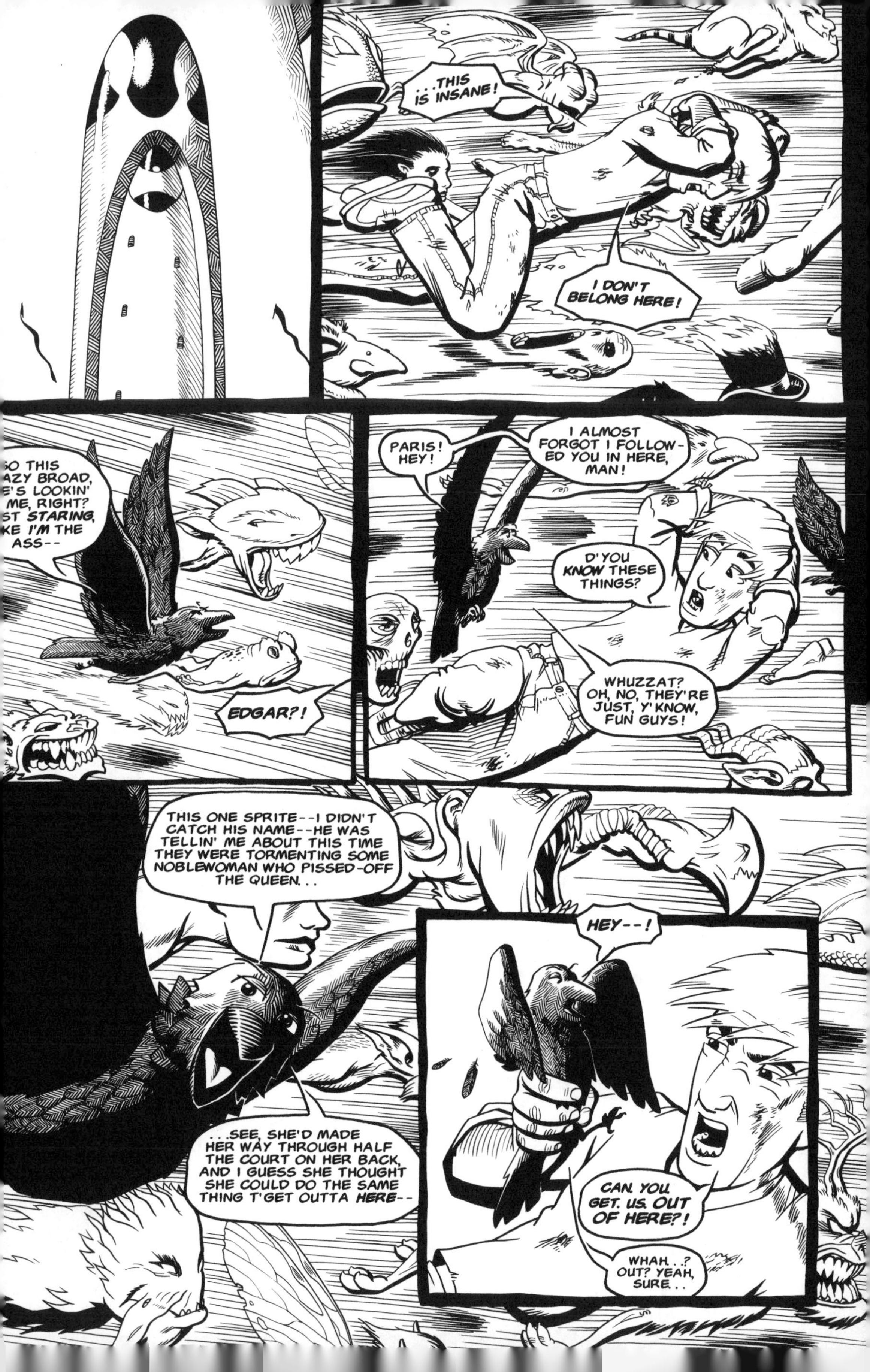
...THIS IS INSANE!
I DON'T BELONG HERE!
SO THIS AZY BROAD, E'S LOOKIN' ME, RIGHT? ST STARING, KE I'M THE ASS--
EDGAR?!
PARIS! HEY!
I ALMOST FORGOT I FOLLOWED YOU IN HERE, MAN!
D'YOU KNOW THESE THINGS?
WHUZZAT? OH, NO, THEY'RE JUST, Y'KNOW, FUN GUYS!
THIS ONE SPRITE--I DIDN'T CATCH HIS NAME--HE WAS TELLIN' ME ABOUT THIS TIME THEY WERE TORMENTING SOME NOBLEWOMAN WHO PISSED-OFF THE QUEEN...
...SEE, SHE'D MADE HER WAY THROUGH HALF THE COURT ON HER BACK, AND I GUESS SHE THOUGHT SHE COULD DO THE SAME THING T'GET OUTTA HERE--
HEY--!
CAN. YOU. GET. US. OUT OF HERE?!
WHAH..? OUT? YEAH, SURE...

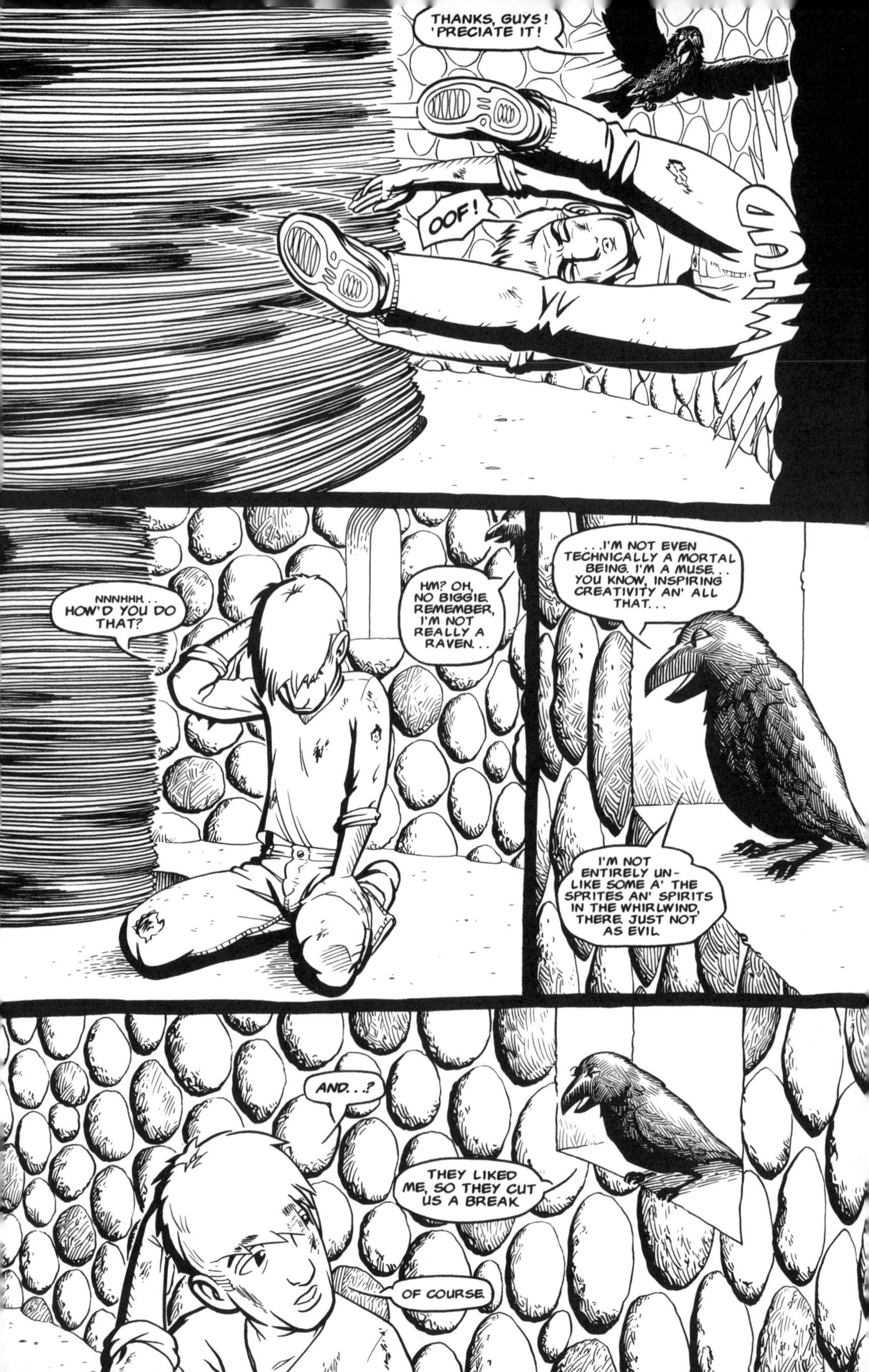
THANKS, GUYS! 'PRECIATE IT!
OOF!
NNNHHH.. HOW'D YOU DO THAT?
HM? OH, NO BIGGIE. REMEMBER, I'M NOT REALLY A RAVEN..
...I'M NOT EVEN TECHNICALLY A MORTAL BEING. I'M A MUSE.. YOU KNOW, INSPIRING CREATIVITY AN' ALL THAT...
I'M NOT ENTIRELY UN-LIKE SOME A' THE SPRITES AN' SPIRITS IN THE WHIRLWIND, THERE. JUST NOT AS EVIL.
AND...?
THEY LIKED ME, SO THEY CUT US A BREAK.
OF COURSE.

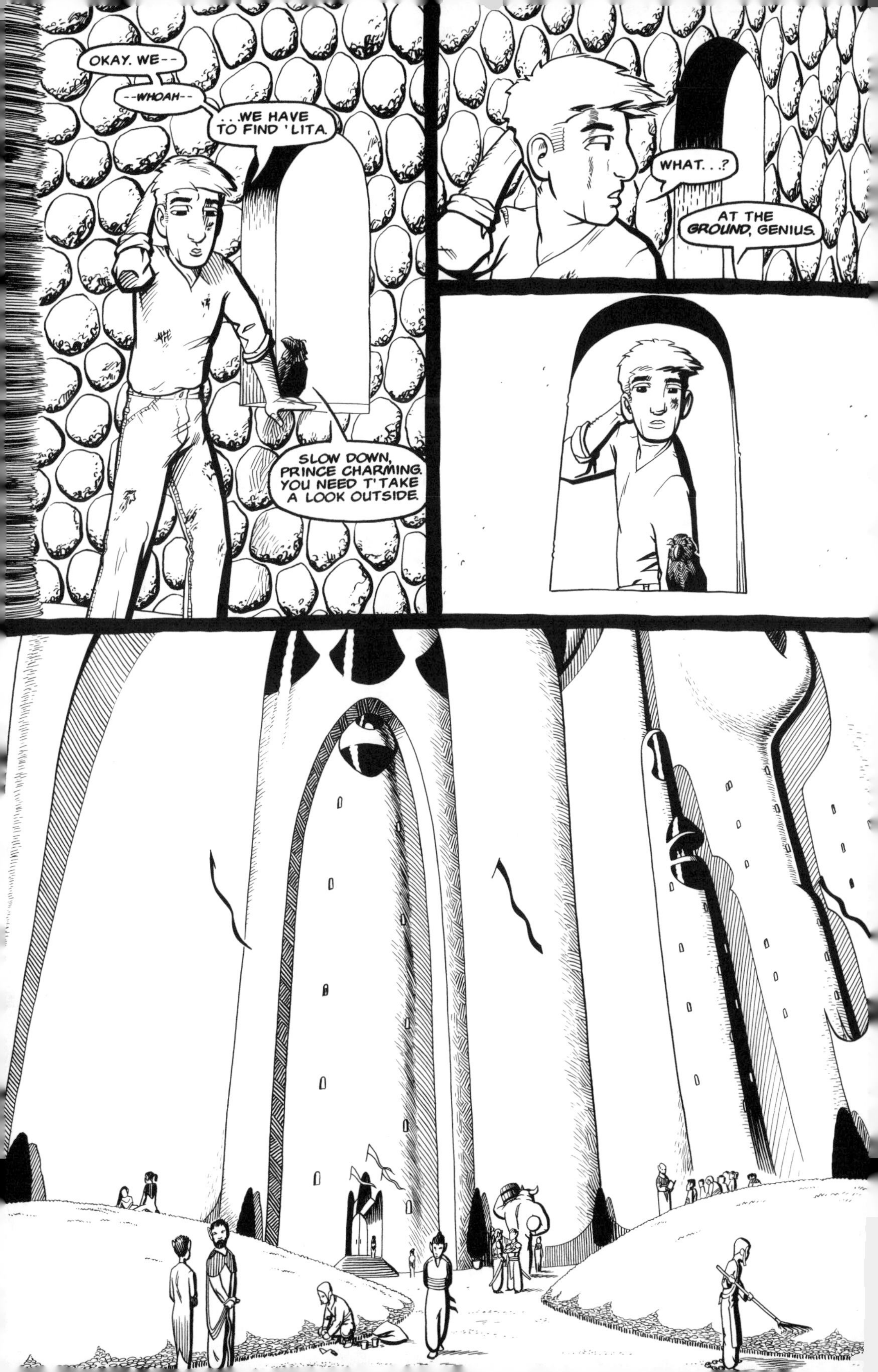
OKAY. WE--
--WHOAH--
...WE HAVE TO FIND 'LITA.
SLOW DOWN, PRINCE CHARMING. YOU NEED T'TAKE A LOOK OUTSIDE.
WHAT...?
AT THE GROUND, GENIUS.

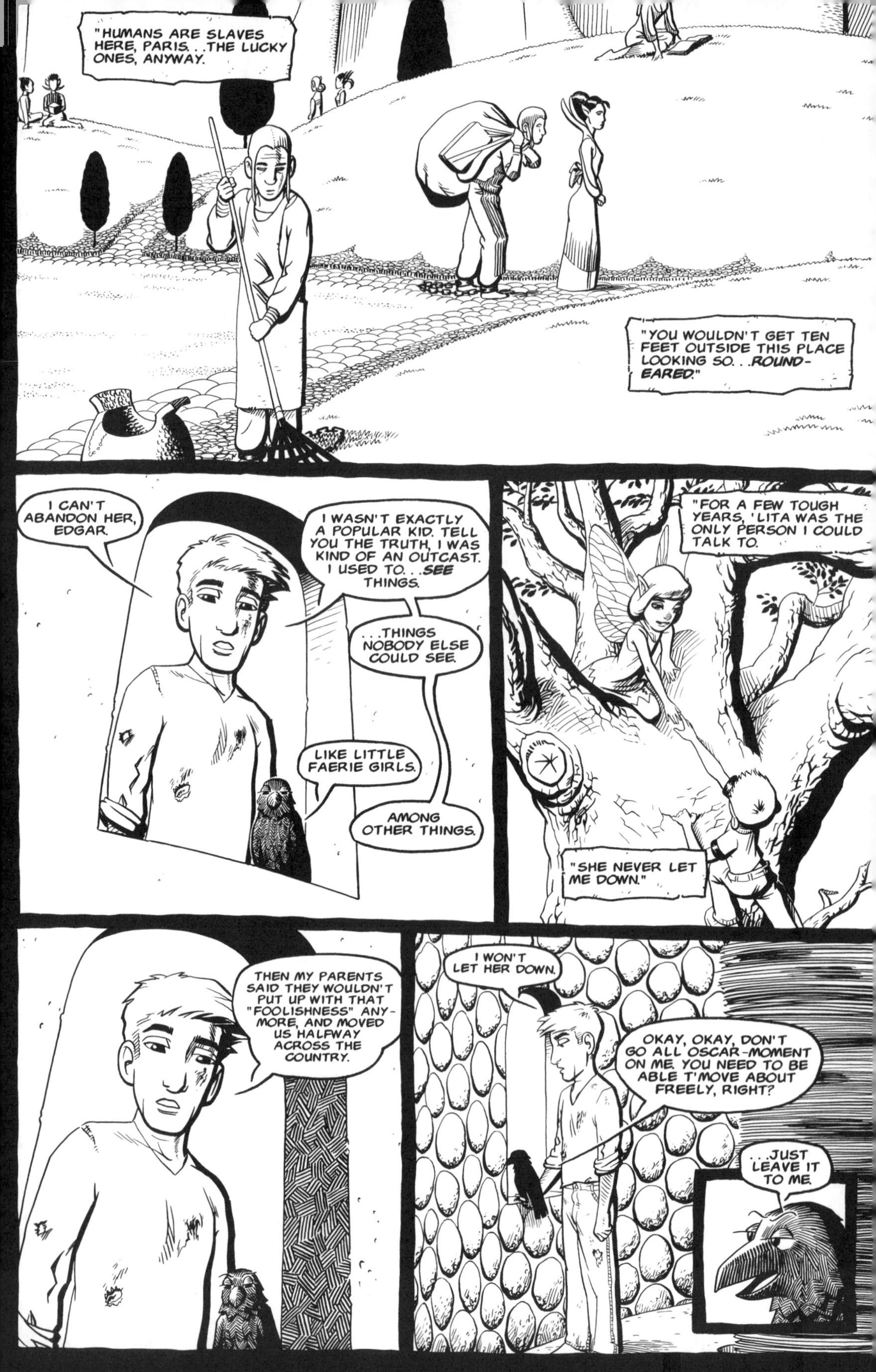
"HUMANS ARE SLAVES HERE, PARIS. . .THE LUCKY ONES, ANYWAY.
"YOU WOULDN'T GET TEN FEET OUTSIDE THIS PLACE LOOKING SO. . .ROUND-EARED."
I CAN'T ABANDON HER, EDGAR.
I WASN'T EXACTLY A POPULAR KID. TELL YOU THE TRUTH, I WAS KIND OF AN OUTCAST. I USED TO. . .SEE THINGS.
. . .THINGS NOBODY ELSE COULD SEE.
LIKE LITTLE FAERIE GIRLS.
AMONG OTHER THINGS.
"FOR A FEW TOUGH YEARS, 'LITA WAS THE ONLY PERSON I COULD TALK TO.
"SHE NEVER LET ME DOWN."
THEN MY PARENTS SAID THEY WOULDN'T PUT UP WITH THAT "FOOLISHNESS" ANY-MORE, AND MOVED US HALFWAY ACROSS THE COUNTRY.
I WON'T LET HER DOWN.
OKAY, OKAY, DON'T GO ALL OSCAR-MOMENT ON ME. YOU NEED TO BE ABLE T'MOVE ABOUT FREELY, RIGHT?
. . .JUST LEAVE IT TO ME.

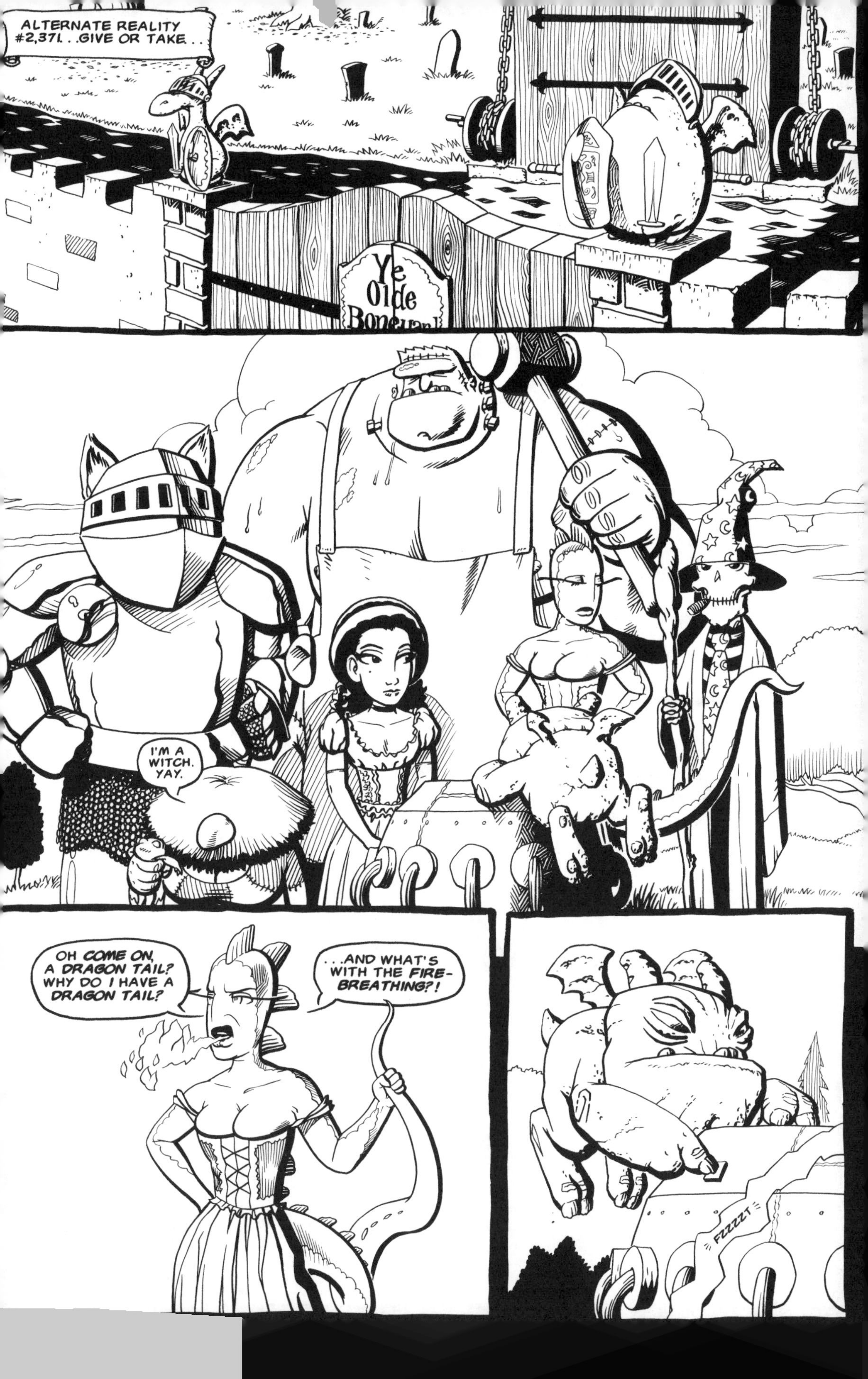
ALTERNATE REALITY #2,371. . .GIVE OR TAKE. . .
Ye Olde Boneyard
I'M A WITCH. YAY.
OH COME ON, A DRAGON TAIL? WHY DO I HAVE A DRAGON TAIL?
. . .AND WHAT'S WITH THE FIRE-BREATHING?!
FZZZZT

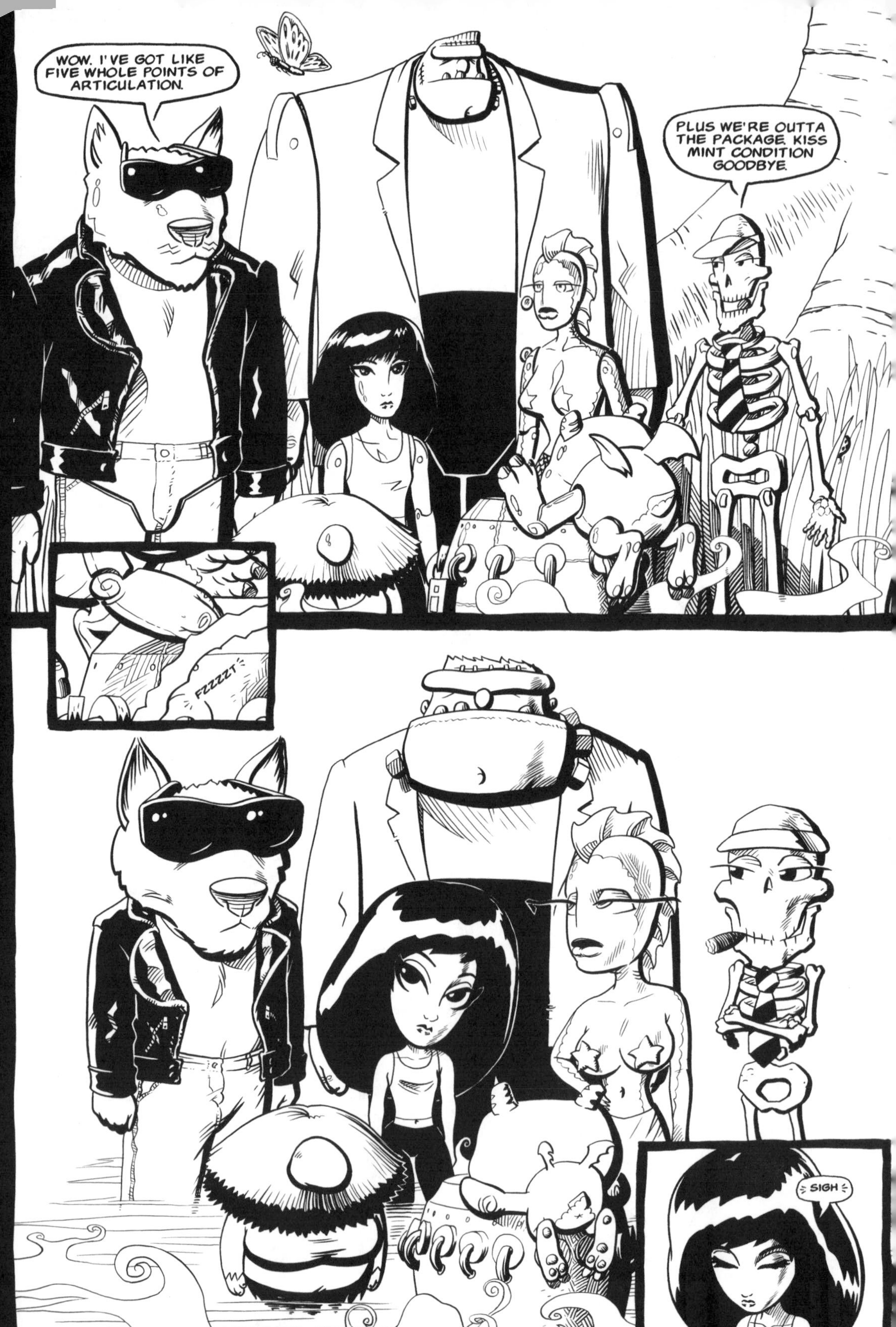
WOW. I'VE GOT LIKE FIVE WHOLE POINTS OF ARTICULATION.
PLUS WE'RE OUTTA THE PACKAGE. KISS MINT CONDITION GOODBYE.
FZZZZT
SIGH

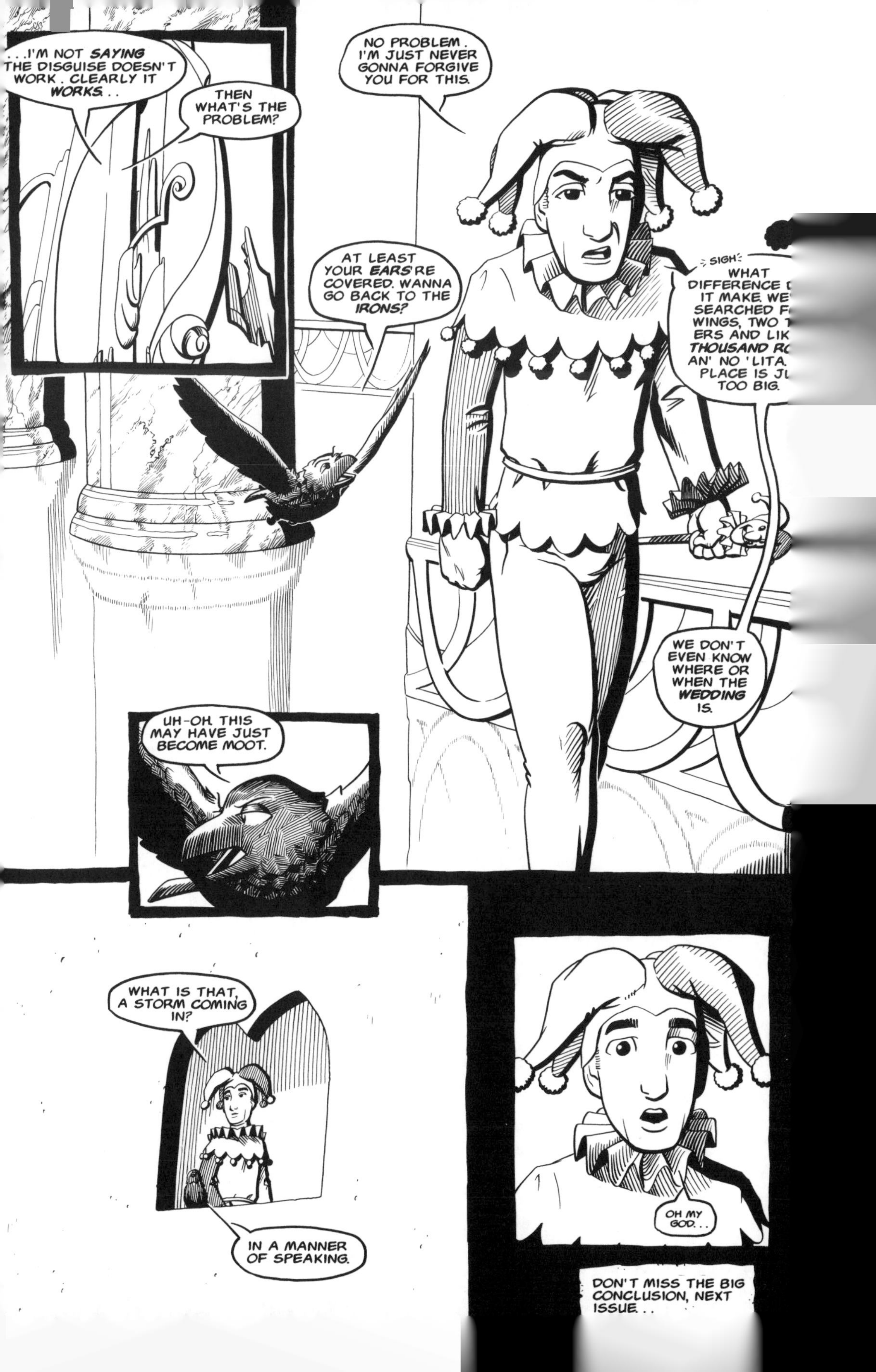
...I'M NOT SAYING THE DISGUISE DOESN'T WORK. CLEARLY IT WORKS...
THEN WHAT'S THE PROBLEM?
NO PROBLEM. I'M JUST NEVER GONNA FORGIVE YOU FOR THIS.
AT LEAST YOUR EARS'RE COVERED. WANNA GO BACK TO THE IRONS?
SIGH
WHAT DIFFERENCE D IT MAKE. WE SEARCHED F WINGS, TWO T ERS AND LIK THOUSAND RO AN' NO 'LITA. PLACE IS JU TOO BIG.
WE DON'T EVEN KNOW WHERE OR WHEN THE WEDDING IS.
UH-OH. THIS MAY HAVE JUST BECOME MOOT.
WHAT IS THAT, A STORM COMING IN?
IN A MANNER OF SPEAKING.
OH MY GOD...
DON'T MISS THE BIG CONCLUSION, NEXT ISSUE...

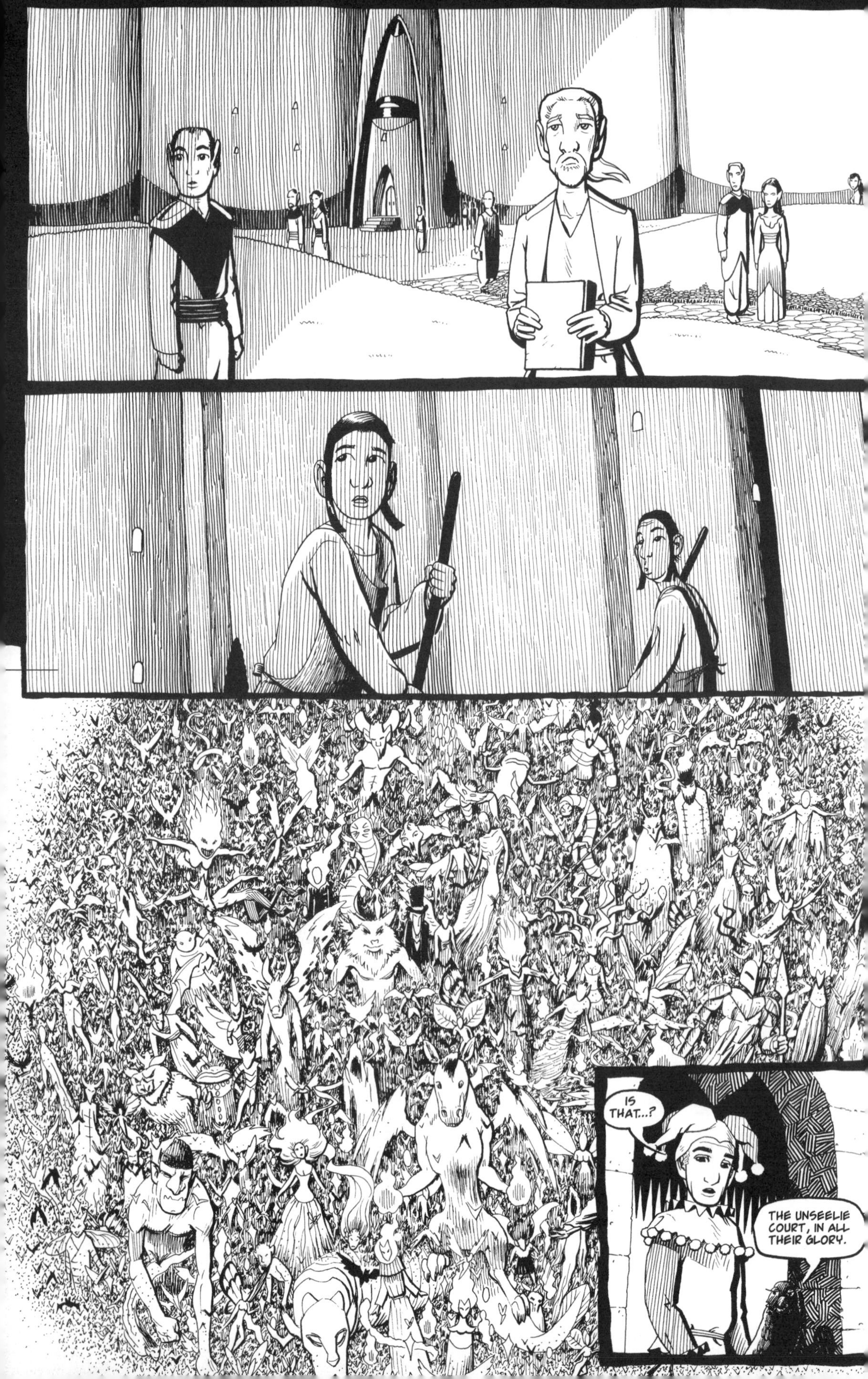
IS THAT...?
THE UNSEELIE COURT, IN ALL THEIR GLORY.

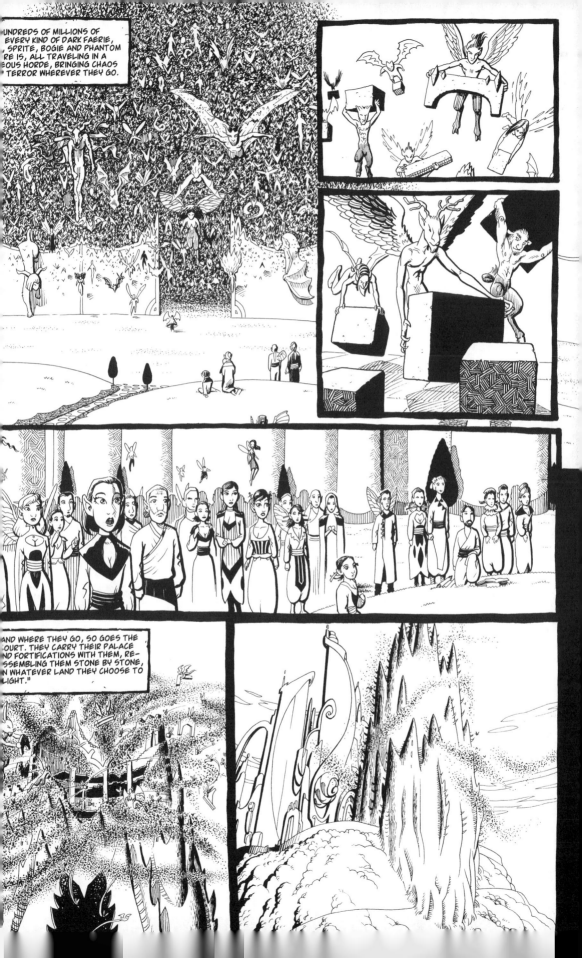

...UNDREDS OF MILLIONS OF
...EVERY KIND OF DARK FAERIE,
..., SPRITE, BOGIE AND PHANTOM
...RE IS, ALL TRAVELING IN A
...OUS HORDE, BRINGING CHAOS
... TERROR WHEREVER THEY GO.

...AND WHERE THEY GO, SO GOES THE
...OURT. THEY CARRY THEIR PALACE
...ND FORTIFICATIONS WITH THEM, RE-
...SSEMBLING THEM STONE BY STONE,
...N WHATEVER LAND THEY CHOOSE TO
...LIGHT."

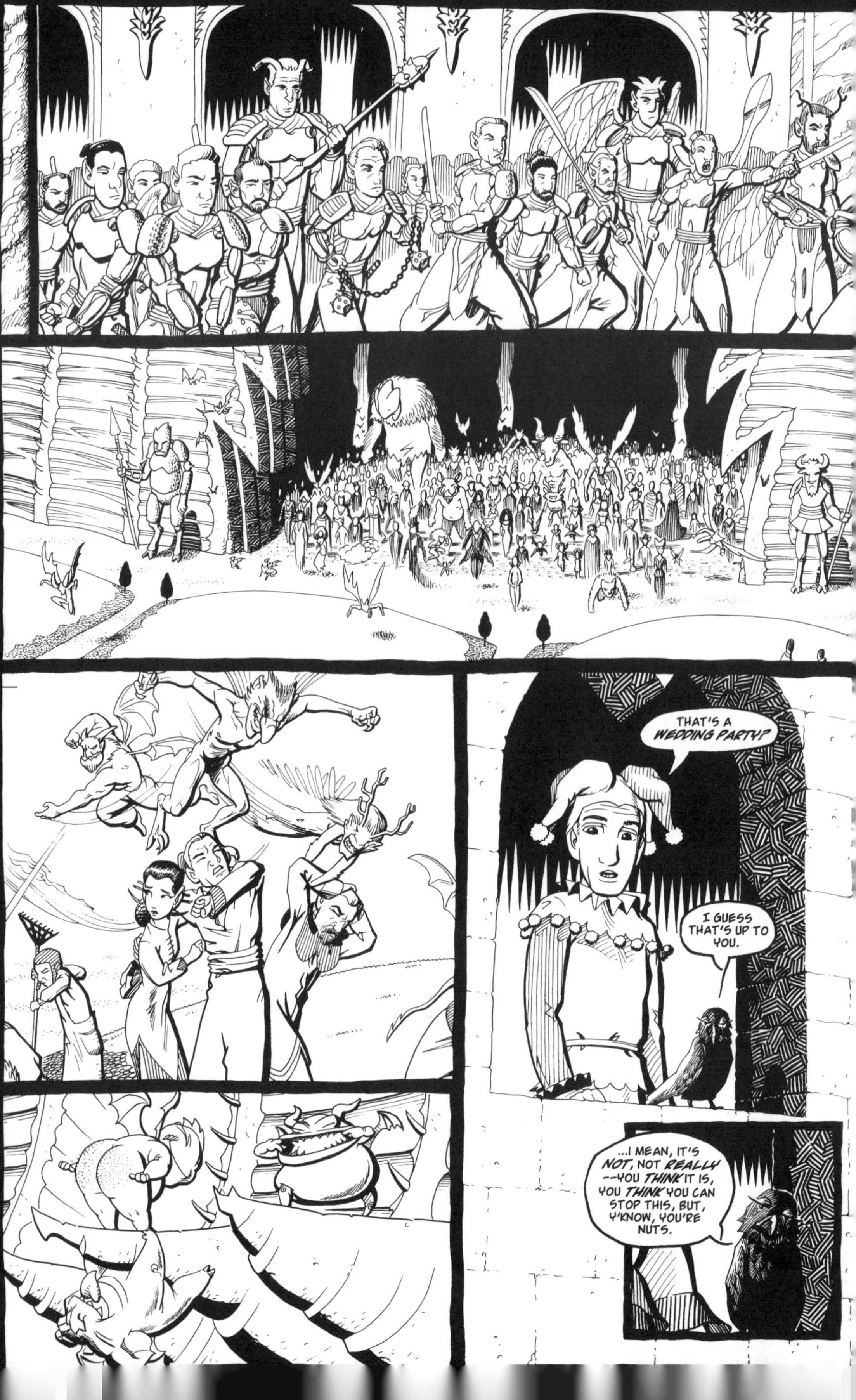
THAT'S A WEDDING PARTY?
I GUESS THAT'S UP TO YOU.
...I MEAN, IT'S NOT, NOT REALLY --YOU THINK IT IS, YOU THINK YOU CAN STOP THIS, BUT, Y'KNOW, YOU'RE NUTS.

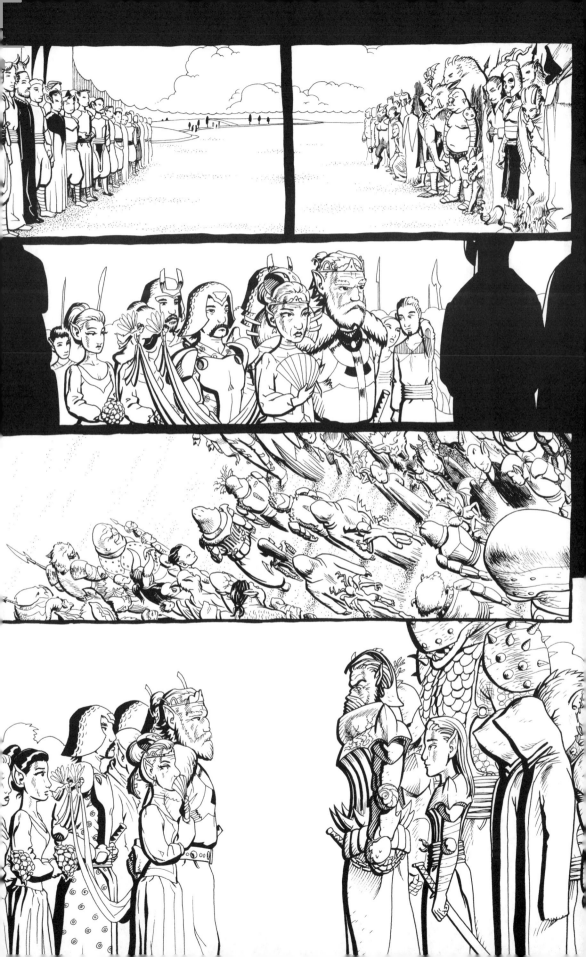

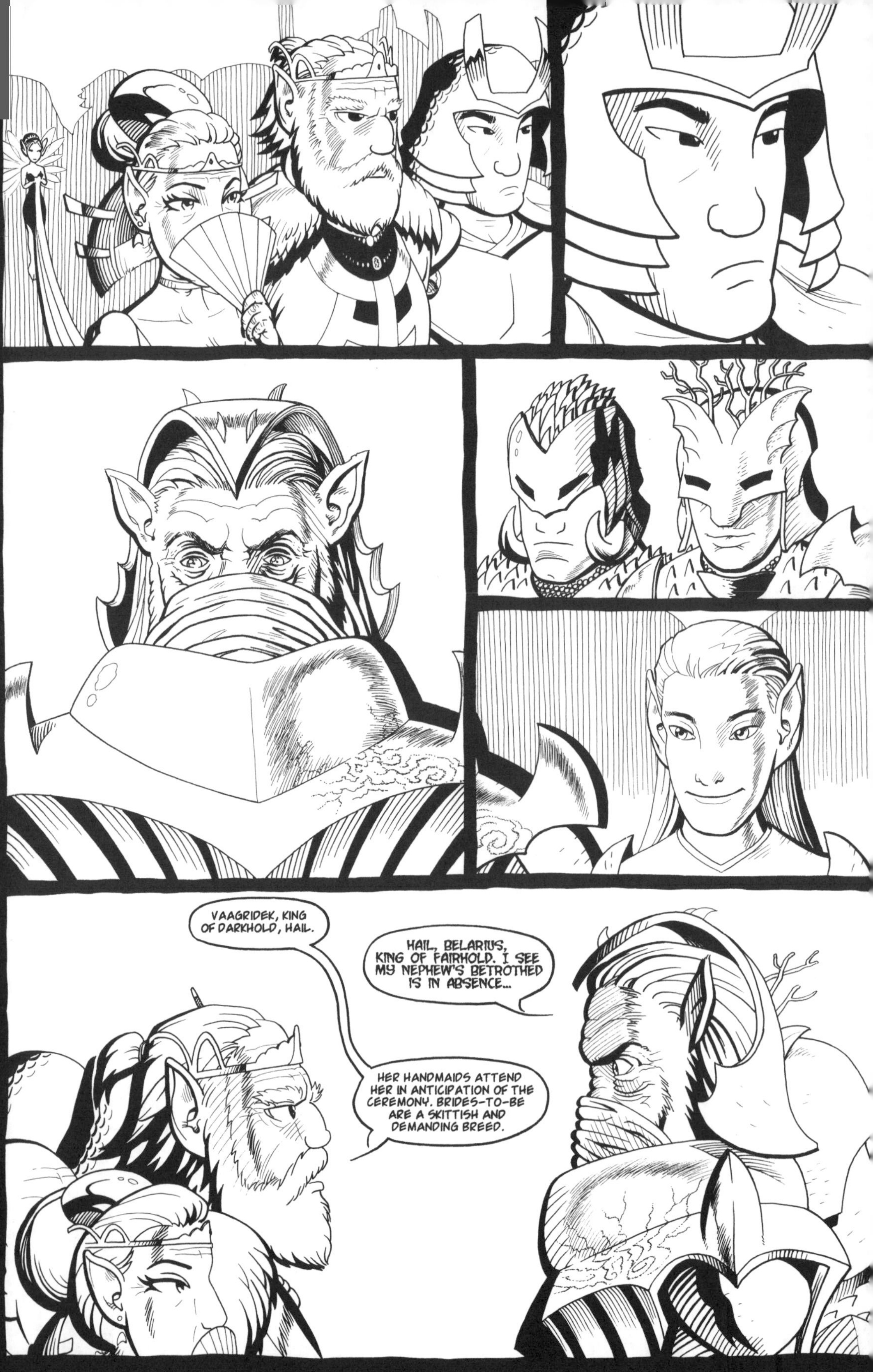
VAAGRIDEK, KING OF DARKHOLD, HAIL.
HAIL, BELARIUS, KING OF FAIRHOLD. I SEE MY NEPHEW'S BETROTHED IS IN ABSENCE...
HER HANDMAIDS ATTEND HER IN ANTICIPATION OF THE CEREMONY. BRIDES-TO-BE ARE A SKITTISH AND DEMANDING BREED.

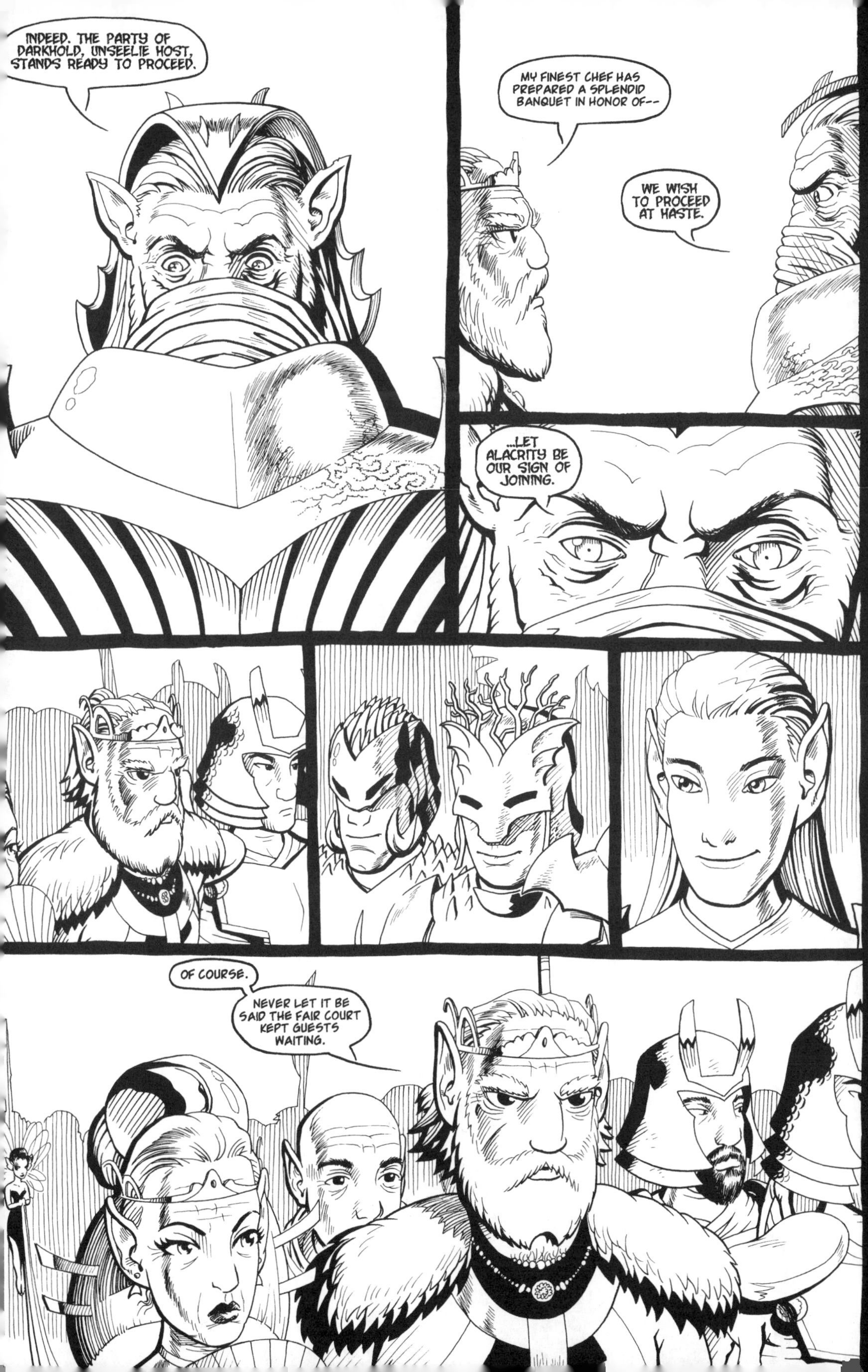
INDEED. THE PARTY OF DARKHOLD, UNSEELIE HOST, STANDS READY TO PROCEED.
MY FINEST CHEF HAS PREPARED A SPLENDID BANQUET IN HONOR OF--
WE WISH TO PROCEED AT HASTE.
...LET ALACRITY BE OUR SIGN OF JOINING.
OF COURSE.
NEVER LET IT BE SAID THE FAIR COURT KEPT GUESTS WAITING.

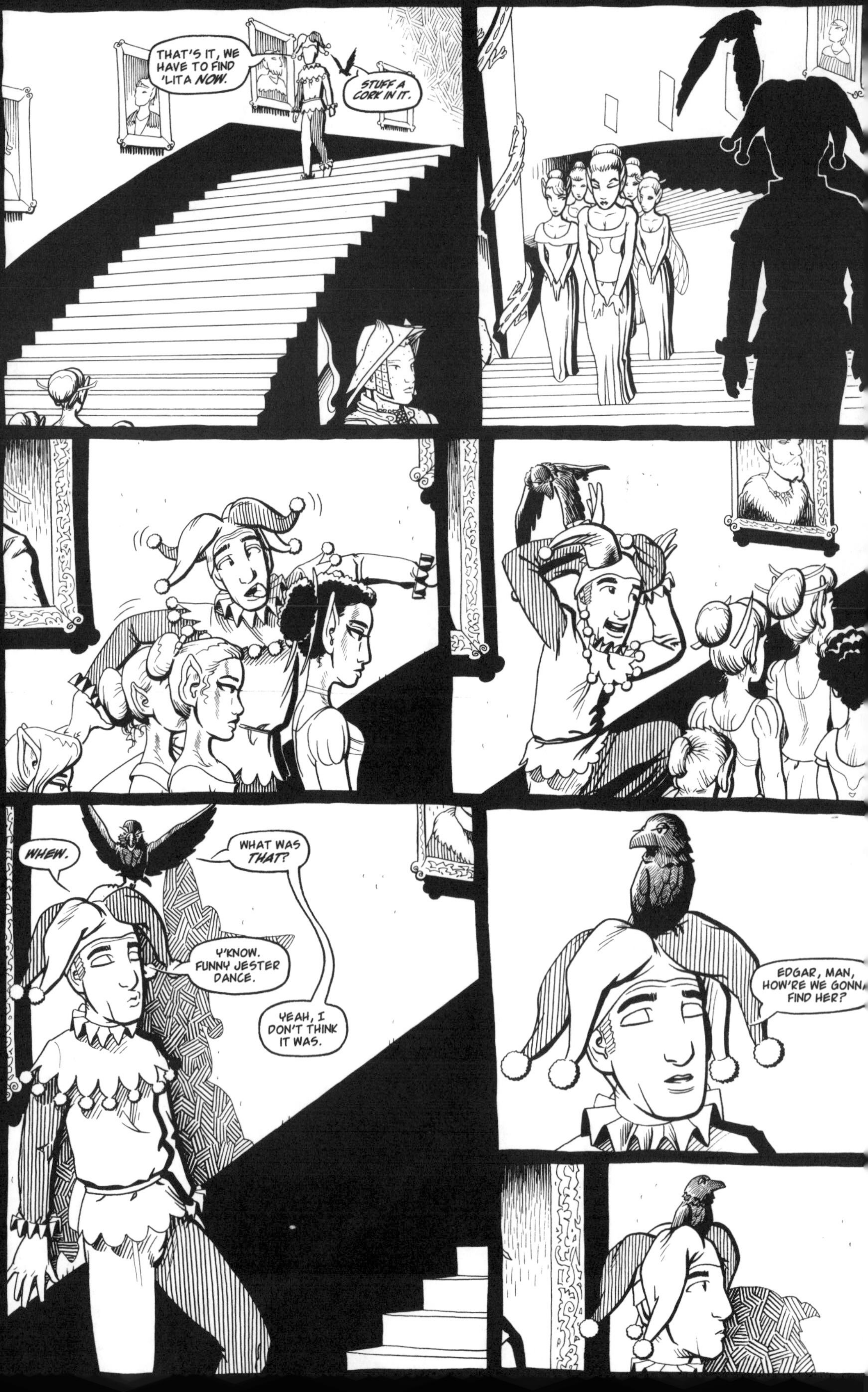

THAT'S IT, WE HAVE TO FIND 'LITA NOW.
STUFF A CORK IN IT.
WHEW.
WHAT WAS THAT?
Y'KNOW. FUNNY JESTER DANCE.
YEAH, I DON'T THINK IT WAS.
EDGAR, MAN, HOW'RE WE GONN FIND HER?

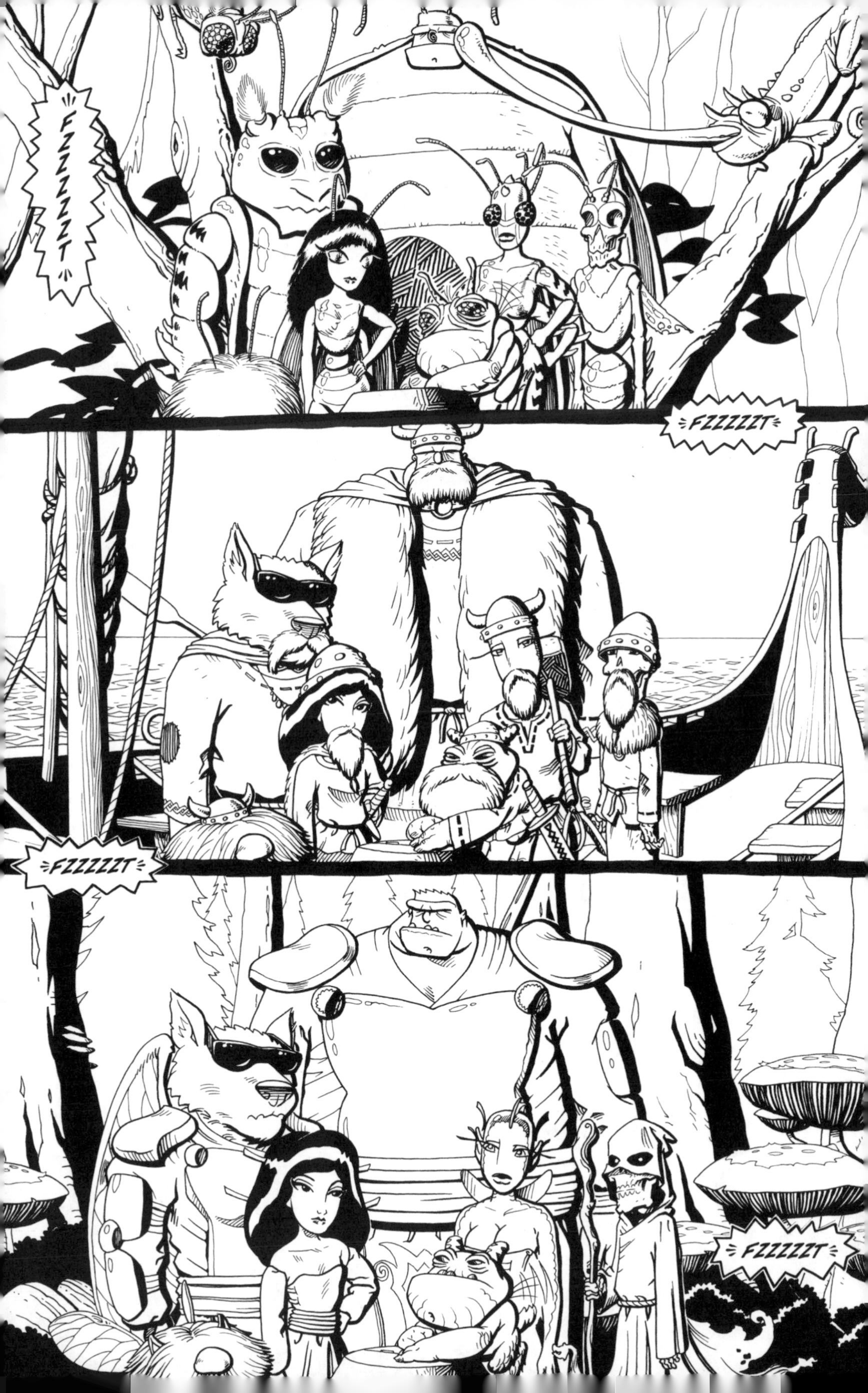
FZZZZZZT
FZZZZZZT
FZZZZZZT
FZZZZZZT

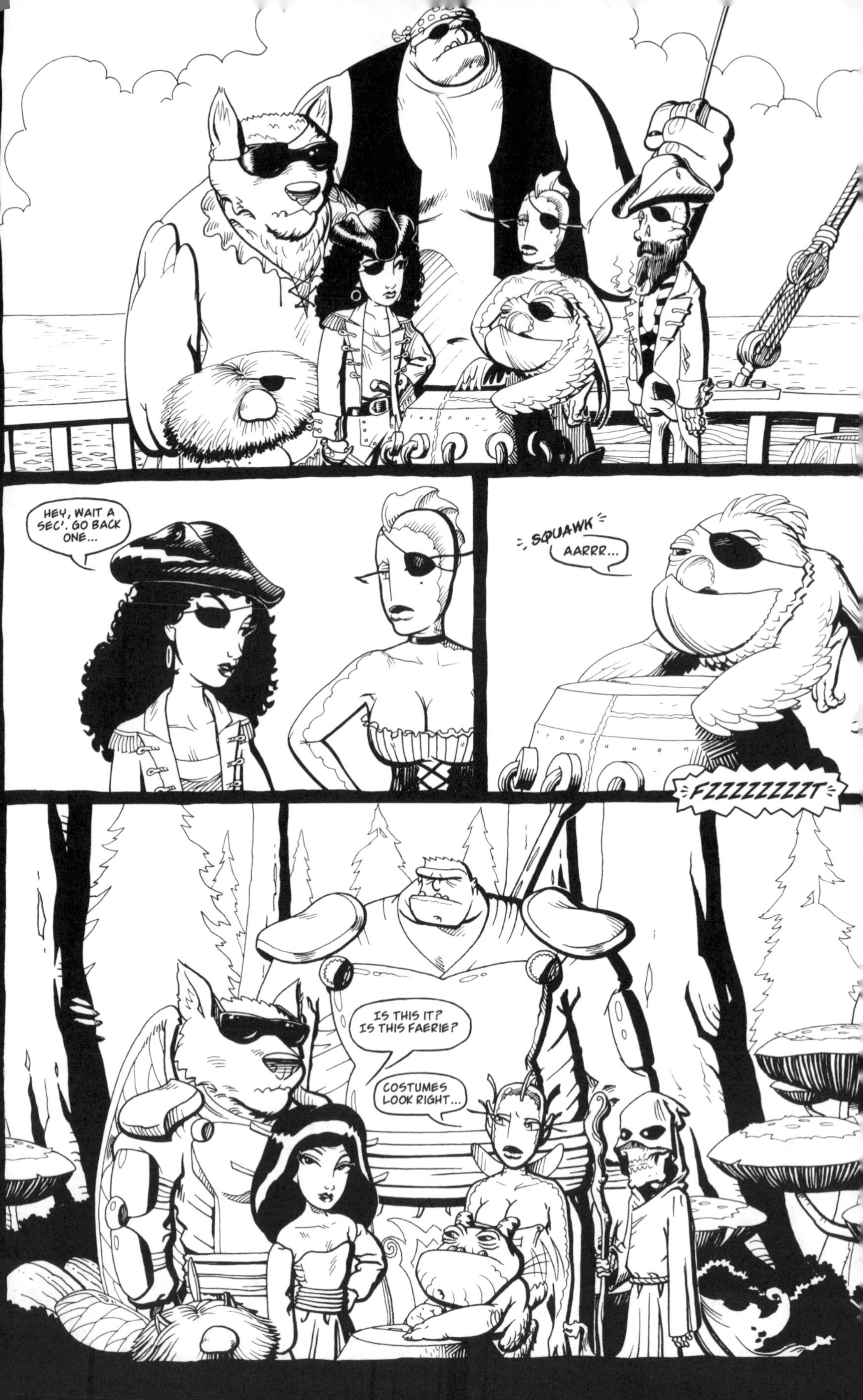
HEY, WAIT A SEC'. GO BACK ONE...
SQUAWK
AARRR...
FZZZZZZZZT
IS THIS IT? IS THIS FAERIE?
COSTUMES LOOK RIGHT...

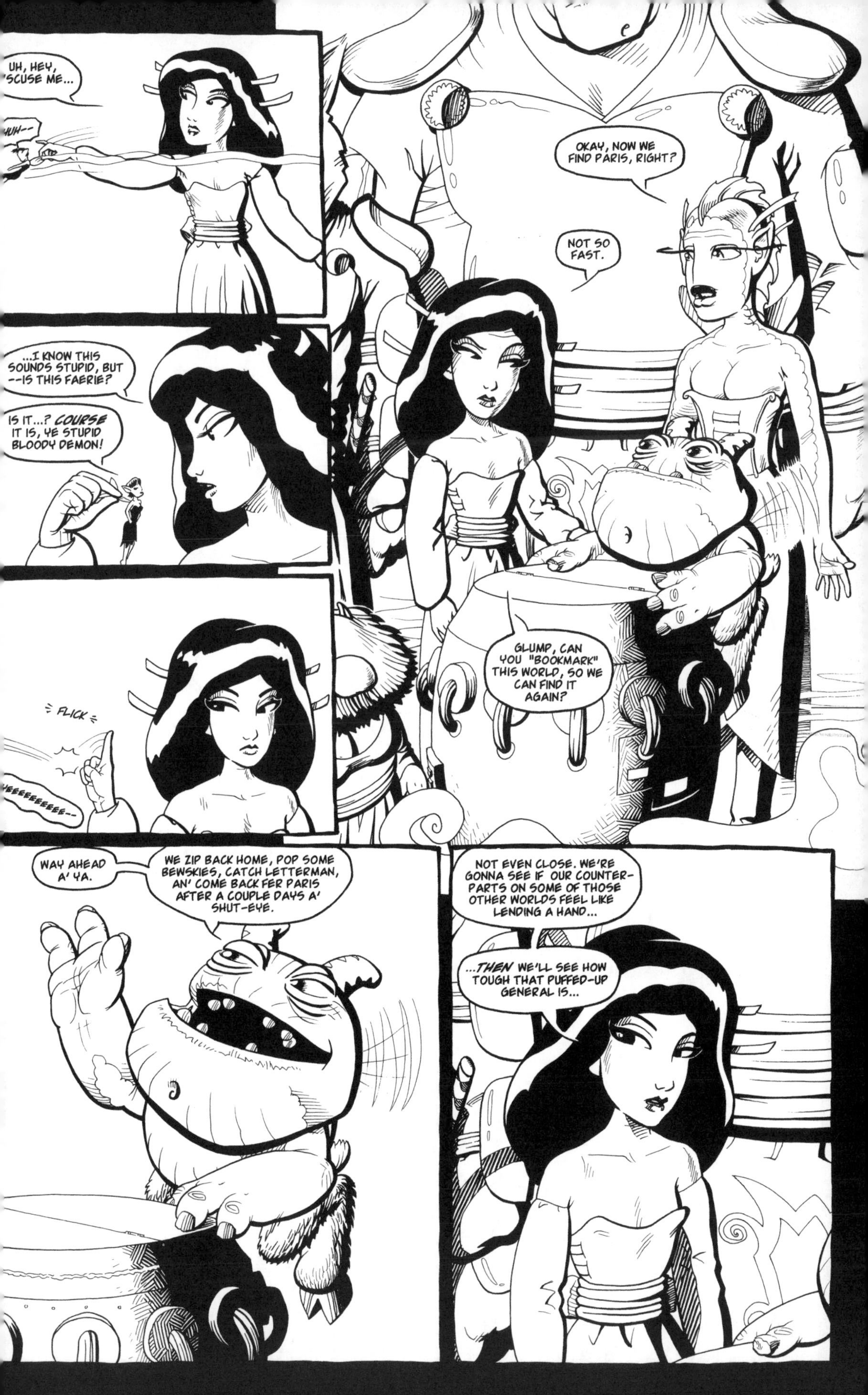
UH, HEY, 'SCUSE ME...
HUH--
OKAY, NOW WE FIND PARIS, RIGHT?
NOT SO FAST.
...I KNOW THIS SOUNDS STUPID, BUT --IS THIS FAERIE?
IS IT...? COURSE IT IS, YE STUPID BLOODY DEMON!
FLICK
HEEEEEEEEEE--
GLUMP, CAN YOU "BOOKMARK" THIS WORLD, SO WE CAN FIND IT AGAIN?
WAY AHEAD A' YA.
WE ZIP BACK HOME, POP SOME BEWSKIES, CATCH LETTERMAN, AN' COME BACK FER PARIS AFTER A COUPLE DAYS A' SHUT-EYE.
NOT EVEN CLOSE. WE'RE GONNA SEE IF OUR COUNTER-PARTS ON SOME OF THOSE OTHER WORLDS FEEL LIKE LENDING A HAND...
...THEN WE'LL SEE HOW TOUGH THAT PUFFED-UP GENERAL IS...

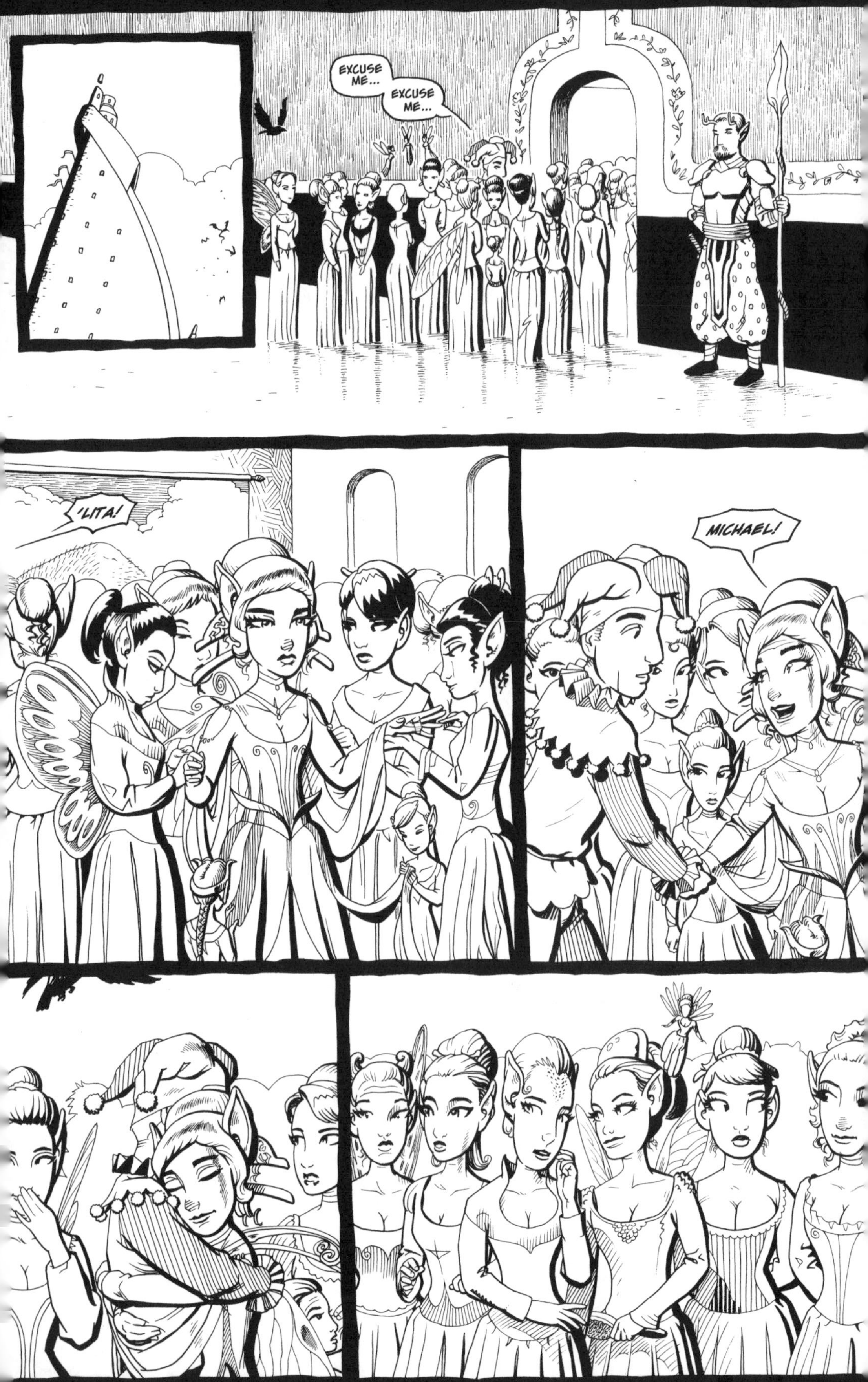
EXCUSE ME...
EXCUSE ME...
'LITA!
MICHAEL!

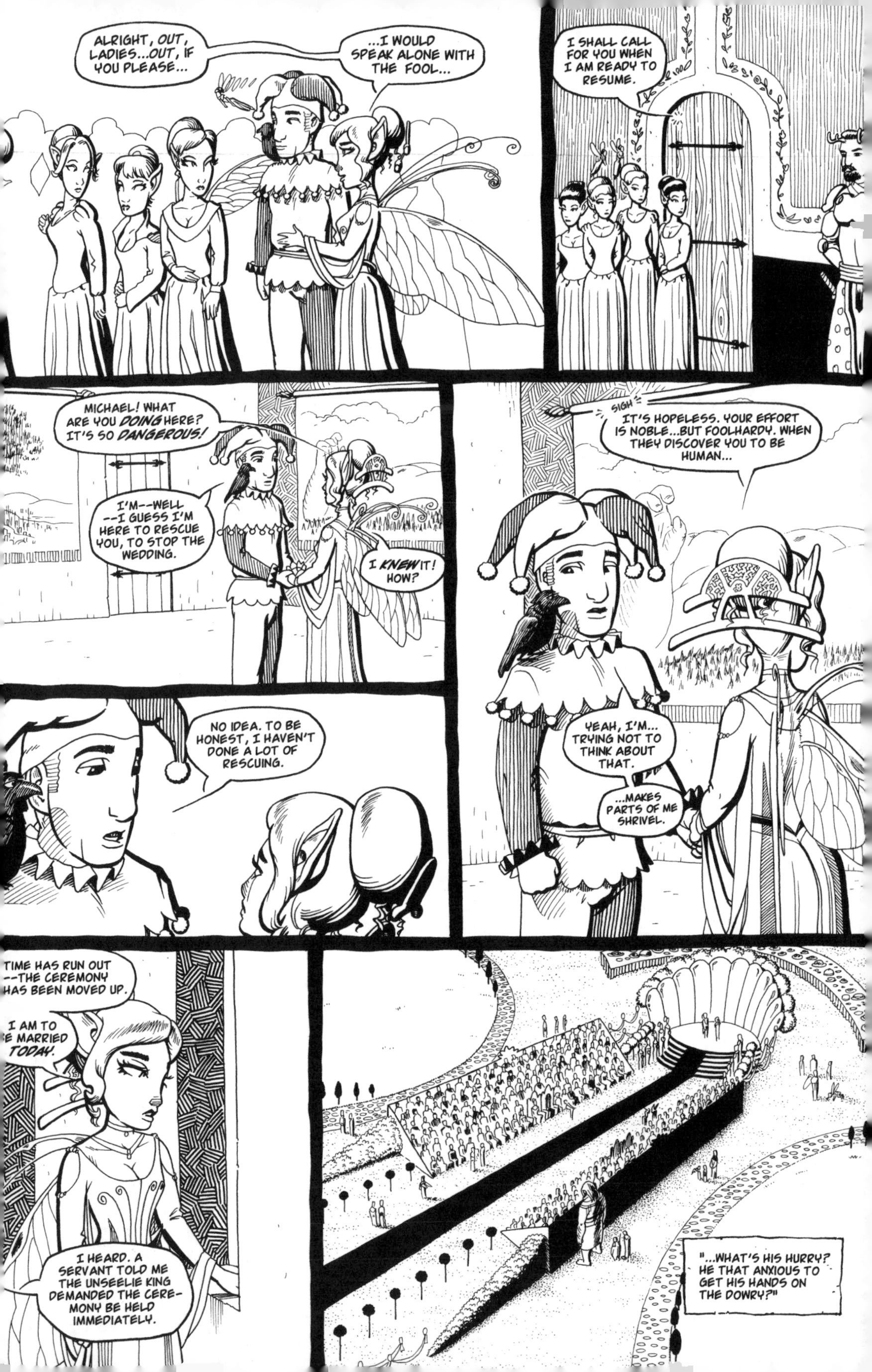
ALRIGHT, OUT, LADIES...OUT, IF YOU PLEASE...
...I WOULD SPEAK ALONE WITH THE FOOL...
I SHALL CALL FOR YOU WHEN I AM READY TO RESUME.
MICHAEL! WHAT ARE YOU DOING HERE? IT'S SO DANGEROUS!
I'M--WELL --I GUESS I'M HERE TO RESCUE YOU, TO STOP THE WEDDING.
I KNEW IT! HOW?
SIGH
IT'S HOPELESS. YOUR EFFORT IS NOBLE...BUT FOOLHARDY. WHEN THEY DISCOVER YOU TO BE HUMAN...
NO IDEA. TO BE HONEST, I HAVEN'T DONE A LOT OF RESCUING.
YEAH, I'M... TRYING NOT TO THINK ABOUT THAT.
...MAKES PARTS OF ME SHRIVEL.
TIME HAS RUN OUT --THE CEREMONY HAS BEEN MOVED UP.
I AM TO BE MARRIED TODAY.
I HEARD. A SERVANT TOLD ME THE UNSEELIE KING DEMANDED THE CEREMONY BE HELD IMMEDIATELY.
"...WHAT'S HIS HURRY? HE THAT ANXIOUS TO GET HIS HANDS ON THE DOWRY?"

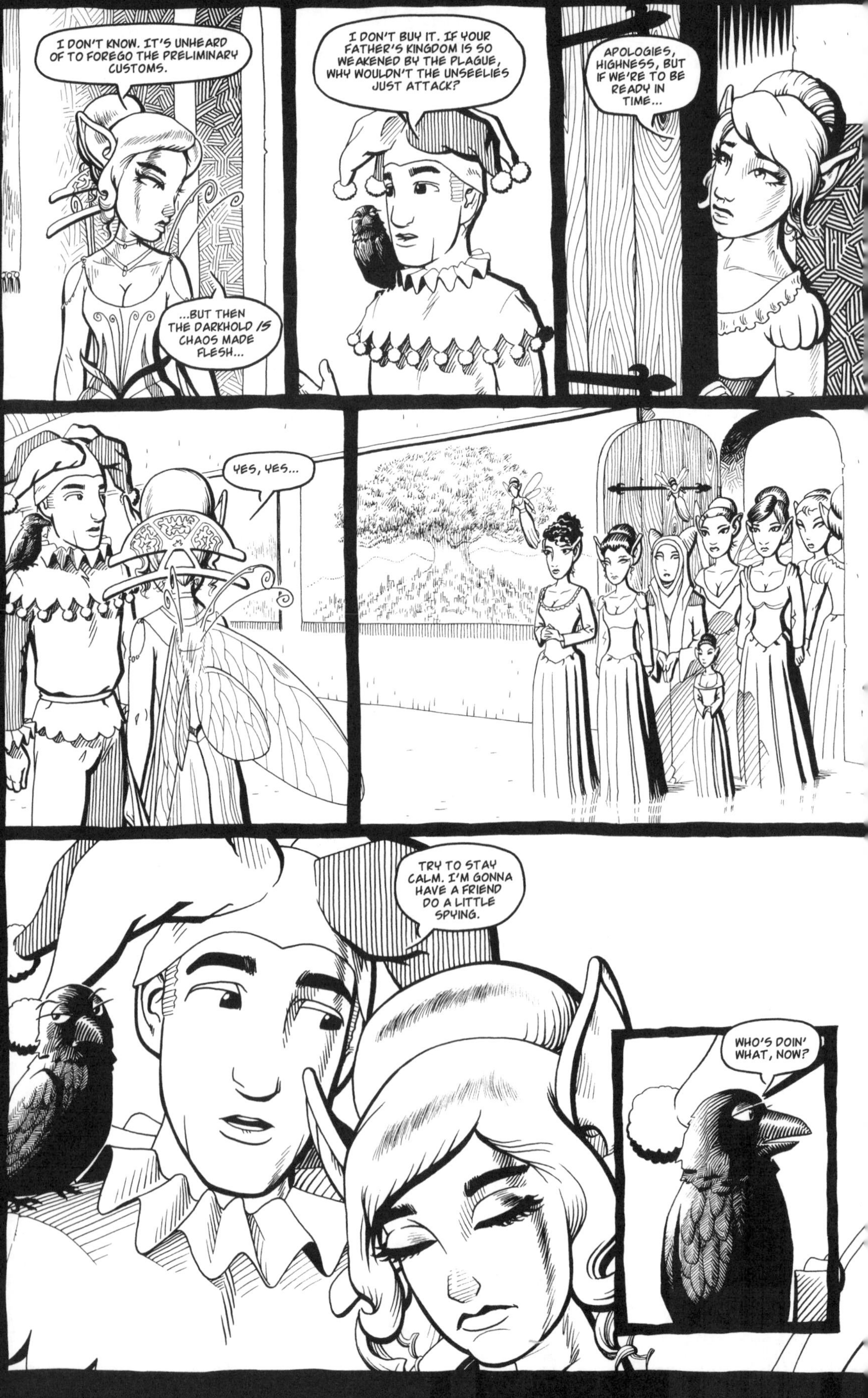
I DON'T KNOW. IT'S UNHEARD OF TO FOREGO THE PRELIMINARY CUSTOMS.
...BUT THEN THE DARKHOLD IS CHAOS MADE FLESH...
I DON'T BUY IT. IF YOUR FATHER'S KINGDOM IS SO WEAKENED BY THE PLAGUE, WHY WOULDN'T THE UNSEELIES JUST ATTACK?
APOLOGIES, HIGHNESS, BUT IF WE'RE TO BE READY IN TIME...
YES, YES...
TRY TO STAY CALM. I'M GONNA HAVE A FRIEND DO A LITTLE SPYING.
WHO'S DOIN' WHAT, NOW?

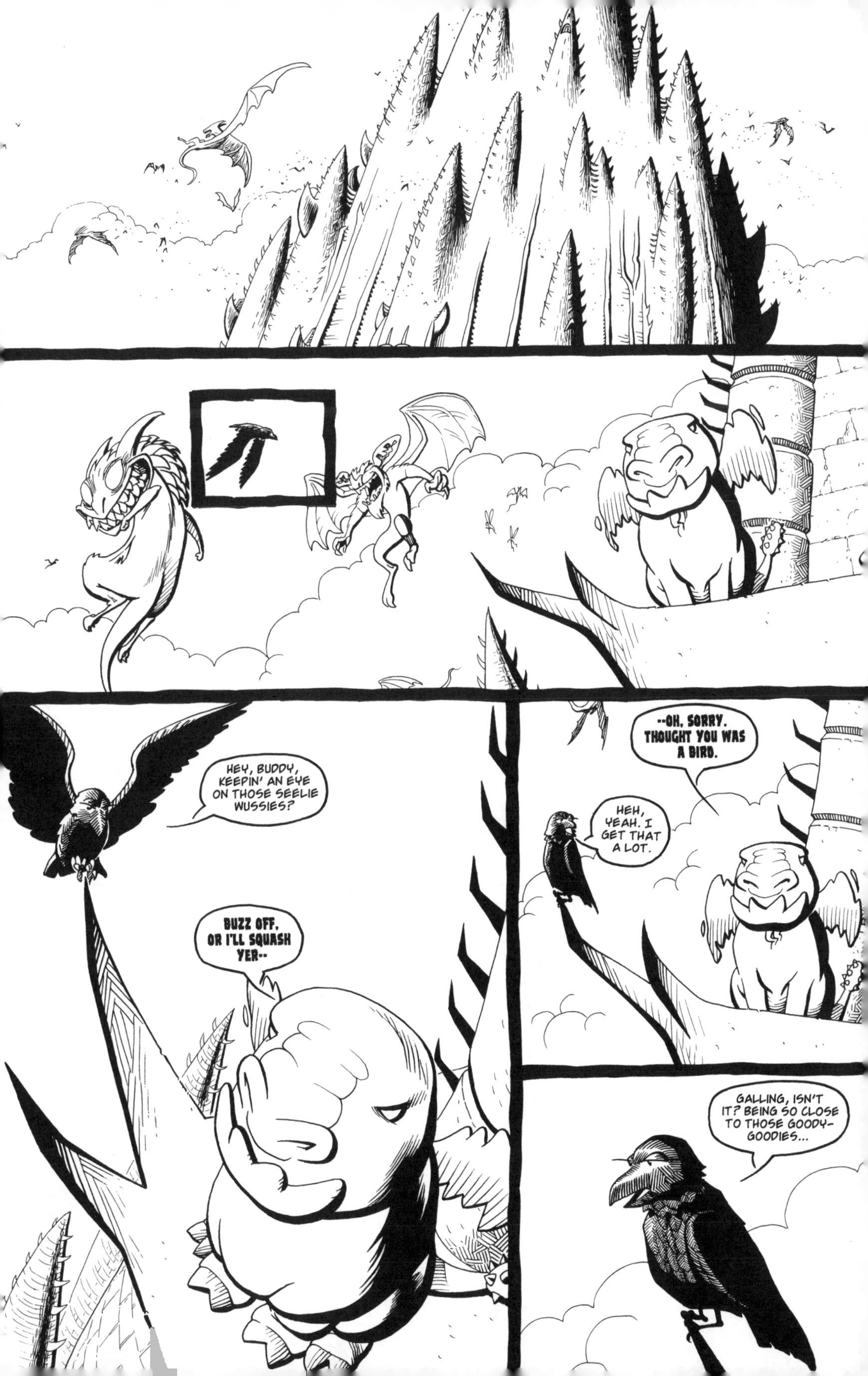
HEY, BUDDY, KEEPIN' AN EYE ON THOSE SEELIE WUSSIES?
BUZZ OFF, OR I'LL SQUASH YER--
--OH, SORRY. THOUGHT YOU WAS A BIRD.
HEH, YEAH. I GET THAT A LOT.
GALLING, ISN'T IT? BEING SO CLOSE TO THOSE GOODY-GOODIES...

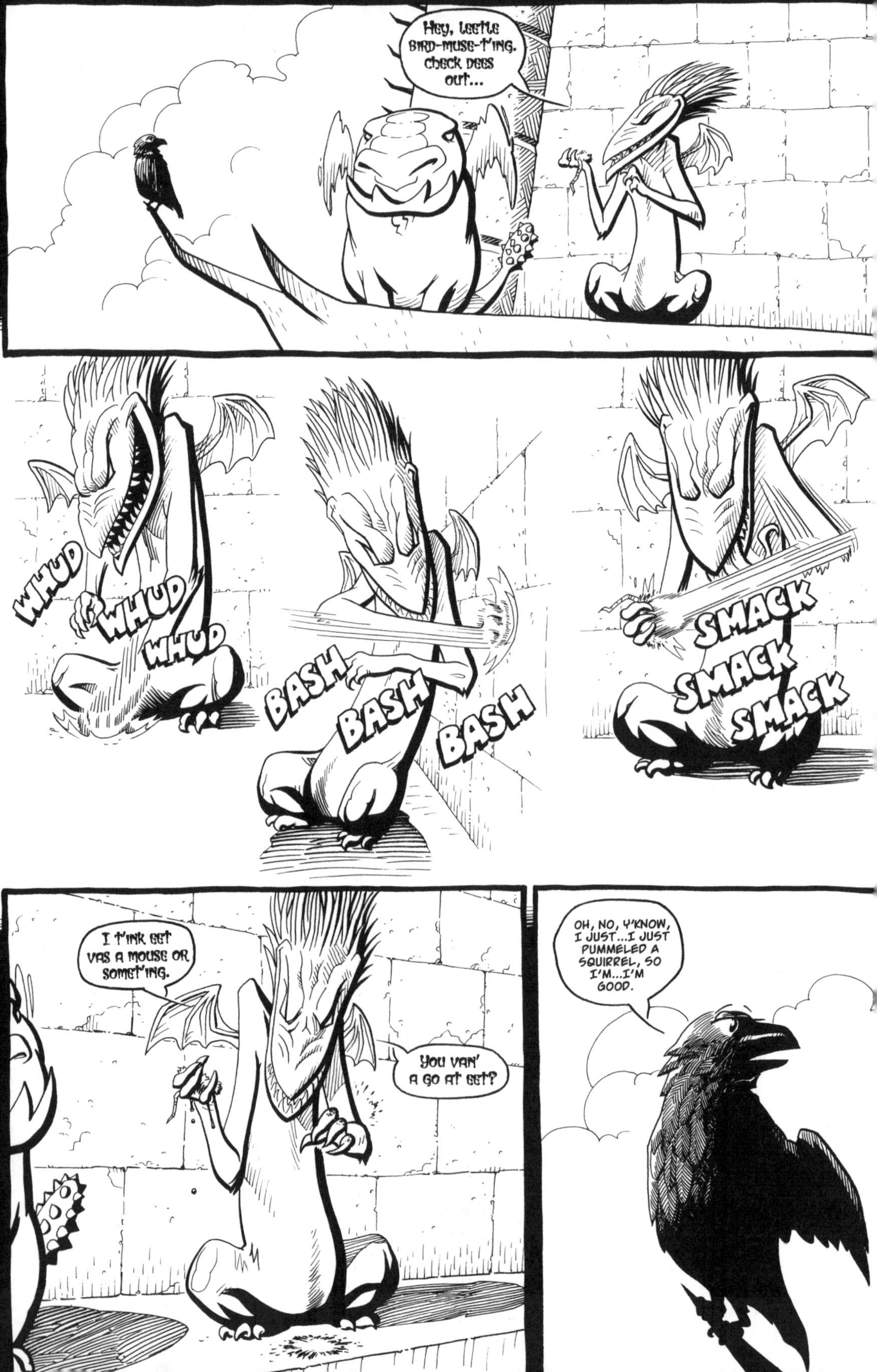
Hey, leetle BIRD-MUSE-T'ING. Check dees out...
WHUD
WHUD
WHUD
BASH
BASH
BASH
SMACK
SMACK
SMACK
I t'ink eet vas a mouse or somet'ing.
You van' a go at eet?
OH, NO, Y'KNOW, I JUST...I JUST PUMMELED A SQUIRREL, SO I'M...I'M GOOD.

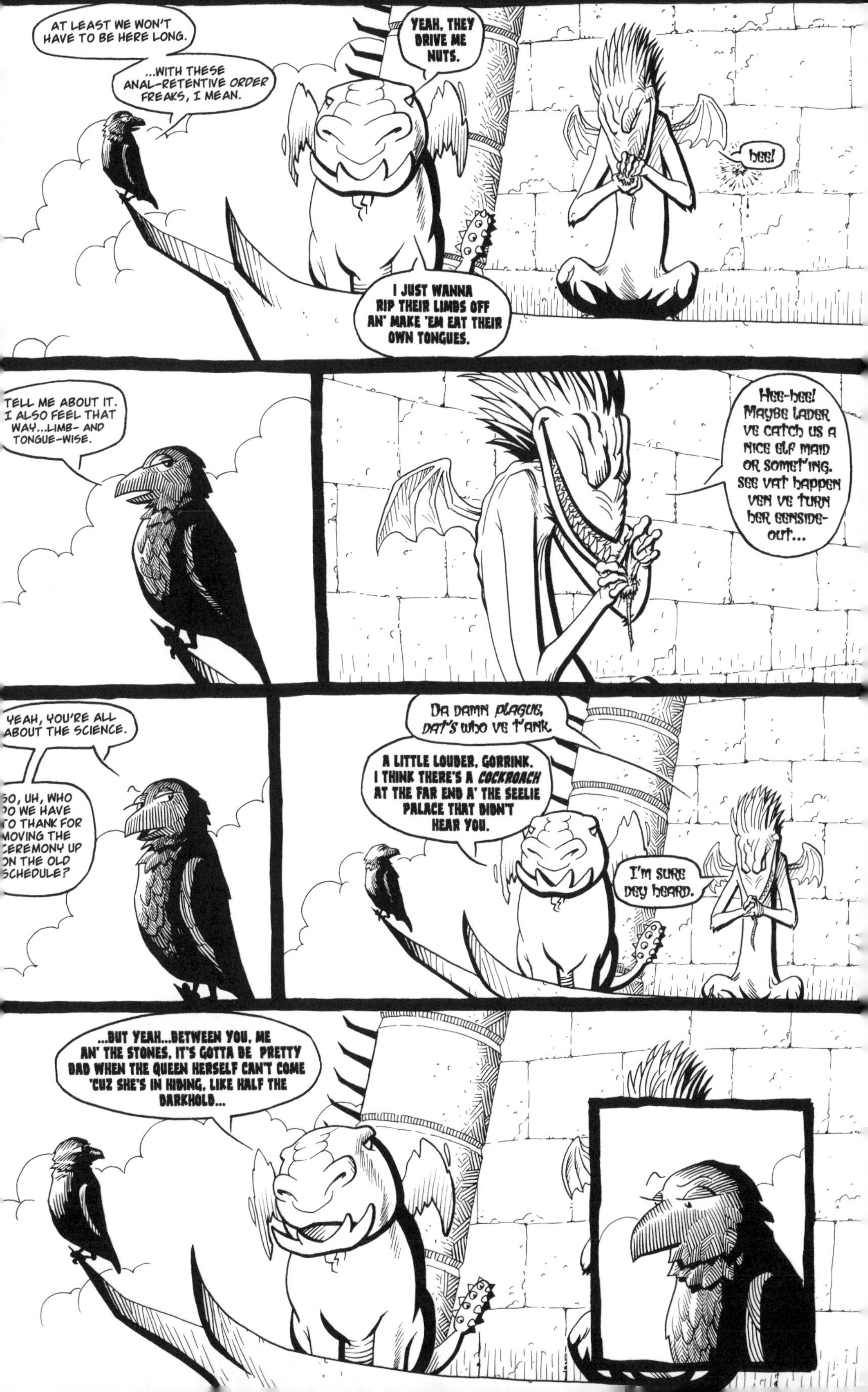
AT LEAST WE WON'T HAVE TO BE HERE LONG.
YEAH, THEY DRIVE ME NUTS.
...WITH THESE ANAL-RETENTIVE ORDER FREAKS, I MEAN.
hee!
I JUST WANNA RIP THEIR LIMBS OFF AN' MAKE 'EM EAT THEIR OWN TONGUES.
TELL ME ABOUT IT. I ALSO FEEL THAT WAY...LIMB- AND TONGUE-WISE.
Hee-hee! Maybe lader ve catch us a nice elf maid or somet'ing. See vat happen ven ve turn her eenside-out...
YEAH, YOU'RE ALL ABOUT THE SCIENCE.
SO, UH, WHO DO WE HAVE TO THANK FOR MOVING THE CEREMONY UP ON THE OLD SCHEDULE?
Da damn plague, dat's who ve t'ank.
A LITTLE LOUDER, GORRINK. I THINK THERE'S A COCKROACH AT THE FAR END A' THE SEELIE PALACE THAT DIDN'T HEAR YOU.
I'm sure dey heard.
...BUT YEAH...BETWEEN YOU, ME AN' THE STONES, IT'S GOTTA BE PRETTY BAD WHEN THE QUEEN HERSELF CAN'T COME 'CUZ SHE'S IN HIDING, LIKE HALF THE DARKHOLD...

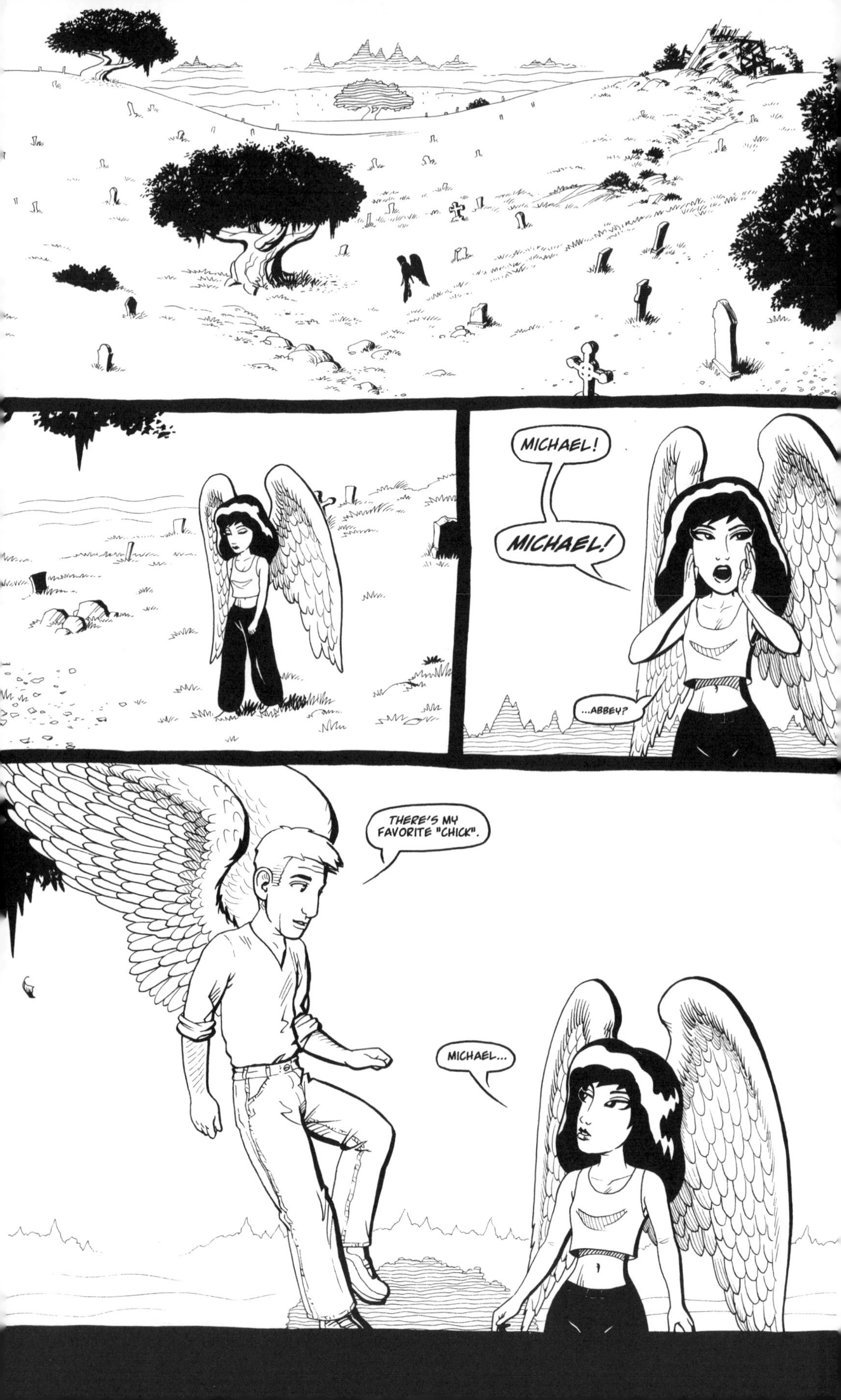
MICHAEL!
MICHAEL!
...ABBEY?
THERE'S MY FAVORITE "CHICK".
MICHAEL...

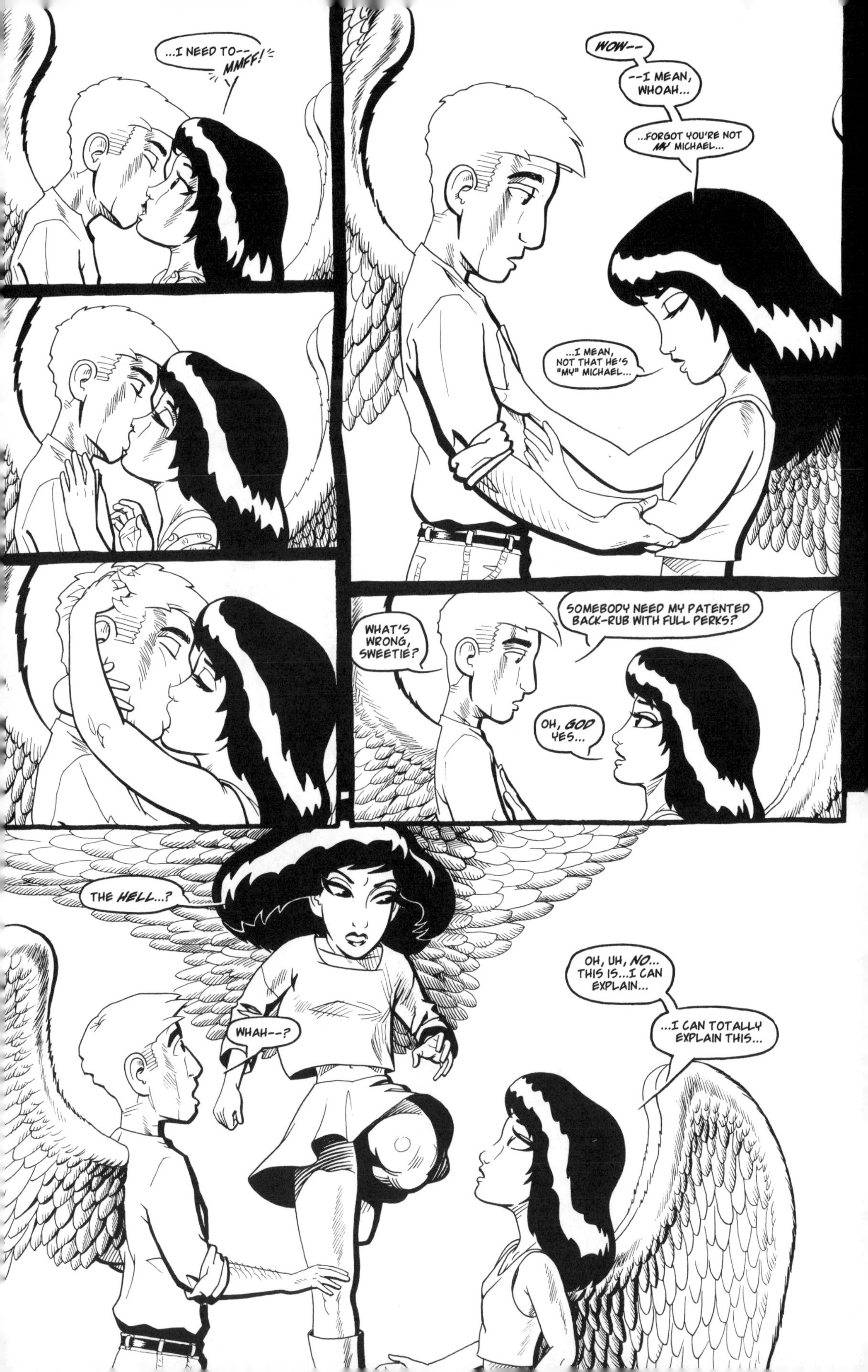

...I NEED TO--
MMFF!
WOW--
--I MEAN, WHOAH...
...FORGOT YOU'RE NOT MY MICHAEL...
...I MEAN, NOT THAT HE'S "MY" MICHAEL...
WHAT'S WRONG, SWEETIE?
SOMEBODY NEED MY PATENTED BACK-RUB WITH FULL PERKS?
OH, GOD YES...
THE HELL...?
WHAH--?
OH, UH, NO... THIS IS...I CAN EXPLAIN...
...I CAN TOTALLY EXPLAIN THIS...

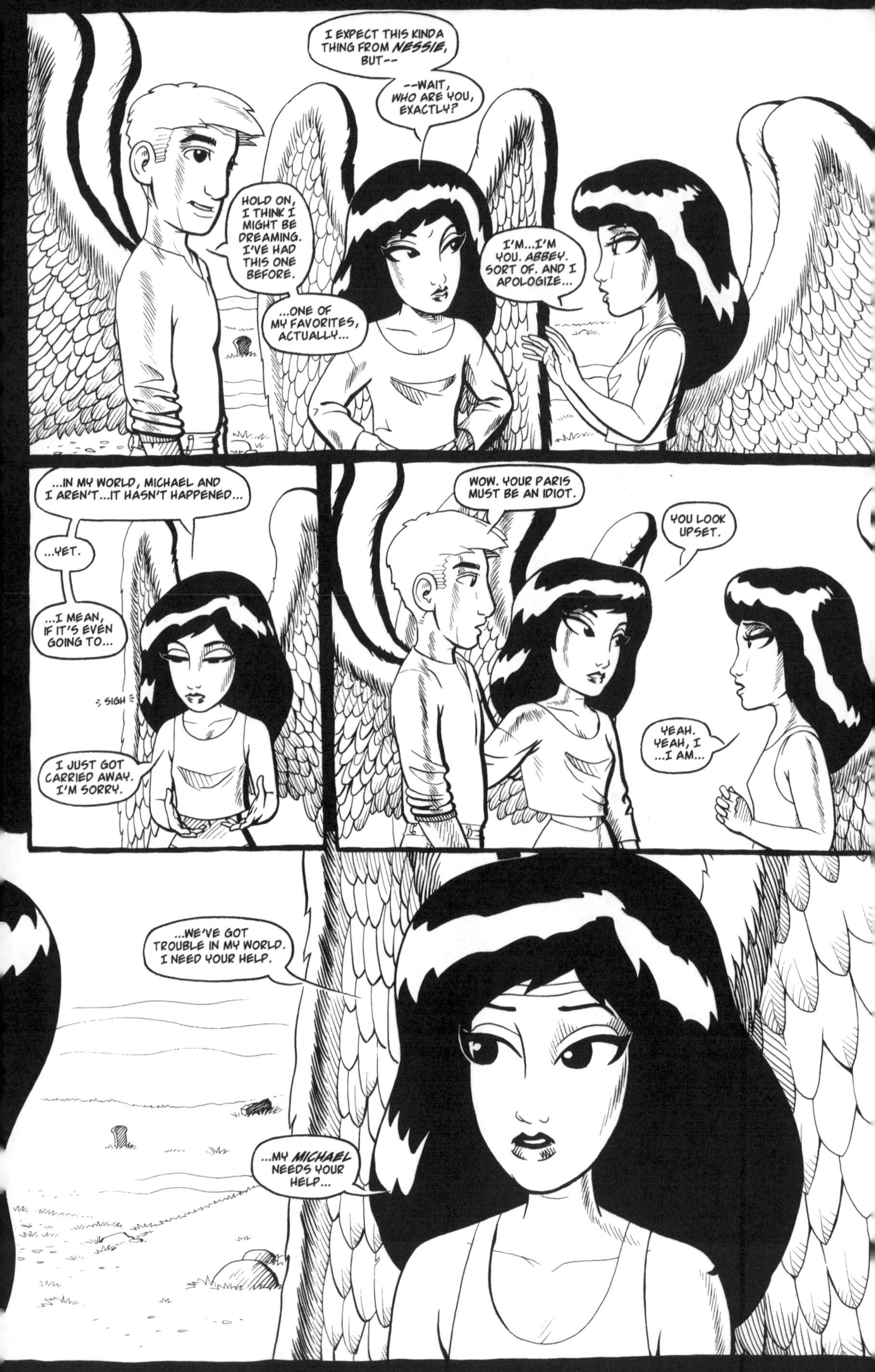
I EXPECT THIS KINDA THING FROM *NESSIE*, BUT--
--WAIT, WHO ARE YOU, EXACTLY?
HOLD ON, I THINK I MIGHT BE DREAMING. I'VE HAD THIS ONE BEFORE.
...ONE OF MY FAVORITES, ACTUALLY...
I'M...I'M YOU. *ABBEY.* SORT OF. AND I APOLOGIZE...
...IN MY WORLD, MICHAEL AND I AREN'T...IT HASN'T HAPPENED...
...YET.
...I MEAN, IF IT'S EVEN GOING TO...
SIGH
I JUST GOT CARRIED AWAY. I'M SORRY.
WOW. YOUR PARIS MUST BE AN IDIOT.
YOU LOOK UPSET.
YEAH. YEAH, I ...I AM...
...WE'VE GOT TROUBLE IN MY WORLD. I NEED YOUR HELP.
...MY *MICHAEL* NEEDS YOUR HELP...

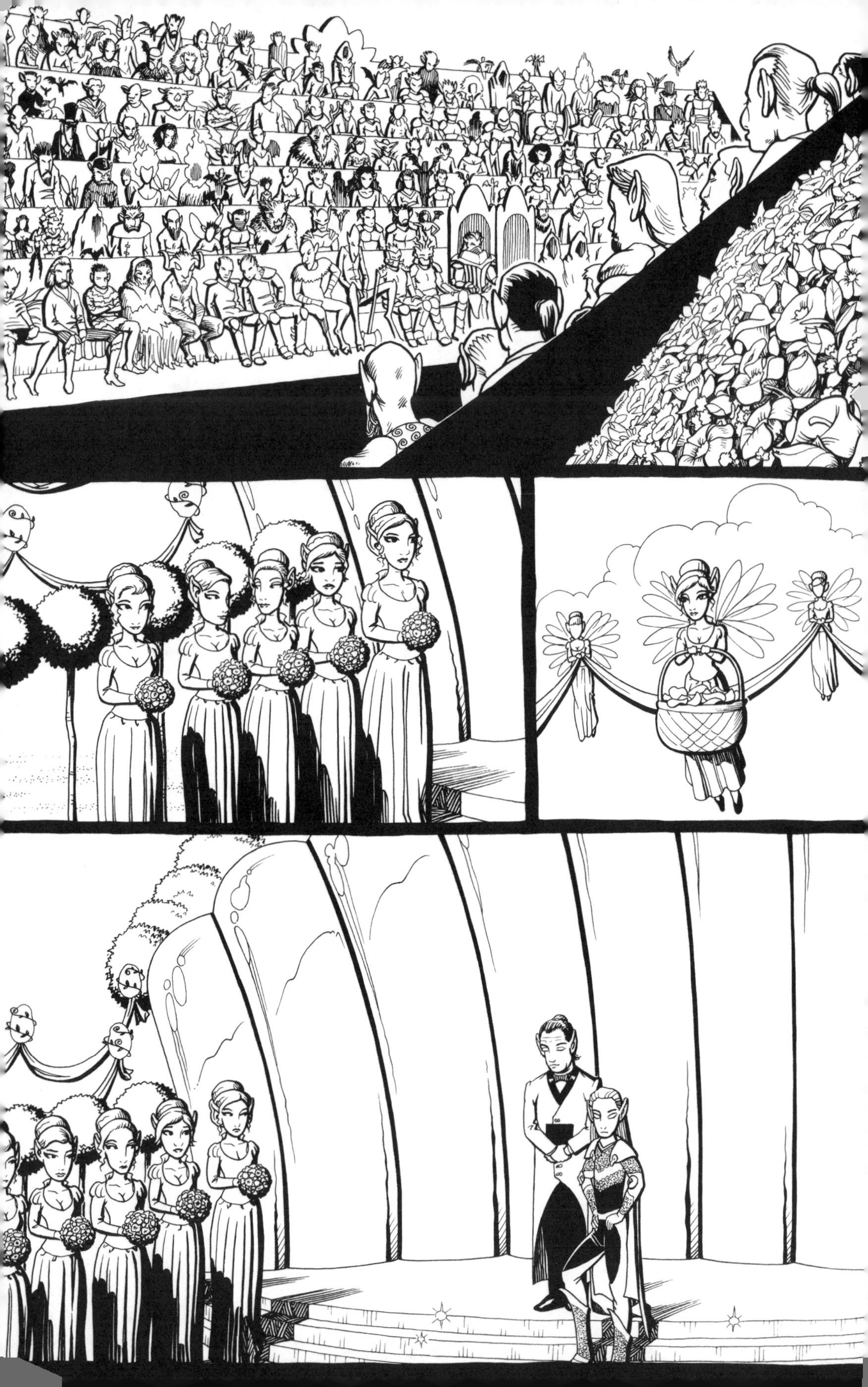

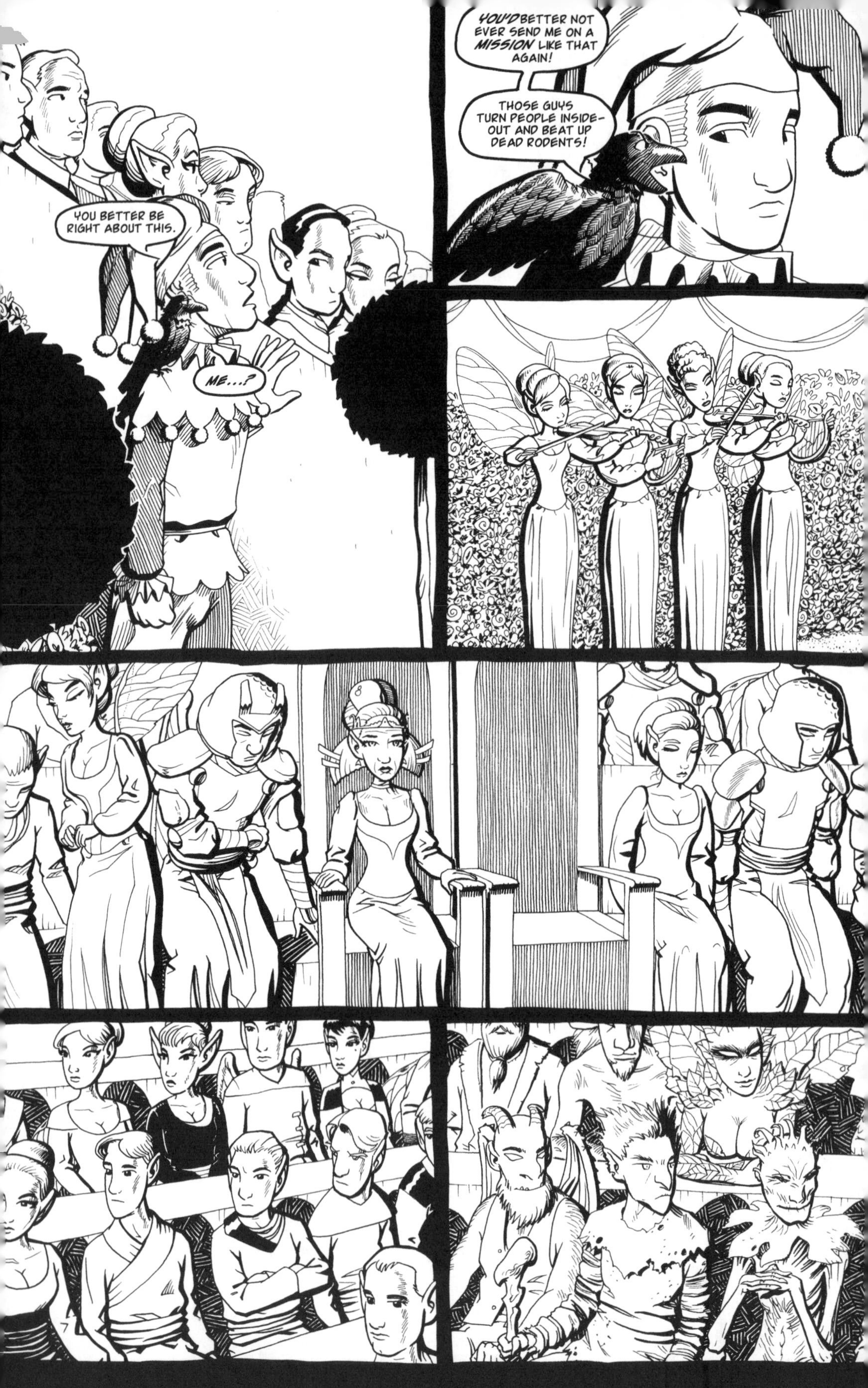
YOU BETTER BE RIGHT ABOUT THIS.
ME...?
YOU'D BETTER NOT EVER SEND ME ON A MISSION LIKE THAT AGAIN!
THOSE GUYS TURN PEOPLE INSIDE-OUT AND BEAT UP DEAD RODENTS!

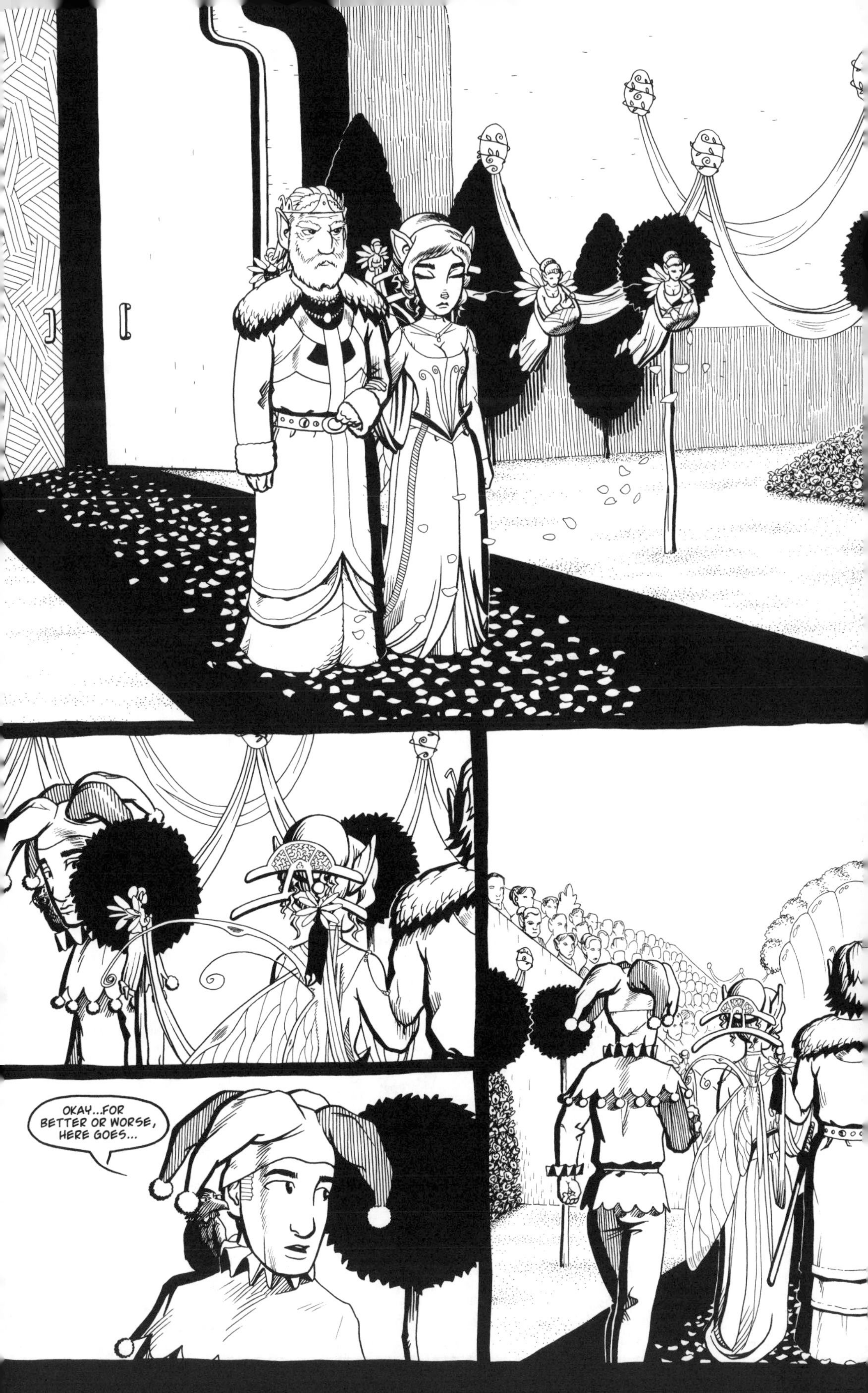
OKAY...FOR BETTER OR WORSE, HERE GOES...

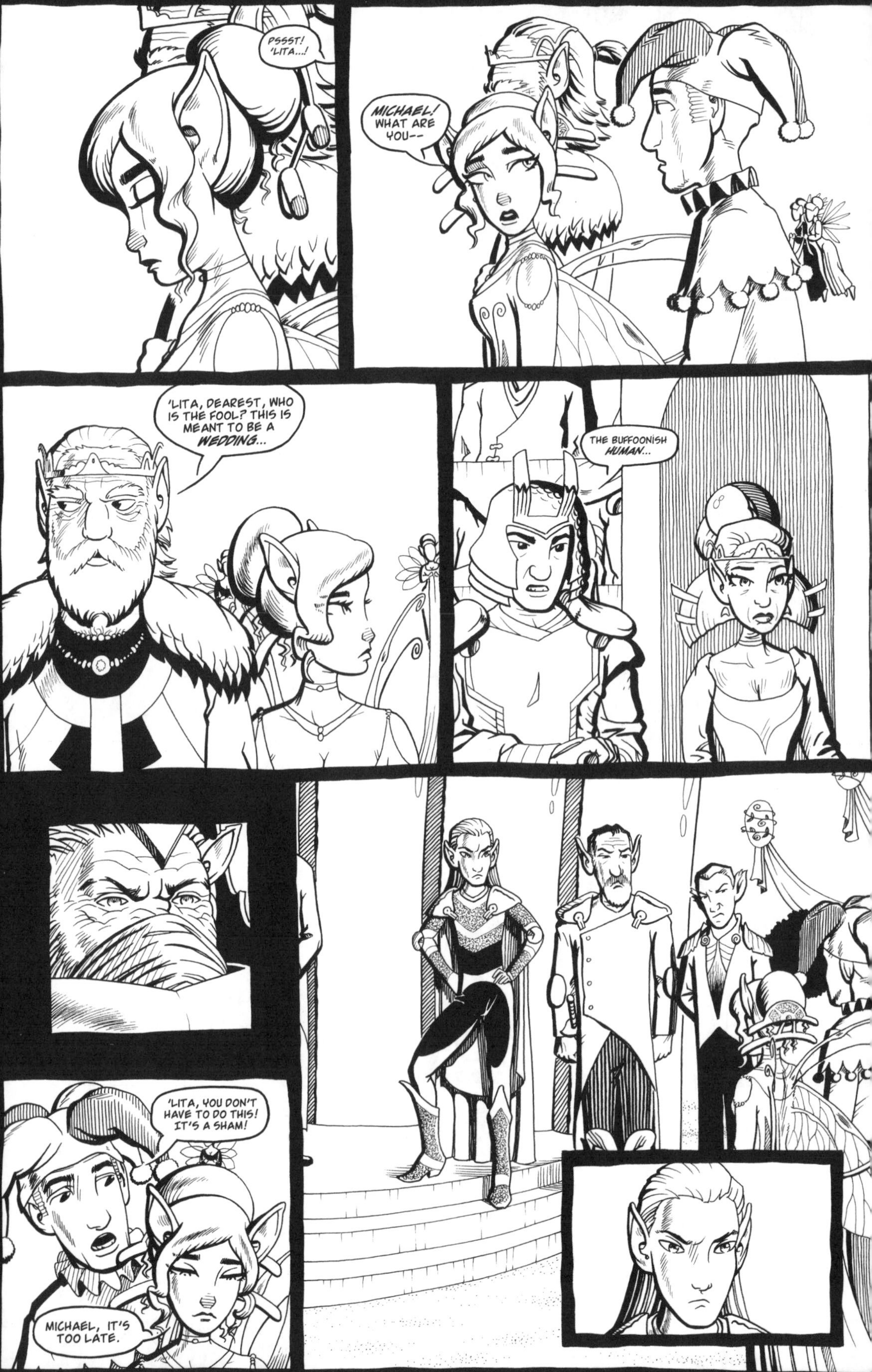
PSSST! 'LITA...!
MICHAEL! WHAT ARE YOU--
'LITA, DEAREST, WHO IS THE FOOL? THIS IS MEANT TO BE A WEDDING...
THE BUFFOONISH HUMAN...
'LITA, YOU DON'T HAVE TO DO THIS! IT'S A SHAM!
MICHAEL, IT'S TOO LATE.

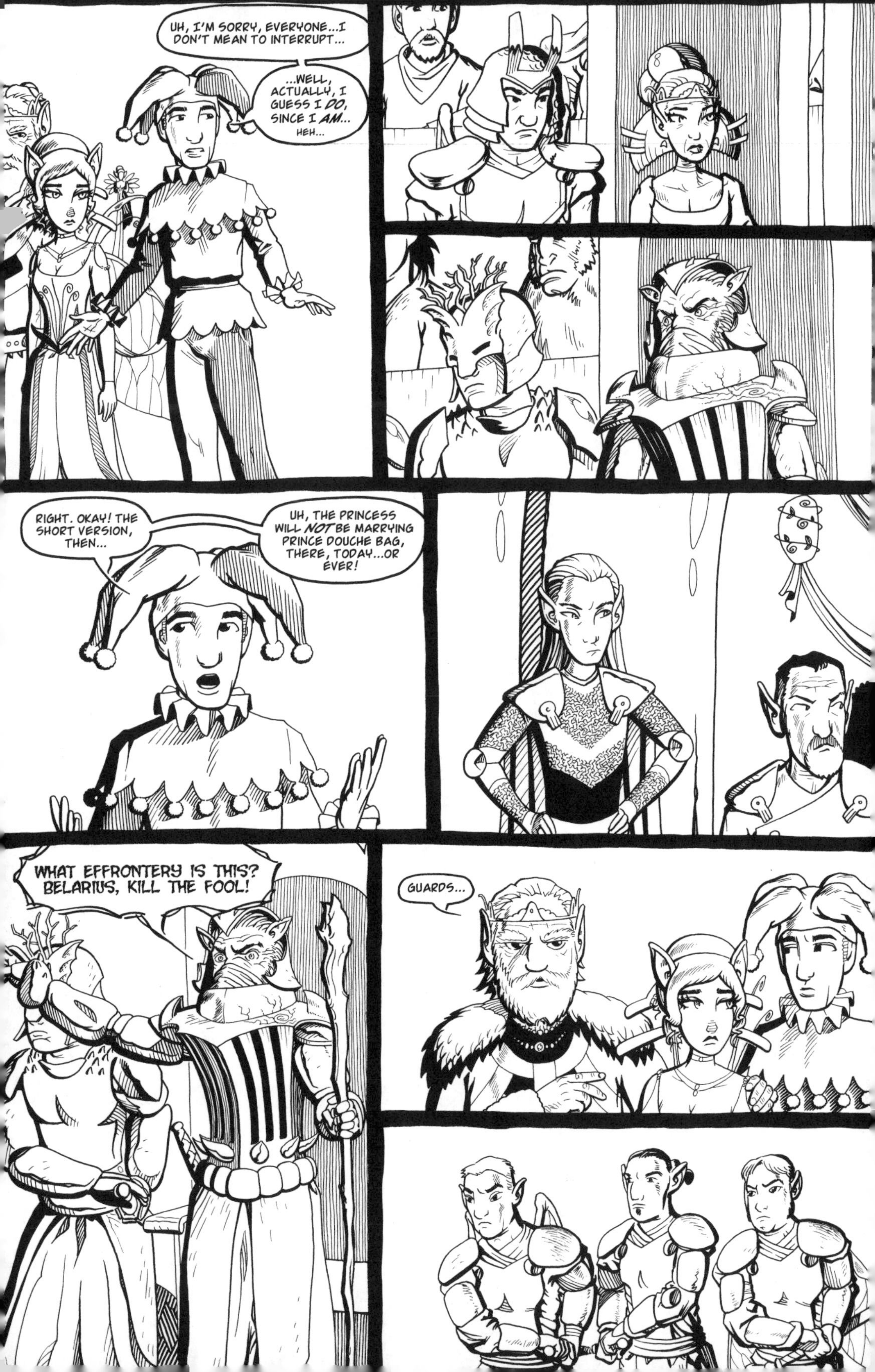
UH, I'M SORRY, EVERYONE...I DON'T MEAN TO INTERRUPT...
...WELL, ACTUALLY, I GUESS I DO, SINCE I AM... HEH...
RIGHT. OKAY! THE SHORT VERSION, THEN...
UH, THE PRINCESS WILL NOT BE MARRYING PRINCE DOUCHE BAG, THERE, TODAY...OR EVER!
WHAT EFFRONTERY IS THIS? BELARIUS, KILL THE FOOL!
GUARDS...

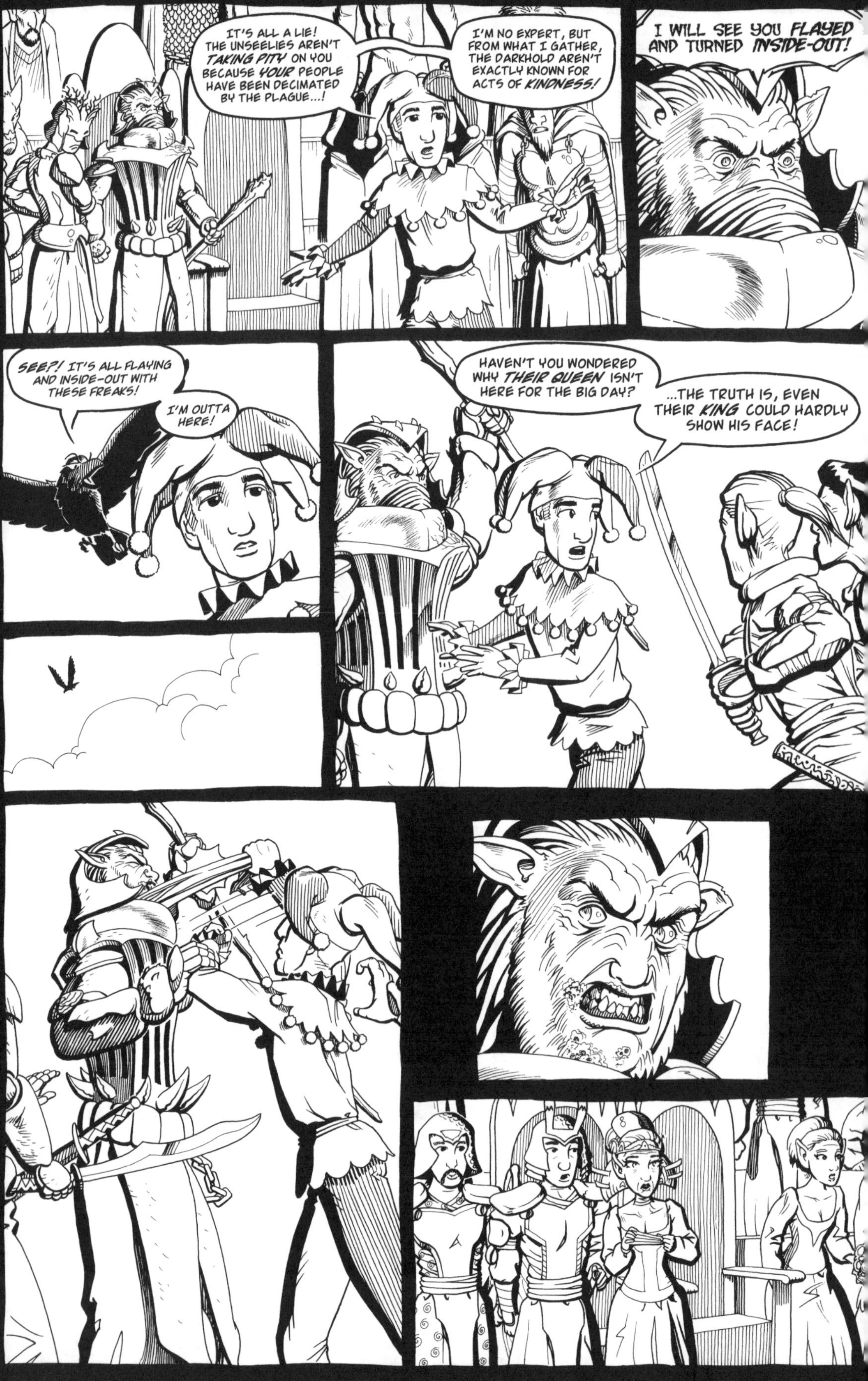
IT'S ALL A LIE! THE UNSEELIES AREN'T TAKING PITY ON YOU BECAUSE YOUR PEOPLE HAVE BEEN DECIMATED BY THE PLAGUE...!
I'M NO EXPERT, BUT FROM WHAT I GATHER, THE DARKHOLD AREN'T EXACTLY KNOWN FOR ACTS OF KINDNESS!
I WILL SEE YOU FLAYED AND TURNED INSIDE-OUT!
SEE?! IT'S ALL FLAYING AND INSIDE-OUT WITH THESE FREAKS!
I'M OUTTA HERE!
HAVEN'T YOU WONDERED WHY THEIR QUEEN ISN'T HERE FOR THE BIG DAY?
...THE TRUTH IS, EVEN THEIR KING COULD HARDLY SHOW HIS FACE!

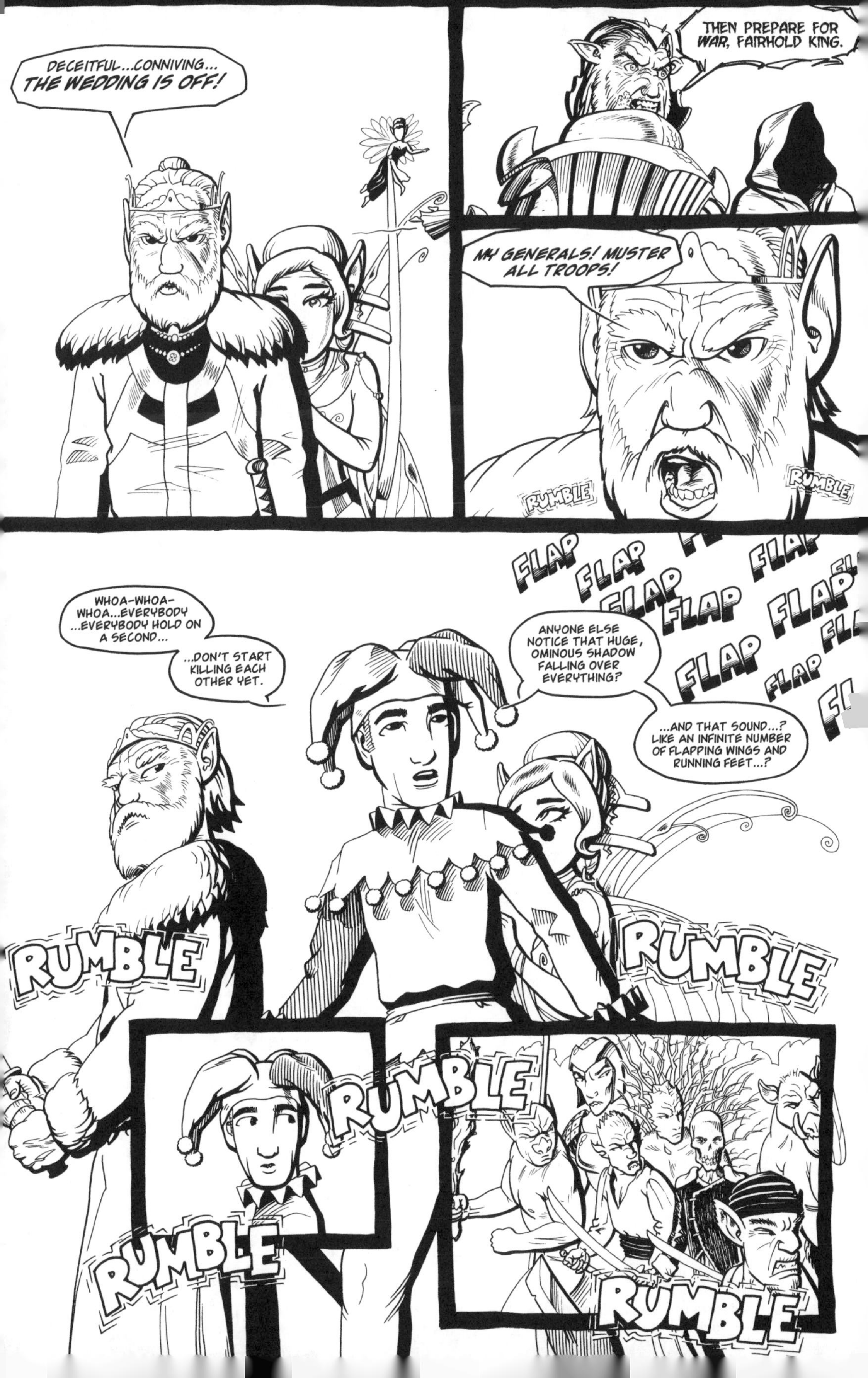
DECEITFUL...CONNIVING... THE WEDDING IS OFF!
THEN PREPARE FOR WAR, FAIRHOLD KING.
MY GENERALS! MUSTER ALL TROOPS!
RUMBLE
RUMBLE
FLAP FLAP FLAP FLAP FLAP FLAP FLAP FLAP
WHOA-WHOA-WHOA...EVERYBODY ...EVERYBODY HOLD ON A SECOND...
...DON'T START KILLING EACH OTHER YET.
ANYONE ELSE NOTICE THAT HUGE, OMINOUS SHADOW FALLING OVER EVERYTHING?
...AND THAT SOUND...? LIKE AN INFINITE NUMBER OF FLAPPING WINGS AND RUNNING FEET...?
RUMBLE
RUMBLE
RUMBLE
RUMBLE
RUMBLE

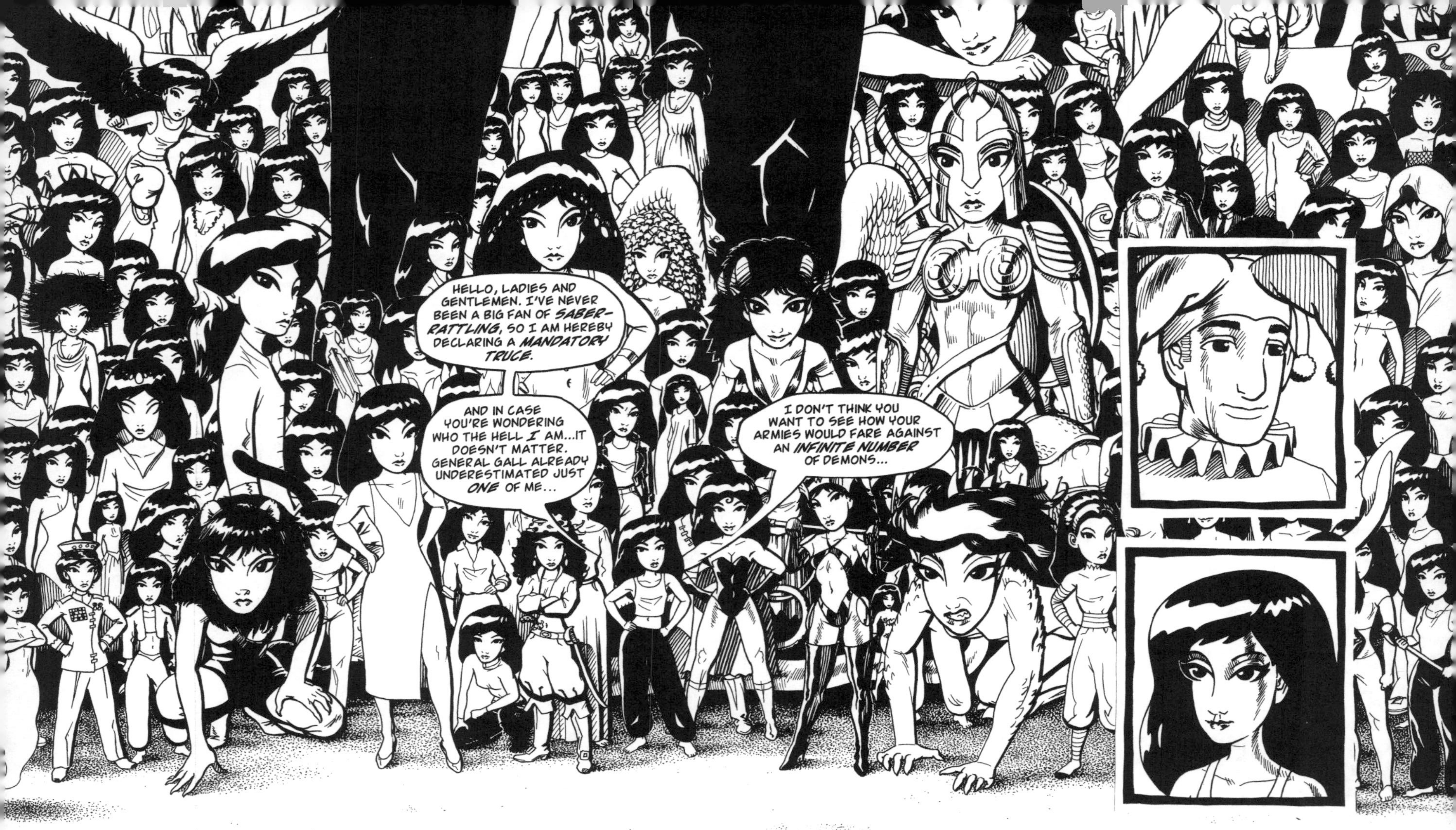
HELLO, LADIES AND GENTLEMEN. I'VE NEVER BEEN A BIG FAN OF *SABER-RATTLING*, SO I AM HEREBY DECLARING A *MANDATORY TRUCE*.
AND IN CASE YOU'RE WONDERING WHO THE HELL *I* AM...IT DOESN'T MATTER. GENERAL GALL ALREADY UNDERESTIMATED JUST *ONE* OF ME...
I DON'T THINK YOU WANT TO SEE HOW YOUR ARMIES WOULD FARE AGAINST AN *INFINITE NUMBER* OF DEMONS...

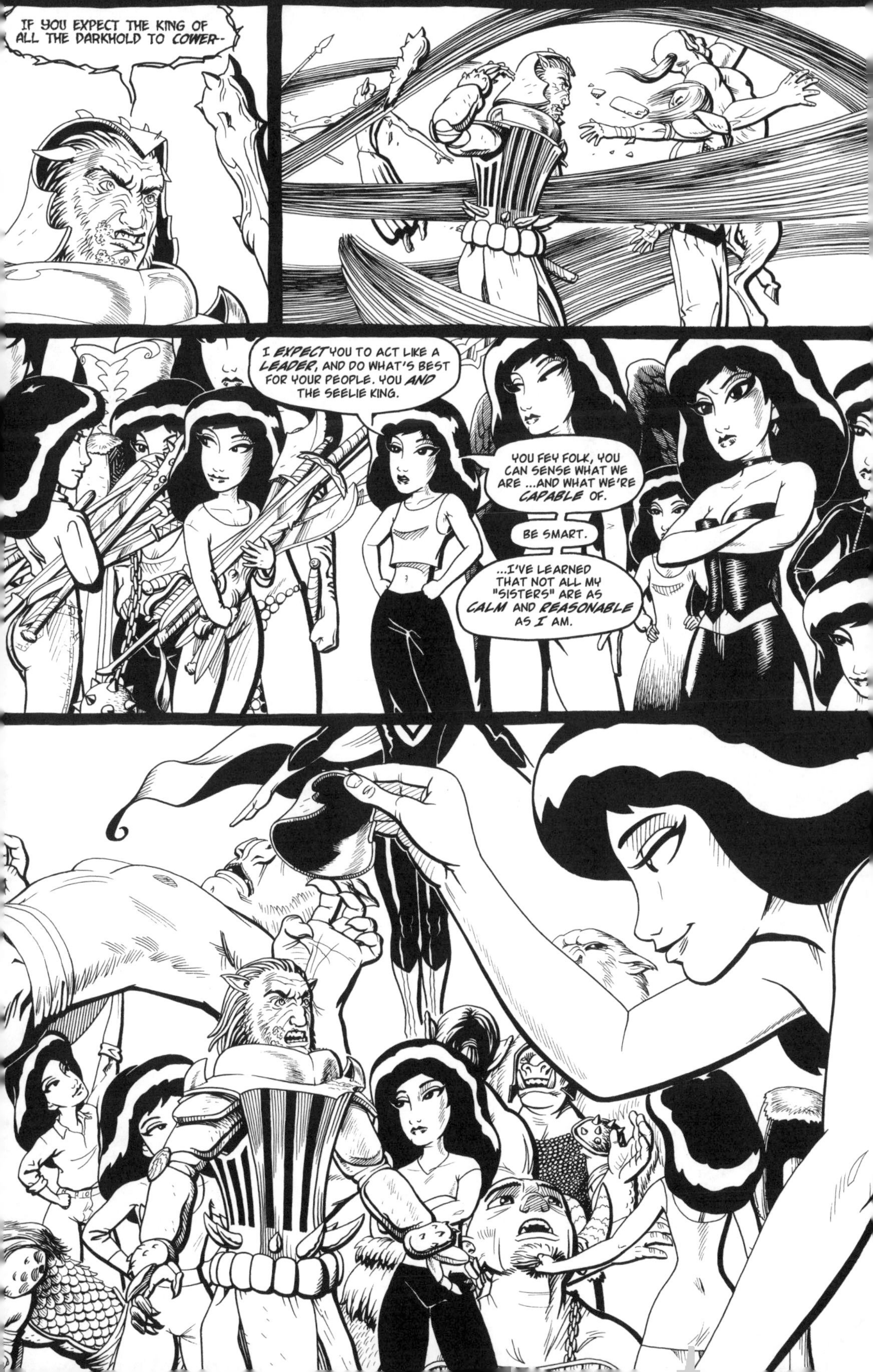
IF YOU EXPECT THE KING OF ALL THE DARKHOLD TO COWER--
I EXPECT YOU TO ACT LIKE A LEADER, AND DO WHAT'S BEST FOR YOUR PEOPLE. YOU AND THE SEELIE KING.
YOU FEY FOLK, YOU CAN SENSE WHAT WE ARE ...AND WHAT WE'RE CAPABLE OF.
BE SMART.
...I'VE LEARNED THAT NOT ALL MY "SISTERS" ARE AS CALM AND REASONABLE AS I AM.

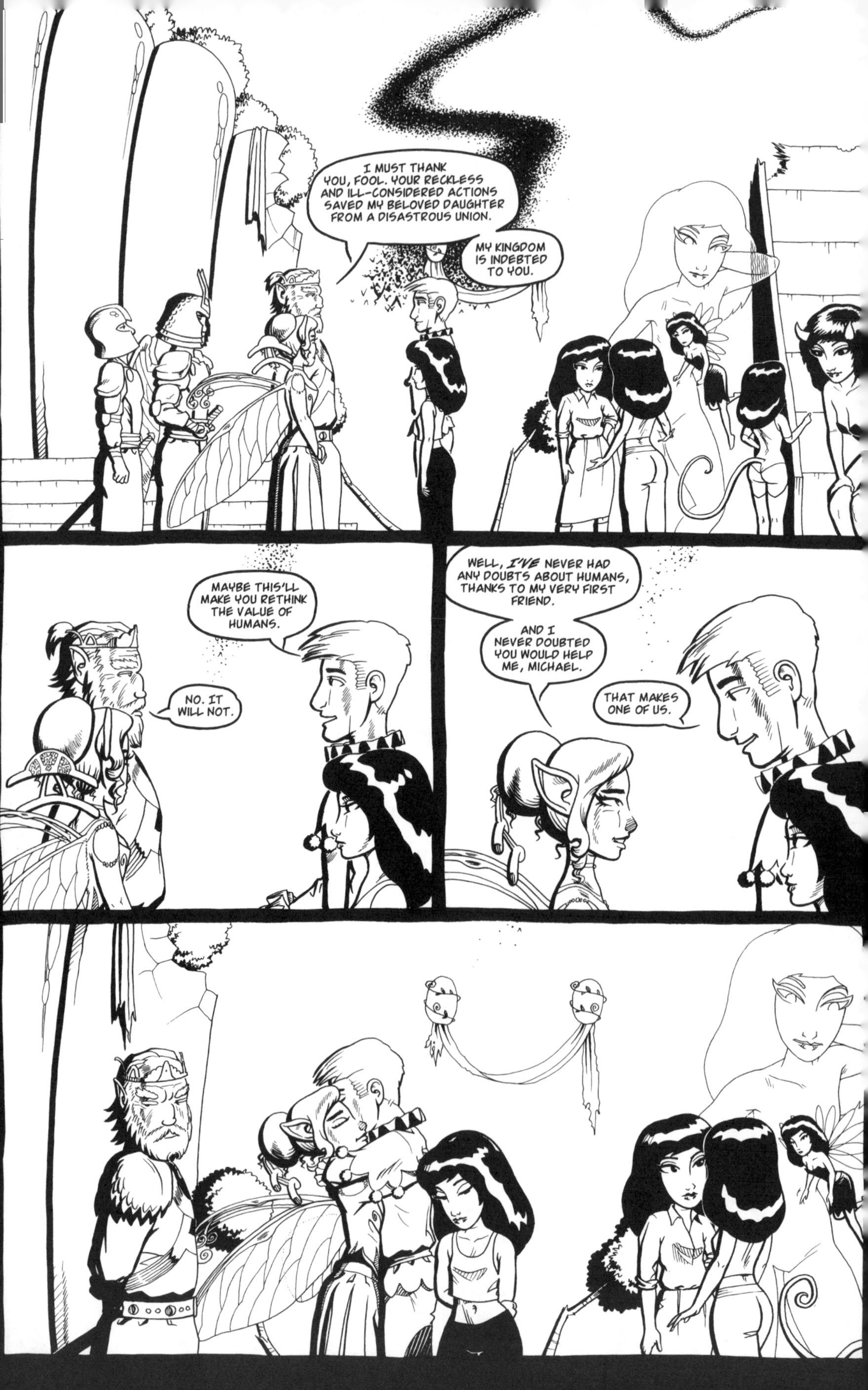
I MUST THANK YOU, FOOL. YOUR RECKLESS AND ILL-CONSIDERED ACTIONS SAVED MY BELOVED DAUGHTER FROM A DISASTROUS UNION.
MY KINGDOM IS INDEBTED TO YOU.
MAYBE THIS'LL MAKE YOU RETHINK THE VALUE OF HUMANS.
NO. IT WILL NOT.
WELL, I'VE NEVER HAD ANY DOUBTS ABOUT HUMANS, THANKS TO MY VERY FIRST FRIEND.
AND I NEVER DOUBTED YOU WOULD HELP ME, MICHAEL.
THAT MAKES ONE OF US.

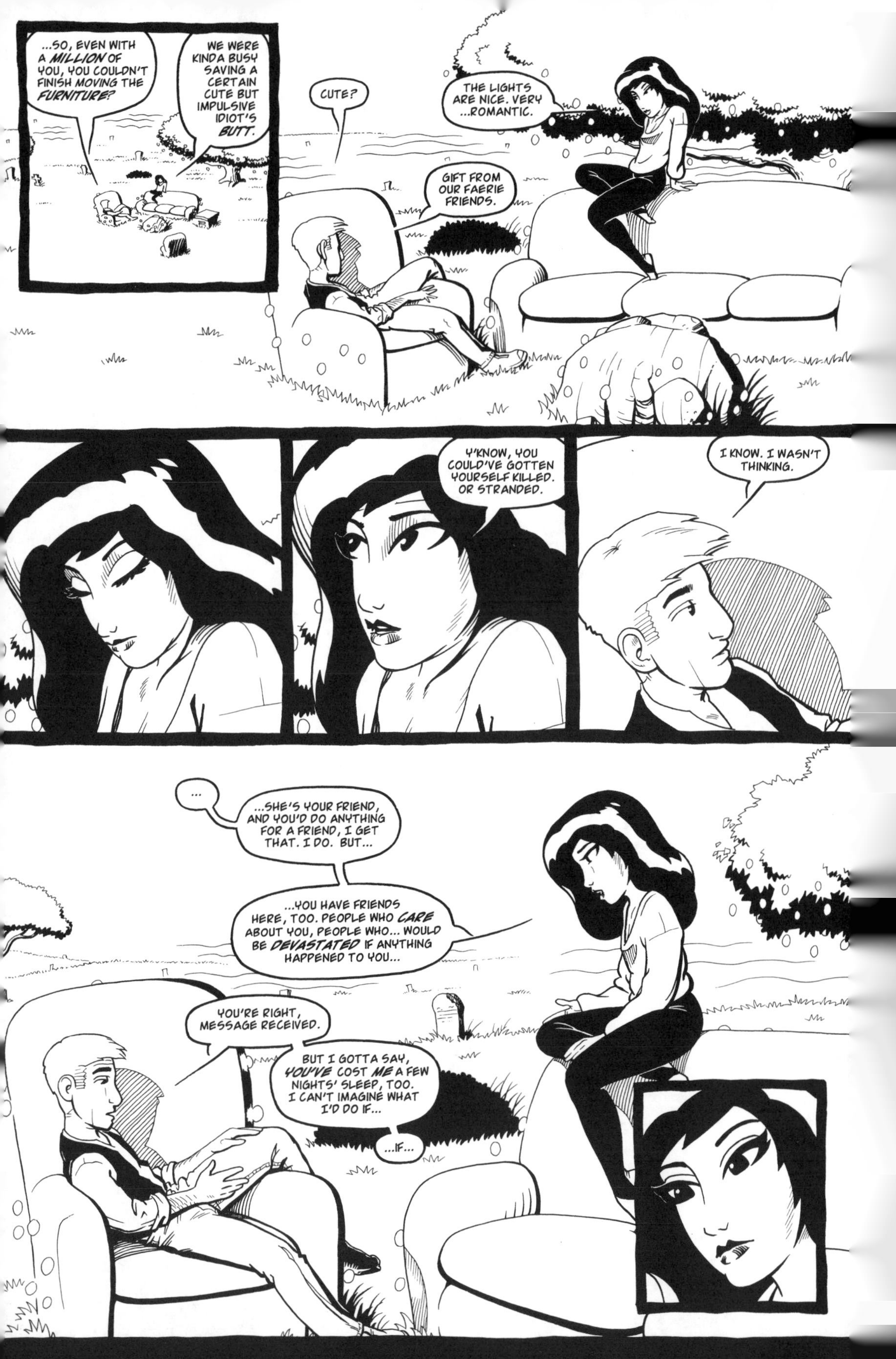
...SO, EVEN WITH A MILLION OF YOU, YOU COULDN'T FINISH MOVING THE FURNITURE?
WE WERE KINDA BUSY SAVING A CERTAIN CUTE BUT IMPULSIVE IDIOT'S BUTT.
CUTE?
THE LIGHTS ARE NICE. VERY ...ROMANTIC.
GIFT FROM OUR FAERIE FRIENDS.
Y'KNOW, YOU COULD'VE GOTTEN YOURSELF KILLED. OR STRANDED.
I KNOW. I WASN'T THINKING.
...
...SHE'S YOUR FRIEND, AND YOU'D DO ANYTHING FOR A FRIEND, I GET THAT. I DO. BUT...
...YOU HAVE FRIENDS HERE, TOO. PEOPLE WHO CARE ABOUT YOU, PEOPLE WHO... WOULD BE DEVASTATED IF ANYTHING HAPPENED TO YOU...
YOU'RE RIGHT, MESSAGE RECEIVED.
BUT I GOTTA SAY, YOU'VE COST ME A FEW NIGHTS' SLEEP, TOO. I CAN'T IMAGINE WHAT I'D DO IF...
...IF...

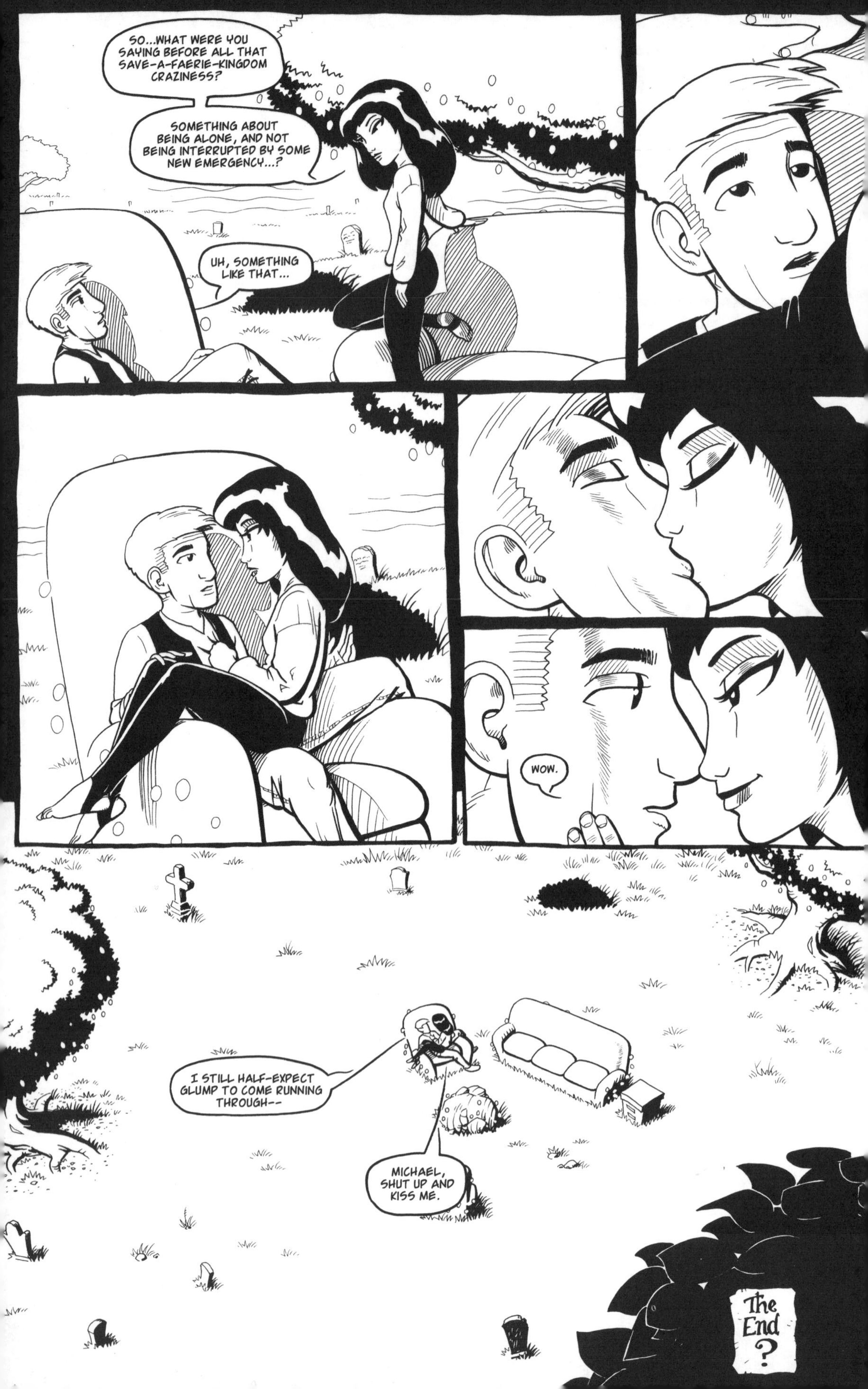

SO...WHAT WERE YOU SAYING BEFORE ALL THAT SAVE-A-FAERIE-KINGDOM CRAZINESS?
SOMETHING ABOUT BEING ALONE, AND NOT BEING INTERRUPTED BY SOME NEW EMERGENCY...?
UH, SOMETHING LIKE THAT...
WOW.
I STILL HALF-EXPECT GLUMP TO COME RUNNING THROUGH--
MICHAEL, SHUT UP AND KISS ME.
The End ?